MIRACLE GIRL

Also by Keith Scribner

The GoodLife

MIRACLE GIRL

KEITH SCRIBNER

RIVERHEAD BOOKS
a member of Penguin Group (USA) Inc.
New York

This is a work of fiction. Names, characters, places, and incidents either are the product of the author's imagination or are used fictitiously, and any resemblance to actual persons, living or dead, business establishments, events, or locales is entirely coincidental.

The poem appearing on page 197 is "Upon Julia's Clothes," by Robert Herrick.

Riverhead Books
a member of
Penguin Group (USA) Inc.
375 Hudson Street
New York, NY 10014

Published simultaneously in Canada

Library of Congress Cataloging-in-Publication Data

Scribner, Keith.
Miracle girl / Keith Scribner.
p. cm.
ISBN 1-57322-250-X
1. Vietnamese Americans—Fiction. 2. New York (State)—Fiction.
3. Deaf women—Fiction. 4. Catholics—Fiction. 5. Miracles—Fiction. I. Title.
PS3569.C735M57 2003 2002037087
813'.54—dc21

Printed in the United States of America
10 9 8 7 6 5 4 3 2 1

This book is printed on acid-free paper. ♾

Book design and title page photos by Meighan Cavanaugh

To Jen

Acknowledgments

For their generosity, their insight, good sense, and precious time, I'm very grateful to Wendy Carlton, Gordon Kato, John L'Heureux, Jason Brown, Tracy Daugherty, Sameer Pandya, James McClenaghan, Suzanne Carey, Anne Cowie, Arlyn Vogelmann, Marjorie Sandor, Colleen Morton, Miriam Richards, Jo Frederic, Robert Schwartz, and at the Oregon State University Center for the Humanities, Peter Copek and David Robinson.

MIRACLE GIRL

NOVEMBER 22, 1963

Just past noon that day, my mother, Catherine Quinn, lay on a delivery table in St. Joseph's Hospital, Chicago, Illinois. My father, Philip, leaned his palms against a candy machine in the lobby, considering gum and chocolate, considering a larger apartment on a quieter street. Squeezing the stainless-steel rails penning her in, my mother felt she was being pried open. How far could her bones bend before they snapped? My father dropped nickels into the candy machine, listening to each one rattle down chutes and slots then chink in the coin box before he inserted the next. "Push," said the nurse. "Harder." My father thumbed another nickel into the machine. "It's too much," my mother screamed. "Push," the doctor ordered. Getting his mind around the taste of a Butterfinger, my father squeezed the corresponding plastic knob and pulled—lubricated levers clunked open a trapdoor. "Good, Catherine. Just one more big push." The Butterfinger skimmed across the smooth steel tray at my father's knees. "God!" my mother screamed out, and she saw the nurse was smiling. A thousand miles away in Dallas, a gunshot crackled in the brittle air. My birth certificate read 12:31. My name, chosen by my parents later that afternoon as Johnson was inaugurated on Air Force One with the young widow at his side, was John Fitzgerald Kennedy Quinn.

I. MONDAY

At dawn, outside my window, a hammered yellow Chevette jimmied into the last free spot. There'd always been plenty of parking on our block, but the miracle in Little Saigon had been going on for a week, bringing in a steady stream of pilgrims whose cars flooded Hudson City. Space had become an issue.

Kids and adults—five in all—spilled out of the Chevette, shirtbacks sweaty and wrinkled. They unloaded a Styrofoam cooler, straw hats, a small lawn statue of the Virgin Mary, then heaped it all in a plastic laundry basket and tramped off, leaving the hatchback ajar.

Rita followed the miracle on the news and kept me up to speed. I tried to show interest, but to me the miracle was mostly about traffic.

I took my coffee into the dining room; my jigsaw puzzle covered the table. I'd completed the border and the left third of a 2000-piece cirrostratus cloud. For fifteen minutes I tried to place ten or twelve pieces—the smokiest of the gray—but nothing fit.

Just before seven, I wandered back into the bedroom and switched off the alarm before it rang. I sat down on the bed in front of the fan.

I couldn't sleep in this heat, and we didn't have an air-conditioner because Rita said they gave her sinus infections. I didn't believe it, but I didn't argue either. She also said she was allergic to shellfish and veal; she feared invisible dust mites eating, mating, and defecating in her pillow.

She lay on her side, the rumpled white sheet draped over her hip, exposing a strip of skin below the hem of her Planned Parenthood T-shirt. I slid in behind her to seduce her from sleep. As I tugged the sheet down her thigh and lifted her shirt above the nook of her waist, her creamy hip seemed to expand.

With two fingertips I traced designs on her skin. When she sighed, I whispered, "What are you dreaming about, lover girl?"

She woke with a start, then groaned and nuzzled into my chest. "You know I don't remember my dreams." She kissed me, missing my lips but catching my chin, then she craned around to see the clock. "Jesus. Why didn't you wake me up? It's after seven." She jumped from our bed and rushed out the bedroom door, "Pregnancy is no accident" printed across her back.

In a tiny room next to the kitchen she switched on her computer, and I lay in bed listening to the bongs and chimes as it booted up. She clattered the kettle, flushed the toilet, and returned, brushing her teeth, to her cluttered office to check her e-mail. The modem screeched. This would be the sixteenth consecutive day that Rita and I hadn't made love.

I showered, dressed, and sliced myself a thick hunk of oatmeal-blueberry bread. Rita kept us in bread. She'd gotten a bread machine from her sister the previous Christmas, and new kinds of bread had become an obsession: olive and sun-dried tomato, Kahlúa and molasses, cinnamon-honey. She seemed to be developing her domestic aspects. Seven years ago when we first met—the first time she invited me into her apartment—I opened her fridge. It glared white. Huddled on the top wire shelf were a carton of Parliaments, a liter of spring water, aloe, and a jar of gourmet mustard in a tiny wicker basket sealed with shrink wrap (also a gift from her sister). And that was all.

"A family in New Hampshire," Rita said as I dropped the bread in the toaster. She was leaning over the newspaper eating yogurt from the container. "They produced only two cubic feet of garbage in a year. A family of four. Plus a dog."

I hung my head in the fridge. There was no blueberry jam. "Just strawberry?" I asked. "Do you know if there's blueberry? Back in the back?"

"One grocery bag of garbage. *In a year*," she added again. "It's in the Smithsonian."

I sat across from her at the table and spooned strawberry jam on my toast.

"I wonder what's in it," she said.

"What's *not* in it? Two cubic feet. Think about it. Impossible." I took a fat bite of toast and washed it down with coffee.

"It says they composted."

"Their poor dog. *He* should be in the museum."

"And didn't buy things with nonrecyclable packaging."

"Here, pooch. My shoe's worn out. Eat it."

"I'm sure they gave their old clothes to Goodwill."

"All that dog wants is a Gaines Burger," I said, "but it's got four strings of dental floss in it from last night. I'll bet these people are big flossers."

"You know, Quinn. It seems to me like they focused their energy on something worthwhile."

"They should X-ray the dog's stomach."

Rita reached for the jar of jam and ate a spoonful. She loved sweets.

"I don't believe them," I said. "I don't trust them."

"You need to go."

"People from New Hampshire," I said.

"They're actually from England. They just live in New Hampshire."

"People from England," I said.

"You're late."

As I pulled away from the curb, the sun streamed through the front windows of our apartment. I could see Rita in her short cotton robe, leafy green with a big Chinese character on the back. I could never remember what it meant. She moved through the living room to her office, where she spent her days selling ad time for radio and cable TV. She was a consultant. At the end of the block I gunned into traffic, heavier than normal. Rita was right—I was late.

At the office I said, "Hi, there," to Patsy at the front desk, and "Morning, Sister," to Rosemary, who was leaning into an open file drawer. I was thinking about Rita—how she was too quick to believe in things, too willing to embrace the good. Standing at the Mr. Coffee I blocked out two cubic feet with my hands in the air. I couldn't believe something so absurd was being hyped by the Smithsonian. And Rita swallowed it whole.

I poured my coffee and took it to my office, where I left the door open enough to show I had nothing to hide, and closed enough that no one could see in. Sitting back with my day planner, I held the steaming cup to my lips. I had to drive out to the old CYO camp for a meeting with Buddy Jensen from Venable Properties, then stop at Li'l Tykes Day Care to give Lilian a new lease. I took a sip.

Suddenly my door swung open wide. Barely eight-thirty and the bishop had already taken off his black suit coat and rolled up his sleeves. His beefy forearms were spiked with thick white hair. Frank was in his late fifties, a big man, as none of the younger priests were. He had the body of a barrel maker or a man who delivered ice, a man who took ownership of the wide swath of space he occupied. I knew exactly what he'd say. "Immaculate Heart."

"I know," I said. It was a property I'd contracted to Venable but hadn't closed. I put the coffee mug on my desk and sat up straighter. I always felt guilty around the bishop.

"June, we agreed. June one at the latest."

"Venable had problems with their numbers," I said.

"What month is it now?"

"They asked me to float it for a little while. I didn't want it to fall through, so I gave them some wiggle room."

"It's August," the bishop continued. "August third. Unload the property. If not to Venable, then to RealCo or those Italians. DiAngio. I want it off our books."

"We did sign with Venable and legally they—"

"I don't need this, John. Not today." The bishop was the only person besides my kindergarten teacher and my grandparents to call me John. "Not with this healing thing."

Patsy's voice scratched through my intercom. "Is Bishop O'Connor with you, Quinn?"

"What is it?" the bishop roared before I could speak.

"Father Floquet is here."

"Have him wait." He took a deep breath and exhaled across my office, his cheeks stretching, eyes moving over my desk, over me, and back to the desk. He tipped a picture frame his way: Rita and me in Jamaica.

He ambled to the far wall and inspected my huge maps of Hudson City. I'd claimed the biggest office in the building—the best office, too, for its proximity to the kitchen, good lighting, and privacy—because I needed lots of wall for the maps. I loved maps, and always made sure my walls were covered to justify the office.

I'd colored current church property on the maps in gold (with a glitter pen, which I'd thought was clever but now worried, as the bishop worked a thumb into his jaw, might seem flip). Church properties I'd sold off were marked with red X's. When I took this job, the diocese was the single biggest property owner in Hudson City, but since then had been edged out by Venable. The bishop leaned in close to a cluster of red that included a hundred-year-old church gone to condos, and he groaned.

He should groan, I thought. The church could lose parishioners and still stake its importance on moral superiority. But without its space—Notre-Dame, the Sistine Chapel, and St. Patrick's Cathedral, schools, land, prime real estate around the world—a claim of dominance, even relevance, was tougher to back up. And selling a church was hardest on the bishop because he knew that selling that space was selling a chunk of his religion—the cross-shaped floor plan with columns reaching toward heaven, the sanctuary, pulpit, and high altar. Catholicism embodied the space it occupied; the space embodied Catholicism.

In the same way, Hudson City had lost some of its soul with the urban renewal of the Seventies. Among the devastated neighborhoods were five blocks of demolished nineteenth-century brownstones that left a pit in the heart of downtown. Development plans fell through, and what came to be called "the big hole" gaped for fifteen years. In 1987, The Galleria partially filled that hole. It opened the day after Thanksgiving, and David Newman, a local celebrity, sang from a balcony above the food court. David Newman was sixteen years old, a junior at Hudson City High. He was also a pop singer, blond and beautiful, who had sung the national anthem for the Yankees and the Mets. He'd been in Broadway shows. His first music video was in production. There was even a rumor he'd sing on *The Tonight Show.*

At the grand opening, halfway through his original song, "This Train Stops for Love," the Galleria balcony collapsed—David fell forty feet to the flagstone below. For the two months he lay in a coma, all of Hudson City monitored his progress. Local TV stations replayed their documentaries: cameras following David from the halls of Hudson City High to the recording studio and backstage at *Les Mis.*

On a dark January afternoon, just before a heavy snowstorm that shut the city down for days, David emerged from the coma—deaf and paraplegic. On the news, teenage girls, who'd kept vigil in the hospital halls, sobbed. But David was serene. He reported that in the coma he'd been visited by the Virgin Mary, who told him that he'd awaken paralyzed and deaf but that one day his hearing would be restored. For a few months people waited with growing impatience for that day, and when it didn't come, David faded from the spotlight. For twelve years no one thought of him.

Then, last week, in his evening computer class at St. Mary's Middle School in Little Saigon, he passed out. When he woke up, his hearing was restored. The teacher immediately phoned his family who rushed to the school. Then she called Father Timothy Floquet, pastor of the adjoining St. Mary's Church. With everyone crowded around him and his hearing aids removed, David responded to his family, formed some words, laughed. The teacher, so excited by what was happening in her class, called the "Tri-City Triumphs!" hotline at Channel 6 News. The cameraman got David to replace his hearing aids, and remove them again for the camera, and on the eleven-o'clock broadcast that night, with Father Floquet by his side, David pointed at his chest and said, "This train stops for love."

But that wasn't all he said. In labored speech, he talked about a deaf woman, herself a former computer student, who had visited their class the previous night. David had recognized her but couldn't remember why. Then, this evening, while he was passed out, the woman had appeared to him, telling him he'd wake up with his hearing restored. The class was for deaf, blind, and disabled people, and the woman had taken it after graduating from college, and now worked in a software job in Providence, Rhode Island. She'd come home to visit her mother and dropped by the class to share the story of her success.

David said she was beautiful. He described her dark skin and lovely features. He described her left eyebrow: elegant and long, reaching in a graceful curve along the strong ridge of her brow, and tapering to a point, where a beauty mark floated at the tip. A beauty mark the same dark chestnut as her eyebrow, so it all looked like one thing, like one of the most elegant shapes David knew: the shape of the sound hole cut into a violin.

He said the woman who had appeared in his coma had had the same shape over her eye. It hadn't been the Virgin Mary twelve years ago; the Virgin had sent a messenger, Sue Phong. And here she was again.

Urged on by the Channel 6 reporter, Father Floquet called Sue Phong's mother and asked that Sue come right over to the school, which she did. Bewildered and obviously uncomfortable, she avoided answering questions, but they got her on film.

"Tri-City Triumphs!" led off the eleven-o'clock news with a fifteen-minute segment including old clips of David Newman as child star, and some history of Sue Phong. Father Floquet's comments were carefully worded so as not to be too suggestive. But that didn't stop the Channel 6 reporter from declaring a miracle. The segment closed with a shot of David Newman—still looking all-American with bright blue eyes and tufty blond hair—hugging Sue Phong, a thirty-year-old Amerasian, the orphaned daughter of a Vietnamese woman and an African-American soldier. Her kinky black hair was tied on top of her head with a colorful silk scarf, her dark skin seemed to glow in the camera lights, her eyes were moody, her lips full and shapely. By anyone's account, she was stunning.

That night, Sue Phong appeared to dozens of Hudson City residents in their dreams. Several minor cures were reported the next day.

Father Floquet had called the bishop's residence before the news aired, and he came to the diocese office first thing the next morning. The bishop had summoned him twice since then.

She was appearing in everyone's dreams now. Bum legs, sinus headaches, acne, and tonsillitis were clearing up all over the city. The sheer mass of claims snowballed.

Then, in response to suggestions that he'd concocted the whole thing, David Newman revealed to the press something extraordinary that would dispel many people's doubts, something that Sue Phong had confided to him: she'd been having strange spells—inexplicable physical sensations accompanied by a voice. Completely deaf since she was a baby, she was now hearing a woman—no words, just the sound of a voice. She'd seen a doctor, David said, who had no explanation. So she'd discussed it with her mother's priest, Father Floquet, which Floquet would neither confirm nor deny to the press. In the course of an afternoon, David Newman was no longer the story. All eyes were on the miracle girl.

On my office map Frank was studying Little Saigon, running his finger over the gold-colored properties. I knew he'd do anything to shut down the healings. Although Floquet didn't seem to be overtly fanning the flames, Frank blamed him for letting it get out of control. Just as the cardinal blamed Frank.

"Have you heard the weather?" he asked me.

"Hot," I said.

"We might need a building," he said.

"What for?"

He took a deep breath and stared at me, trying to decide whether *I* could be blamed. "I want you in this meeting."

I followed Frank to his office; he called in Father Floquet. "One," Frank began, thumping his desktop with two rigid fingers. "What are you trying to pull?"

Floquet's congregation at St. Mary's was almost completely composed of Vietnamese and Amerasians, and was the only growing congregation in the Tri-Cities—in the whole diocese actually—which seemed to make the young priest a little cocky. He gazed with complete serenity at the bishop.

"And two, why haven't you done as I've told you?"

Floquet sat forward in his chair and thoughtfully tapped his lips. "In what manner have I disobeyed you?"

"The streets are clogged with pilgrims. That's how."

"I've counseled the girl. I've suggested she recant. I've talked to David Newman. But what is my counsel compared to what they've experienced, compared to the evidence?" Floquet's head fell to the side. "We are only men." Floquet was as spindly and meek as the bishop was large and powerful. If the bishop held more space than he occupied, Floquet held less, as if he might turn and reveal that he was only two-dimensional.

"What about this crucifix turned to gold?" the bishop demanded.

"Something the pilgrims cooked up."

"Alchemy"—the bishop slapped his desk—"as we enter the twenty-first century."

"There's lots of rumors, Bishop. The pilgrims are frustrated."

"Send them home."

"But they're drawn here. The girl's aura, if you will. . . . They *believe.* I think a statement from the church would help. To take control."

The bishop shook his head. "It'll only give the thing credibility."

"With all respect, Bishop, maybe this *thing* deserves—"

"I told you I want it squashed. This hysteria makes the faith look ridiculous."

For all his apparent calm, Floquet's legs were flapping open and closed, back and forth, which the bishop couldn't see from the other side of the desk. He wore scuffed black shoes, a scrap of shoelace in each one, just long enough to knot across the top eyes. No socks and knobby ankles, reddened, like his fingers—nails bit to the bone. "Hysteria?" Floquet said. "Or raw passion?"

The bishop seemed to be chewing a hunk of gristly steak deep in his molars. "Before I bump you to a cow town outside Utica, remind me why you think there's something to this."

Floquet's legs stopped flapping. He reached forward and touched the bishop's desk. "In my seven years for Jesus," he said, "I've never experienced the passion of this woman. I haven't felt anything even close since my early days in the seminary. A fluttering in my chest, like music, from long hours of prayer. I'd forgotten the feeling. I've become nothing but an administrator, which the Lord needs, certainly. But a life needs the balance.

"They're visitations she's having really. She described them in all the physical detail, and as I've told you, Bishop . . . well . . . very direct and physical. I feel blessed, honored really, that this would occur in my parish, that she'd come to me. You're angry with me, Bishop, for not stopping it. But I'm part of it—"

"Vanity!" the bishop bellowed. "Hubris!"

My heart was racing, but Floquet appeared more placid than ever. "My weekday Masses are drawing hundreds, maybe thousands." He put a hand to his chest. "When *I* preach—"

"You report here tomorrow morning at eight, and tell me what you've done to shut this down. You're on a tight leash! You may go now."

The bishop propped his elbows on the edge of his desk; his head dropped. He stared at the crucifix beside his phone like a man at a bar staring into a bourbon.

"What did you want me for?" I ventured.

"Oh, cripes." He winced like he had heartburn. "I forgot." I'd never seen him so distraught. "I was thinking about St. Mary's Middle School. Opening the gym to get people out of the heat. Nothing that could be taken as an endorsement. We could provide water, maybe Kool-Aid." He let out a long sigh. "These things do nobody any good. Indignity all around. People want to believe, and a bishop can only seem vicious."

He was a fighter, a no-nonsense, old-fashioned man's man. It embarrassed me to see him so demoralized.

"I could have left the Tri-Cities last year, you know," he said. "They would've given me anything. A little parish in the Catskills. A cush job on the cocktail party circuit in Manhattan. A teaching position. Put me to pasture in a monastery." He slumped back in the chair, staring at the hard fold in his gut stretching the buttonholes of his black shirt. "But I wanted to stay here and get the diocese in order, get the cathedral restored. That cathedral will be my death. Plaster's falling . . ." He shook his head. "It's like a hailstorm. One transept is roped off. And my niece's wedding is less than a month away. The cardinal comes just after that. All I wanted was a little order."

"We'll straighten it out," I said, trying to be upbeat. I knew he desperately wanted the cathedral fixed up for his niece's wedding. Sister Rosemary had told me about Frank's mother's funeral a few years back: Frank looked out from the altar over his mother's casket at the pews packed with his extended family from all over the country and from Ireland, huddled in their coats, shivering in the cold damp cathedral. Paint was peeling, water stains defiled the walls, the artwork was dirty and damaged, you couldn't hear Frank's eulogy over the banging steam pipes. He'd been ashamed, and his niece's wedding was his chance for redemption.

"Maybe we could all pitch in. Slap a little paint around."

His Irish blue eyes glared dangerously in my direction. With the fake Italian accent he put on to indicate deep exasperation, he turned his pink Irish face to the heavens and intoned, *"Madon-na!"*

Then he punched his intercom. "Patsy," he said. "I want this miracle girl in my office. One o'clock."

I left the building, two-story brick, formerly a Catholic elementary school. An art deco stainless-steel awning fanned out over the front doors, kind of like a diner except for the cross rising from its scalloped edge. To the left of the doors, stainless-steel letters spelled out "Tri-Cities Roman Catholic Diocese."

The bishop had hired me to inventory building space for the diocese. I'd taken the job in a panic—laid off and deep in debt without any other prospects in a hard-up city. I figured I'd work there for a couple months, and always had my eye out for something more rewarding, but five years later I was still working for the diocese in a job that had shifted from space management to sales: unloading property that wasn't utilized directly by the church or earning at least sixteen percent per year. The bishop gave me a relatively free hand. He seemed to like me, in a disapproving paternal sort of way.

From the river I drove north on Route 7, up through the Heights, passing by Rita's old elementary school. P.S. 4 was boarded up now, a small building, 20,000 square feet, too close to the new highway. Venable owned it. When the market was right, they'd pull it down and build apartments or, more likely, a retirement home. "Trust me on this one," Buddy Jensen had told me. "Put your money anywhere having to do with old people. Next twenty years, old people are going to be huge."

Another mile north, I passed the dairy farm that even in my childhood was getting swallowed up by the city. I pulled into an Arby's drive-thru and ordered a coffee that came in a Styrofoam cup almost too big to hold in one hand. This was a sad fact of the Tri-Cities: Starbucks fever was sweeping the country—in Kansas City and El Paso you could buy first-rate cappuccinos in strip malls—yet here, one hundred fifty miles up the Hudson from Manhattan, one hundred sixty miles west of Boston, you burned your tongue on Arby's coffee—bitter and thin—from Styrofoam buckets.

I lived in Hudson City despite the coffee, despite the fact that Bill Clinton had planned to visit on a tour of cities that the economic miracle of the Nineties had passed over, but canceled when he learned Hudson City didn't have a prayer of revival before the next election. I stayed because of Rita, who stayed in a tangle of her family's roots. And there were my roots, too. Maybe I stayed to untangle and sort and inventory what it was that kept me here.

When I finished college, I went right to work at that renowned American institution, Monticello Furniture, as an inventory analyst. Not to inventory product, but space: production space, shipping and office space, storage space. I calculated available square footage in the two factories and fourteen nonproduction facilities, from design and raw-material ordering to receiving, production, shipping, sales, marketing, accounts payable, maintenance, and food service. Why should shipping in the Mechanicville plant with ninety-seven container units shipped weekly be confined to 11,000 square feet, when shipping in the Scotia plant moved only eighty-two container units per week, yet they stretched their legs comfortably to fill 15,000 square feet? Such were the inefficiencies and inequities I spent eight years ironing out. Most simply, I counted space.

I had majored in business, and in my senior year I discovered inventory theory. It was incredible to me that nine-tenths of a problem could be solved by counting. Solutions became obvious with a good inventory of wetlands or fish and wildlife in the Northeast, or the skills of nurses or air traffic controllers in New York State.

But finally it was space planning that got me excited. Space is often a company's most valuable asset—its real estate and the space within its real estate. Space has a value beyond its monetary value, just as money has a value separate from what it can buy. The amount of space you own or control, its adjacencies, and whether it's the company's "better space" determine your leverage and prestige. Space is a tool. Space is power. Those who understand space are destined to control space. And controlling space means money. Big money. My starting salary at Monticello Furniture put me in Armani suits, a 320i, and the stock market.

But just over a year later the '87 crash took everything I'd invested. Then Monticello Furniture dropped into its first slump in a hundred and sixty years of business, and I became an unwitting downsizer—my business models, employee surveys, space plans and layouts were used by my bosses to slash employees. And in the end they used my data to build their new factories in South Korea and Vietnam. That colonial jointer on Monticello Furniture's famous logo decked out in a tricorner hat, knickers, and buckle shoes as he skims a wooden plane over a gate-legged tabletop is now a South Korean woman operating an edgebander and membrane press, or a Vietnamese teenager in a gas mask and goggles shooting a polyurethane spray gun.

I'd say the only thing I took from my years at Monticello was a love for making furniture. There was a 2200-square-foot wood shop at the Mechanicville plant used to develop new designs. State of the art. A six-foot cast-iron Delta table saw, a twelve-inch lathe, an 8000-rpm planer, a shaper with drop-in spindles, a hollow chisel mortiser, hand tools, clamps, and jigs to make you weep. Given the man-hours per day in the shop, the space should have been squeezed down to 1400 square feet. But I enjoyed staying on for an evening or going in on a Saturday too much. Fudging those numbers was perhaps my first real act of corruption.

After another ten minutes of farmland—the smell of manure and grasses heated by the morning sun—I turned down a side road, then another. These turns were etched in my memory—it was the route to the day camp I went to for nine summers, ages five to thirteen, a CYO camp owned and operated by the diocese. Five years ago the camp closed, and last summer I sold it to Venable. They tore down the arts and crafts cabin, the dank locker rooms, and the rec hall. Swing sets, backstops, and flag poles were ripped up, and the docks were dragged from the water. The camp was subdivided into three-quarter-acre lots around the lake. Venable was building two houses on spec. Several lots had been sold, and construction had begun on three more homes.

Buddy Jensen was the Venable broker I sold to, and I'd been after him for months about getting me an interview. My job at the diocese had shifted to real estate sales, and I wanted to get back to space planning. The pure stuff. Venable was the only entity in the Tri-Cities that owned more property than the diocese, but their old-fashioned approach to space management was holding them back. They needed a space planner—they just didn't know it. I'd called Buddy again a few nights ago, and he'd told me to come out to the camp to talk it over.

I parked my Land Rover at the end of a line of pickups next to Buddy's Seville—white with a soft blue top, gold-spoked wheels, the green and gold Venable crest on the doors—and I walked toward the lake. Years ago, carting around my Monkees lunch box here at Camp Tekewitha, I'd lost my first tooth and planted my first kiss. I'd learned to hold my breath under water, crafted pot holders and Popsicle-stick art, graduated from T-ball to slow pitch, taken my first toke of pot.

There had been a stage partway up a grassy slope where we'd put on plays. Now, a contemporary with wrap-around decks was going up on the spot. A roofing crew slapped on shingles with air-staplers, and four men were popping in vinyl windows below. They'd thrown up the house in six weeks.

"You didn't believe it could be done," I heard in the distance. "Ye of little faith." Striding over the old Wiffle ball field, Buddy Jensen—gleaming white hard hat with the Venable crest—came at me. "You said we'd never get these homes up so fast."

Right away, I wondered what he wanted. Ever since I'd asked him to help get me on at Venable, he'd wanted more favors—a peek at properties the church hadn't listed yet, big escrow accounts for minor code violations, agreements to recalculate square footage, and, in the case of Immaculate Heart, endless stalls before closing. "How's it going, Buddy?" He'd dangled the interview for months.

"Good. Real good. You look good."

"When's the heat breaking?" I said.

"It's getting worse."

"It was never this hot when I was a kid. It rained sometimes is all." After a few minutes standing in the sun I'd sweat through my shirt. Sunlight glared off two construction trailers sitting on the level grade where the chapel used to be. "We can talk in my truck," I said. "In the AC."

"Let's take a walk instead. There's something you need to see."

I wiped my face with a sleeve. "How are you not sweating?" I said. He wore a crisp white polo shirt, blue Dockers, and the hard hat.

"I never sweat. Never have." His face was sallow. His wrists were thin. "How could we know each other so well and you don't know this fact about me?"

The truth is that Buddy had been good to me—he took me to lunch to talk career goals, put in a good word at the dealership when they balked at financing my Land Rover, arranged for Rita and me to get an incentive trip to Jamaica that was reserved for Venable brokers and agents, helped me prepare my tax returns (and saved me a bundle).

"I don't want to take a walk," I said. "I'm dying in this heat."

"In the shade," he said. "In the woods. It's cooler in there."

Sweat trickled down my chest.

"We need to talk about you and Venable," he said, and I relented.

The path circled the lake. A wide pine-needle-cushioned path in places, pinching between two trees, over a root or rock, then opening up to a Cadillac trail again. I'd walked it hundreds of times. There'd been picnic tables under the trees where we ate lunch.

"What do you suppose a matching Monkees lunch box and Thermos from around nineteen-seventy would be worth?"

"Oh," Buddy said. "All that stuff. You can't put a value."

"With pictures of the four guys, Davey Jones in the little sunglasses, and 'Monkees' spelled out in the shape of a guitar."

"Put it on eBay. There's punk-kid millionaires in Silicon Valley who'll pay anything to pretend they had this loot first time around."

"When the Beatles were breaking up, I went around camp with my lunch box telling everybody it was the Monkees who were breaking up."

"So it's in good shape? Collector's quality?"

"No idea. Haven't seen it since I was probably ten or twelve."

"So what are we talking about?"

"I'm just remembering."

Buddy was a half-step ahead of me. He stopped and turned. "Why'd you say that? I mean about the Monkees breaking up."

"I got it confused. I was a kid."

He resumed walking, more slowly now. "How's Rita?" he asked.

"Working hard. Good, though."

"You two doing good?"

"I count space, she sells time. Never a shortage of raw material." I'd said this before.

"Apartment good?"

Another favor from Buddy. Our rent hadn't gone up since Venable bought our building. "Good enough."

We passed lot markers—wooden stakes pounded into the ground with orange ribbons stapled to their tops. Buddy surveyed the lots as we walked.

"She probably works too much," I said.

"Stop here a minute, Quinn." We were a third of the way around the lake. "What do you see?"

The sound of air-staplers skimmed over the water. The lake had seemed so much bigger when I was a kid.

"Do you know what I see, Quinn? Backyards with grass and swing sets. Decks, cedar-shingled roofs, dogs sleeping in the sun. I see homes, families living the dream. Getting their slice. I don't see men saying, 'She works too hard.' I don't see a young couple living in—let's face it, Quinn—a ghetto. I see a couple snuggling on a hammock overlooking the lake, sirloin tips sizzling on the Weber."

He definitely wanted something. Most likely a property. A favor. Favorable terms. I said, "I see a beautiful natural setting morphing into a subdevelopment."

"You can't turn a city around without attracting quality business," he said, "and you can't attract quality business without custom homes. You need to envision, Quinn."

"I envision shoddy construction." There was a tiny island formation in the middle of the lake—three protruding rocks—just big enough for us, when we were campers, to bump up against in a rowboat and feel like we'd reached the edge of the world. Sunfish no bigger than our hands collected in the shallows between the rocks; with a hook and line and a pinch of bread we could snag one in minutes. I smelled the lake—the smell of summer, of fish slime on my hands. The smell of pinecones. "I envision lawn chemicals leeching into the water. Three-eyed fish."

"You should be seeing your life here," Buddy said. "You *always* say Rita's working too hard, that your job's not what you want, doesn't pay enough. That you need a move. Venable'll take a serious look at you when you're ready, but you're not ready yet. Trust me on that one. You don't know enough. Experience. You come on now, you'll get eaten alive. What aren't you getting from your job? Stability? Security? God, Quinn, you're in your mid-thirties, living in a crappy apartment with a woman you don't even talk to about marriage who'd rather stare at a computer screen than go to bed with you."

I couldn't believe I'd confided in Buddy. "Stick to the topic. When can I come on at Venable?"

"Dammit, Quinn. You're jumping the gun. That's the problem with young people. I want it now. MTV. Fast food."

"A minute ago I was rotting away in my mid-thirties."

"Why do you want to come on board now?"

"I'm thirty-five years old. I've got to—"

"Earn some security. Am I right? Some equity? A place to raise a family? Am I right? What would you say to point-seven-three acres in Lakeshore Estates with one hundred ninety feet of waterfront? What would you say to lot sixteen?" Buddy withdrew a contract folded in thirds from his breast pocket. "What would you say to twenty-five-hundred dollars?"

"It's worth ten times that."

"It's worth twenty times that."

"What do you want from me?"

"Don't be so suspicious. I'm in a position to help you and Rita get serious. Get to the next level."

I stared him down. "What do you want?"

He slapped me on the back. "Hey, listen," he said. "When's the lease up on Eighteen-Ten Hoosick Street?"

I had to think for a minute—Lilian at Li'l Tykes Day Care. He'd mentioned the property before; other than 1810, Venable owned the whole block. He obviously knew the lease was up next week. "It doesn't matter," I said. "It's not for sale."

"Not until you say it is."

"Stop it, Buddy. I can't add properties to the list. I give the bishop the data, and the list comes back to me. You know that."

"Vacant properties go on the list, don't they?" He bent over to read a number on a lot marker and noted it on his clipboard. "If the rent went up, they might have to move."

I shook my head. "I knew you were aggressive but . . . not a chance."

"You owe it to the Church to get what you can. The market sets prices, not you. You shouldn't be giving special deals to old girlfriends."

"Let's just cut this now." I looked over my shoulder into the woods, toward the distant rumble of heavy machinery. "I should go. And I need you to sign on Immaculate Heart. The bishop's really riding me."

"This is a beautiful lot," he said. "If you don't keep it, you could turn it over for a quick fifty K."

"It's not right, Buddy," I said. "It's wrong."

Buddy unfurled the contract with a snap. The diesel rumble grew louder. "We've signed. Do you have your checkbook?"

And suddenly the rumble was on top of us, like choppers appearing overhead in a Vietnam War movie. "Who do you think you are?" I said.

Trees were shaking, dropping leaves and needles. The ground vibrated. Buddy raised his voice: "Your best friend." He waved the contract at me.

Ripples echoed across the water. Buddy was smiling and nodding, looking up the incline through the woods. Over the crest, fifty feet back on lot sixteen, the blade of a Venable bulldozer rose into view tearing up small trees and rocks.

"Your easement," Buddy shouted over the noise, holding out the contract, but I didn't take it. Finally he shouted, "Over breakfast. We'll talk about your interview."

Neither one of us budged until he looked at his watch. "Ten-thirty. At the Miss Hudson." He shouted something else, thumping his finger on his clipboard and pointing down the trail, but I couldn't hear him.

The bulldozer stopped and raised its blade. Black smoke blew from its stack and it roared in reverse.

. . .

Traffic was oddly heavy on the drive back to town. This stretch of upstate New York two-lane highway felt more like Vermont—cows grazing in rutted pastures, old wooden houses with front porches toeing the road. It was a vast stretch of open country less than ten miles from the congestion, the housing projects, the failed urban renewal of downtown Hudson City.

Just past Arby's, traffic slowed to a crawl. I was stuck behind a minivan with a Christian fish on the bumper. The goddamned miracle. I punched the steering wheel and dialed Rita to get the latest, rolling past a locksmith and barber in a half-vacant commercial strip. The low-profile building was dwarfed by a billboard on its roof reading "I'M AVAILABLE" with a phone number.

Rita didn't like me to call during the day, interrupting her work. Voice mail picked up on the first ring. She was on-line. I thought she maybe did this on purpose—stayed on-line all day—so that I couldn't disturb her. "Hi, sweet cheeks," I said. "I'm stuck in traffic in the Heights if you can believe it." I was switching ears with the phone when the rear end of the minivan was suddenly right in my windshield. I slammed on the brakes and looked in my mirror, bracing against the seat. The car behind me screeched but stopped in time, the crucifix hanging from its rearview mirror slapping the windshield. The phone fell between my seat and the door, and I waved an apology through my rear window as I fished it out. The guy's dashboard, I could see now, was lined with statues of Mary. "Jesus," I said to the voice mail. "Damn pilgrims."

A few blocks later I came to the light in front of my own former elementary school. It was built just after the First World War, brick and bulky on a small hill rising up from Hoosick Street. Protruding from the front of the building was a bronze clock, enormous and ornately scrolled, topped with a bronze acorn the size of a basketball. The doorways were classical—Doric columns and pediments molded from concrete. Inside, the floors were chestnut, ceilings were twenty feet high. The teacher used a long pole with a brass hook at the end to open the windows. Venable bought the school five years ago, after it sat vacant for ten. The basement and ground floor became School House Market-Place—gift shops, a florist, two cafés, the Earring Tree. The second and third floors were high-priced apartments. The lawn was fenced in with iron rails; the playground was a parking lot.

The Catholic schools I was unloading had none of the character of the old public schools. They were all built between the Fifties and Seventies—single-level brick face, aluminum framing, beige and powder blue spandrel panels. Classrooms were stingy with low, sound-tiled ceilings. No view. No light. They were only good for mid-rent office complexes—insurance salesmen and bail bondsmen.

The light went green and the sluggish line of traffic lumbered ahead. I flipped on the radio, switched to AM, and hit Scan. A woman on a call-in show was saying, . . . *God did it, I believe it.* I was about to hit Scan again when the host cut in. *WTCR Skywatch: traffic is jammed. My advice if you're going out for lunch today is,* Do not. *Steal a co-worker's sandwich from the office fridge and sit tight. Stay tuned to WTCR for nonstop Miracle Mania.*

I was almost to Li'l Tykes Day Care now. I dialed Buddy's cell phone. "What bullshit," I said when he picked up.

"It's just bringing the rent in line with the market."

"No," I said. "The miracle. The city's being overrun."

"Overrun by what?"

"Where are you?"

"Lot nine," he said. "Seasonal stream, southern exposure, unique rocks—"

"And a wet basement."

"What's overrunning?" he asked.

"Catholics, I guess."

"Dammit," Buddy said. "Visions of the Virgin Mary are not the image we want for Hudson City."

"You can't bribe me. This is totally out of line."

"Catholics are *not* new economy."

"I'm calling to tell you that Lilian's getting a new lease in five minutes."

"As fast as I can I'm buying out the Catholic Church, but we'll never beat this stigma with pilgrims rolling in like gypsies."

I swung into a meter spot just beyond the day care. "Just so you know. In case you don't want to have breakfast. And with this traffic you're going to be late anyway."

"Okay, let's make it eleven o'clock," he said. "And I just had a conference call about you with the office. They gave me the okay to talk job prelims."

My foot was on the brake. I'd never shifted into Park. I wasn't sure I believed him, wasn't sure I could trust him anymore. "Don't make me wait." Then I nosed back into the line of traffic.

The Miss Hudson was an old stainless-steel trolley car diner. On the roof a huge dour cow head was flanked by the grill exhaust. The diner was squeezed between two brick warehouses. The one on the left had a shiny sign on its sheer brick wall: "For Lease. Venable"; the one on the right was ours. Buddy's car wasn't there.

I waited by the racks of Doublemint next to the cash register. The booths and counter stools were full, much busier than usual. "Hey, Joanie," I said when my favorite waitress went by, plates of eggs stepping up her arms.

"Can't you stop this, Monsignor?" which was what she called me. She dealt out the plates at the first booth then slapped my shoulder. "Should I thank you or the bishop for this?" She was filling coffees behind the counter before I could answer.

What had I gotten myself into with Buddy? The little favors we did each other had always seemed so innocent—there was never real money involved, never any cash. It had seemed like a well-oiled business relationship. Suddenly, there was 50K on the table and Lilian was getting the shaft. Suddenly, it was oily.

Buddy showed at eleven-thirty, and Joanie snagged us a booth, skimmed her cloth over the table, and clattered down cups and saucers. The smell of sour coffee and ammonia made me hungry.

The sooner I got on with Venable as a space planner, the sooner I'd be done selling to Buddy. I was sure he could get me in the door if he wanted to; then once within the company, I'd distance myself from him. I just had to proceed cautiously.

"I did some rethinking on the drive," Buddy said. "The zealots are not new economy, but they are new consumers."

"They're a new pain in my ass," I said. "And now you're a convert, too?"

"I didn't appreciate the numbers. There's potentially thousands of them. They gotta eat. They gotta sleep somewhere." Joanie leaned a hip into our table, pencil and pad ready. "They might want a drink, new shoes, jewelry, suntan lotion. Spending is spending."

"They're bad tippers who linger," she said.

"Think tax base," Buddy said. "Think big picture. Always big picture. I'll have the S&L."

The omelets were named for New York State scandals. "Nelson's Weak Heart," I said. She wrote it down as she walked away.

"Maybe now these Catholic fathers of our city will embrace Little Saigon as an asset," Buddy said.

"The mayor's a Protestant," I corrected.

"She doesn't run this city and you know it. It's the commissions—master planning, health and welfare, schools and parks—passed on father to son. This city's run by Catholic pot roast."

"You sound paranoid. Like Nixon."

"Can we please have a conversation without you bringing up Nixon? Once?"

This wasn't true. I only mentioned Nixon occasionally. I sipped my coffee.

"Whoever calls the shots," Buddy said with a sweep of his arm above the table, "he-she-it needs to spruce up Little Saigon, get some fine food in there for tourists. Americans don't like to see people squatting on the sidewalk with soup."

"But people want authenticity." We'd had this argument before. "Why do you think this diner is so popular? It's got history, it's got—"

"History's only worth something if it's renovated. Besides, tourists won't flock to Little Saigon for boiled vegetables and fish sauce no matter how authentic it is. French-Vietnamese is what people want. Maybe some dancing. Put the waitresses in *ao dai*."

"Think about the old mills," I said, "with twenty-inch beams. They're screaming out to be converted to lofts. Raw desirable space."

"Who's going to buy them?" Buddy said, and he was right. Venable was buying up Hudson City at fire sale prices, but most of their income came from rentals and complicated schemes to snag second-rate manufacturers with federal grants, state-insured loans, and local tax credits. There weren't many yuppies looking for lofts.

"There's architecture here that's been torn down most places," I said. "You admire a façade then step into a room with a plank floor and pressed-tin ceiling, and you feel good. You want to own the place, or work there. Authenticity sells."

"We've got twenty thousand of the most authentic Vietnamese this side of the Mekong Delta, and I don't see who's buying that. Look," he said. "You see that brown bagger." He pointed out the window to a man in a summer suit on the sidewalk. "You know who he is? Tri-City Cadillac money. Plus collar money. His granddad owned the collar mills where the new jail is. He's worth five million easy, but does he spend a little on a nice lunch? No." We watched the man cross the street. "I've taken him to lunch half a dozen times. Otherwise he eats egg salad on white bread that his wife puts in the fridge the night before. How do you keep good restaurants where this is the attitude? We need a paradigm shift." He shook his head. "Five million and he spends lunch hour checking out haircut prices."

Joanie set down our plates and filled our coffees. We dug in. "People are going to Van Rensselaer Arms and paying thirty-four ninety-five for surf and turf. Surf and turf, for Christ's sake! A rubbery frozen lobster tail and overcooked fatty sirloin. I swear there's no chef. The cook and dishwasher trade off." He pointed behind the counter at the grill. "This good man here is an artist by comparison. *He* can do magic with a couple eggs, ricotta, homemade sausage"—he stabbed at his omelet, ate a bite—"diced pepper and mushroom. You don't attract new-economy business to a city where people plod to the trough and pay thirty-four ninety-five for surf and turf, Snickers pie, and a watery cup of hazelnut decaf. Do you think there's a single restaurant in San Francisco serving surf and turf? They've got waitresses with pierced navels who talk seriously about the wine list and whether the Thai sauce is better on the ahi or the mahimahi. Van Rensselaer is a beautiful historic building. Authentic Dutch architecture. Fine. It was a brothel once and a bootlegger got shot there. Spectacular. But cook a goddamned meal!"

He filled his mouth with omelet then swallowed it with coffee. "And hotels," he went on. "The university has conferences, and people cross the river to stay in Albany. They go to Albany restaurants. They spend free time shopping in Albany stores. We need them to stay here. But at the Ramada? Gold shag carpeting, chrome chandeliers, flags of the world hanging over the reception desk. Flags of the goddamned world?! The Ramada's on par with the best hotel in Da Nang."

"Look," I said. "Authentic Seventies sells. You said so yourself about my Monkees lunch box. If they laid some fresh shag carpet in the Ramada and served fondue, the place would be a retro gold mine."

"I'm trying to make this city world-class, and you're thinking kitsch. Maybe you're not the right match for Venable."

I wondered if I'd been tricked. "No way, Buddy. I've got ideas for this city and ideas for Venable."

"I don't think you have the commitment. Deep in my bones I want to make Hudson City great again."

"So do I."

"Why do you still live here, Quinn? Why didn't you bail out? Someplace where you don't have to work so hard to scrape a living."

"I'm committed to this city."

"I have a standing offer at Coldwell Banker in Westchester County. Do you know the commissions I'd make down there?"

"This is where I was born," I said. Which it wasn't.

"I'd triple my income overnight. *That's* how you measure commitment, my friend."

"And Rita wants to stay."

"What for? Do you want this city to succeed like you want your children to succeed? Do you weep for this city, I shit you not, when it fails? You don't even *have* children. You probably want to stay near your parents. It's just easier to stay."

"You don't know about me and my parents."

"So you're here because you *resent* your parents. People act in lots of screwed up ways. You're not immune."

"Will you just twist some arms at Venable and convince them they could use a space planner? That's all I'm asking. You guys *need* me."

"Ha!" A smile broke over his face. He made a "come here" motion with both hands, meaning, *Tell me.*

"Fine." I wiped my mouth. "Looking at Venable's operation it's obvious . . ." I cleared my throat. "Okay. One example. Much of Venable's competitive advantage comes from the full range of disciplines you offer clients. Right?" Buddy looked out the window. "Full-service realtor, brokerage, acquisition, development, property management, finance." He showed no response. "But the Venable offices don't encourage business development across the disciplines. You and the other brokers are buying up properties and as you look at a building, I'll bet finance doesn't know what you're thinking. And that's what's holding Venable back."

"Nothing's holding Venable back. We own everything."

"But you could own it more. You could own it better. 'Cross-functional teaming,' Buddy. That's what it's called. Your company is very Eighties—separate silos of production won't make it in the next century."

He laughed. "Where do you dig up this crap? We take a cut of every real estate dollar that changes hands in the Tri-Cities. Those silos are stuffed with cash." Sliding out of the booth, he grabbed the check.

"I'd design the Venable headquarters like a series of interlocked rings that intersect at open teaming-collaborative areas with white boards, comfortable chairs, a cappuccino cart, water bubblers, a computer. . . . Then the development folks bump into the brokerage folks and—"

"You want to do a Martha Stewart on Venable? That's the great proposal?" He hung his hand on the coat hook at the end of the booth.

"They're called bump spaces."

He laughed and pulled out his wallet, turning to go.

"It's what the dot-coms are doing. Cyber cafés in the building to get programmers bumping into each other and exchanging ideas. You've got to be talking."

He turned back. "I like you, Quinn. You know that." Then he pulled the contract for lot sixteen from his pocket and dropped it on the table. "If you don't take your piece of the pie . . ." He was shaking his head. "And these ideas of yours—maybe they're fun. But we work in the trenches at Venable. Tough decisions, tough negotiations, and a deep belief in Hudson City. We're not talking 'let's decorate the office.' We're talking faith." He gave Joanie some cash and was gone.

I drank the last cold slug of coffee. As I pushed myself out of the booth, my tie skimmed a swipe of butter on the table. The table was too tight to the bench. Standing, I nearly caught my eye on the coat hook. Nothing was designed right.

I have *faith,* I thought, as I grabbed the contract and stepped out into the dense heat, heavy in my lungs. *Faith in the form and function of space; we shape space, and it shapes us right back.*

Traffic back to the office was horrible. I parked in our small lot next to the bishop's old Honda Civic, set The Club and the alarm. Heat radiated off the pavement and up the legs of my pants. As I passed the bishop's office window, I saw him standing there, staring out at the stop-and-go traffic on the street.

"Hellfires are burning," I said to Patsy, and was almost to my office when she called me back.

"He wants you."

The bishop didn't turn from the window. His arms were folded across his chest; his thick back stretched his shirt. As a kid he'd declined a football scholarship at Notre Dame, but now he looked more like a retired heavyweight boxer. "I expected you back hours ago."

"I had a meeting with Buddy Jensen from Venable."

"So you closed on Immaculate Heart," he said, finally turning around.

He hadn't phrased it as a question—more of an *expectation*; he waited—not for an answer but for the inevitable disappointment.

I didn't say anything. If he wanted to ask, he could ask. I got sucked into his Catholic trips too often.

But he stared me down until I looked away at the little bronze Jesus, the size of a lead soldier, hanging from a red oak cross on his desk.

Patsy's voice came over the intercom. "A call, Bishop O'Connor," and he looked away from me at the phone. Bless her. "It's Rome." I could hear the excitement in her voice as I backed toward the door. The bishop picked up the phone and pointed at me, then at the chair. I sat down.

"*Buona sera*, Cardinal. It's been too long." The receiver looked small in his big hand. He nodded as the cardinal spoke.

Over the bishop's shoulder, out the window, traffic was at a standstill. On the sidewalks people were all walking in the same direction—toward Little Saigon—pulling children in wagons loaded down with lawn chairs and coolers. It was a couple miles from here.

"I understand," the bishop said. "Certainly. This time tomorrow at the latest." He hung up.

I uncrossed my legs and slid up in the chair.

"I've just promised the cardinal we'll squash this thing. The millennium's got them stretched real thin with priests to investigate. They've got miracles all over the world. If it's real, it won't go away. But it's not real, and we need to send the crowds home before this goes any further." He popped a can of Diet Coke and took a long drink. "I'm not unrealistic. It'll take a couple days for the streets to clear, and we've had some heat strokes, so first I want you to go ahead and open up St. Mary's Middle School. It has to be done quietly, without arousing the sense that the diocese is endorsing this. And then, if pilgrims keep showing up, where are they going to spend the night?" He took another sip, staring at me.

"Are you asking me?"

"No, John. I'm asking the Oracle at Delphi."

Was it possible, I wondered as the bishop's hand clenched the edge of his desk, that he'd ever slug me? I ventured a guess. "Hotels?"

He took a deep breath and exhaled as he sat slowly back in his chair, dragging his fingertips, squeaking along the surface of his desk. "Son. I'll share a statistic with you: there are exactly eight hundred seventy hotel and motel rooms in Hudson City, with a capacity of roughly two thousand. Vacant? Roughly none."

"Extraordinary," I said. "All from the miracle thing?" No model could've predicted it. Supermarkets stocked forty percent more charcoal for July 4th; charcoal producers increased production as early as February to reach the bubble for shipping in early June. With a good model they can figure it to the briquette. But a miracle? I raised my eyebrows at the bishop. "It defies any reasonable expectations," I said.

As he often did, the bishop looked at me, had a few thoughts, and with a barely perceptible shake of his head, set them aside for later, for final judgment. "How many people could sleep in St. Mary's Middle School?"

"Well, do we put people in the halls? Does the fire department restrict us to legal room occupancy? Do we consider sanitation facilities?"

"Give me a number."

"It's a small school. Twenty-one thousand square feet, I think. About fifteen classrooms, half a dozen offices. If we allow eight feet by four feet for each person—"

"For the love of God—"

"Three hundred?"

The bishop gently punched his forehead.

"Four?"

"A drop in the bucket. We'll need—"

"Excuse me, men." Sister Rosemary was rapping on the door as she entered. She always looked exactly the same—never a wrinkle or spot on her gray habit. Her hair never seemed to grow or get cut. She was fifty-five years old, as healthy as a woman half her age. Day in and day out she looked like she belonged on the cover of *Redbook for Nuns.*

"The Red Cross can get us two thousand cots, blankets, and pillows," she told the bishop. "And they'll set up first-aid stations. They just need to know where." She set a plate with an apple, cored and quartered, on the bishop's desk, which he didn't acknowledge.

"John," he said. "You let them know by three o'clock."

Under her breath Rosemary muttered, "Thanks for the apple." She rolled her eyes. "Who'll say grace?"

Patsy's voice called again: "The mayor's office, Bishop." He picked up the phone. "Yes," he said, and folded his arms with the receiver pressed to his face.

Sister Rosemary sat on the edge of a straight-backed chair. She had the firm footing of the very devout that allowed her to toy with irreverence. I never knew for sure if she was being coy, confiding her skepticism, or testing mine. Once in the office kitchen, measuring out scoops of decaf from a five-pound Chock Full o' Nuts can, she put her lips to my ear and whispered, "I drink a cup of coffee every morning before receiving communion. Religiously." I didn't know if she was being heretical, naughty, or flirtatious.

She picked up the plate of apple and held it out to the bishop, but he ignored her. Then she offered it to me. I declined with a wave and a smile. She gave me one of her eye-piercing looks that could have meant anything (*Why are you involved in small-scale corruption with Buddy Jensen and church property?* or *Why don't you make a pass at me and we'll go nuts?* or *Why don't you want some apple?*), then she took a wedge herself and chomped it dramatically.

When the bishop finally spoke, his fist tightened around the receiver. "Young man. The church will do everything in our power to put a roof over the heads of these visitors to our diocese. We will expect the city, at the very least, to provide some security and crowd control, to provide water stations, and to haul away refuse. If the mayor has a problem with any of this, she may call me herself. I'm finished speaking with you." He slammed down the phone. "Weasel!" he said through clenched teeth.

"Bishop O'Connor!" Rosemary gasped, and winked at me.

"The Protestants are in control of this city!" He threw his arms up.

"No need to use such language." She really was cute, in a sassy, older-woman way. Truthfully, I found the virgin thing intriguing. She *had* to be curious.

"John," the bishop said. "Draw up a list of buildings we can open. Just the ones we can get into immediately."

"What about buildings with the services shut off?"

He gave me a blank stare.

"Water. Power."

"Take some responsibility, John. Make some decisions."

I closed my office door, tossed my suit coat over a chair, and opened my briefcase. The Li'l Tykes lease and the Lakeshore contract were on top. Shit. I really wanted a job with Venable. But I'd known Lilian since grade school. And it was a day care. I dialed Rita and voice mail picked up. "Call when you can," I said.

Despite what Buddy claimed about Hudson City being run by a Catholic pot roast, the bishop's fears were closer to the truth: the Irish Catholic grip on the city was slipping. Vietnamese and African Americans were winning district elections; there were three languages of instruction in the public schools. Although many of the newcomers were

Catholic, their social concerns weren't always in line with the Church's. As the Church slipped from the foreground, Venable surged into the vacuum on their way to proclaiming themselves the new Hudson City royalty.

I turned my rattling air-conditioner higher, then pulled some files and tried to work up a model: toilets and exits per square foot, degree of code compliance (safety versus nonsafety violations), relative proximity to St. Mary's. I felt a little of the old excitement. Every event needed a space planner.

Every company did too. If not for Venable, I didn't know who I could work for in Hudson City. Monticello was gone, and any other company would want the same thing as the diocese: inventory, then sell off to make a few bucks before bankruptcy. There was the prison or the government, but I'd give up on space planning before working for them. I could try to convince Rita to move, but I knew she'd resist. Besides, I think I really was a little committed to the city. No, I didn't weep when another local shoe store failed or when Wal-Mart gave us a cursory look then built across the river, but my memories were invested here, and right along with Hudson City my personal history had gone bankrupt. I wanted a little solvency—private and civic—before I moved on.

And I had to pay off my debt, which I wasn't doing in this job. The Land Rover was killing me. I'd consolidated my debt a few times so I really didn't know what I was paying for every month. But I'd never gotten ahead of the BMW payments, not to mention the car stereos, stolen twice. I thought of selling this damn Cartier watch every day (plus the one I bought for Rita that she never wore). I'd gotten us great US Open seats a few years in a row. A Soloflex. Weekends at Saratoga Springs and Lake George. After leaving Monticello, I tried to set up my own wood shop and bought all new machines—a nice one-and-a-half-horsepower table saw with extension wings, a 3-knife cutterhead jointer, and on and on, all of which I sold at a tremendous loss two years ago.

I started on an equation isolating numbers of rooms and available square footage per building, allotting what seemed like a generous thirty-two square feet per cot. I phoned the apartment again—*Sorry, I'm unavailable right now* . . . "Hey," I said at the beep. "I'm in the office."

I'd heard Rita's message thousands of times. She'd had to rerecord it once or twice for various reasons, but it had never changed from the years before I moved in. Not "we." Not "Rita and Quinn." The phone was in her name, and she paid it. I paid for groceries. We kept our vehicles separate. The computer was definitely hers. I never even used it. I bought the fans and controlled air flow. She wrote her name in her books and remembered who bought what: she'd say, "My blender. My VCR. Your stereo." And six years after I'd moved in, she still said, "My apartment." Buddy was right: we weren't moving to the next level.

If I had a job with Venable and chipped away at my debt, I could buy a nice lot like the one on the lake. With some financing I could build something small—a cottage that could later become Rita's office. If I started providing the space, maybe things would balance out between Rita and me.

But working for the Church I could never afford it—I didn't have the down payment, and with my debt I'd never get a loan. I swiveled my chair around so the AC blew in my face. I'd known Lilian my whole life. We went to P.S. 19 together. Between fifth and seventh grades, I must've kissed her hundreds of times. We played spin the bottle with our after-school gang in Mike Malone's parents' garage. Lilian kissed the softest.

The summer before ninth grade, by the blue water tower that sits like a spacecraft on the highest hill in Hudson City, Lilian and I and a few other kids smoked a joint. I went to take a leak in some weedy trees, and when I came back out into the sun, the others were gone—all but Lilian—and a moment later we were lying on the ground, making out. It was hot and muggy, our skin sticky. My eyes were closed, but I remember the pissy smell of humidity in the weeds as I reached my hand under her tapestry skirt, along her thigh, and our tongues darted faster and her breathing deepened until I fingered her: her breath caught in her throat as if, from inside her, she'd been bit.

I yanked my hand away. For a moment we looked into each other's eyes, and then she hugged me. With her kinky hair hot against my face, I started counting pull tabs and bottle caps scattered on the ground, and chips of green glass. I noticed a flattened Marlboro pack with condensation beneath the cellophane. She hugged me in a way that seemed at the time very mature and womanly, as if she was offering forgiveness, or asking for it.

I opened the file on St. Joseph's School, empty now for five years. I'd tried to sell it to Buddy, but he wouldn't touch it. I wondered about bathrooms. If there were five hundred people to twenty toilets and each person went six times a day for an average of three minutes . . . Was I giving favorable treatment to Lilian? The Heights *was* one neighborhood where real estate had appreciated in Hudson City. I shook my head—*No way*—and went to the workroom for coffee.

A man in a dark suit was standing with his back to me, his hand on the photocopier, talking to Sister Rosemary. "Mr. Quinn," she said as I approached, and I knew she was up to something. "May I introduce you to Mr. Miller?"

He turned and I shook his hand. He was in his early twenties.

"Mr. Miller tells me," she said, touching my arm, "that he's sure our copier probably gets the job done. Do you think, Mr. Quinn, that our copier gets the job done?"

The poor guy. I lifted the pot of coffee to my nose and sniffed.

"But Mr. Miller says our copier is like Kmart, whereas if we get a Xerox copier from him, it will be like Brooks Brothers. He said we need to ask ourselves whether we want to be Kmart or Brooks Brothers. Isn't that right, Mr. Miller?"

"Yes, ma'am." He nodded. "Sister."

"It involves some real soul-searching," she said.

The coffee was burnt, but I poured a cup anyway.

"Mr. Quinn," she said. "Would you rather be Kmart or Brooks Brothers?"

"Banana Republic," I suggested.

"Ah, ha," she said. "Does Xerox have something in Banana Republic?"

The salesman nodded. "You could think of most of our copiers as Banana Republic."

"The bishop is a big golfer, so he might be interested in more of a collating Arnold Palmer Collection," she said. "As for me—" She held her arms out at her sides. She wore a gray dress with a white short-sleeved blouse underneath, a wooden cross on a wood bead necklace, white tights, and well-worn navy flats. I always suspected that those blue shoes—not black—were the expression of her wild side. "I buy my clothes through a clerical catalogue. I'm sure you don't have a copier in *that.*"

"Not exactly."

"Well, this is what we'll do. If Brooks Brothers is what you recommend, let's draw up the papers for Xerox to donate one to the diocese."

"Actually, ma'am—"

"No, don't say a word. You're right. Kmart doesn't reflect the diocese's image."

"I understand, but—"

"Please, Mr. Miller. You've convinced us, and we're not offended." She took him by the arm and led him into her office like a boy she was scolding.

I drank the old coffee, and for the next several hours worked on finding the pilgrims a place to sleep. By four o'clock I had a preliminary list on the bishop's desk. "I've still got to rank each property for availability and whether the services are turned on. There's also issues of traffic flow. Plus liability."

"That's fine, John," he said.

"How'd it go with the miracle girl?"

He ignored my question. "When can you have the lists final?"

"An hour," I said. "By five."

"We'll have the armory for tonight. The Red Cross is setting up cots right now. Much better really because the diocese isn't involved. But we'll be stretched there, and if this doesn't let up, we'll need another building."

"Is it getting worse? I mean, are there more of them?"

He didn't look up. "Thank you, John."

In the foyer I asked Patsy about the miracle girl.

"She didn't come," Patsy said. "She refused."

Just after six, I put my lists on the bishop's desk. It sounded like he was on the phone with the mayor. Patsy had already left. I got out quick before he could call me back.

When I pushed through the glass doors—the art deco awning and cross over my head—throngs of pedestrians stopped to stare at me. A few waved; a few made the sign of the cross. I waved back, and I thought I heard a tiny roar rise up from the crowd.

I started my truck and blasted the AC. Buddy was never at his office so I called him there. I wanted to get it over with. "Buddy," I said to his voice mail. "No go on Eighteen-Ten Hoosick. It's not the right thing. Don't take it personally, but I couldn't force her out. We've made some good deals, but this would have left a bad taste. So we'll need to close on Immaculate Heart by the end of the week. And let's get together so I can explain my ideas for Venable more clearly. What's essential is that Venable capitalize on its—" The voice mail cut me off.

Traffic crawled through downtown, past entirely vacant blocks. It killed me to think of the money waiting to be made in Hudson City. Venable was buying, but they sat on too many properties—inventory inefficiency. I had ideas for pumping up the demand side of the equation: just as the city didn't take advantage of potential tourism in Little Saigon, the university was resented as a hulking tax-exempt gorilla. But these were high-tech graduates, the same talent Buddy wanted to attract from Seattle, Boston, and San Francisco, and they were already here. The problem was that they left every spring after graduation. For very little investment, public and private, the vast raw space in lofts, warehouses, old mills, and brownstones could be made so attractive to start-up dot-coms, that the talent would be compelled to stay.

The ten-minute drive home took half an hour. There was no parking, so I pulled onto the sidewalk and tossed the clergy permit on my dash. Our apartment overlooked Burden Park, an entire block of grass and trees, enclosed by a wrought-iron fence. The gate was locked, and only the residents in the surrounding buildings had keys. I'd heard that Gramercy Park and this one were the last of these arrangements remaining in the state. It was no surprise that Venable was methodically buying up the buildings with access—accumulating keys.

I unlocked our apartment door. The TV was turned toward Rita's office. She was sitting at her computer. "Just a sec," she called. "Let me get off-line."

The Channel 6 Action Team was live on Broadway in Little Saigon. In the top left corner of the screen, a box showed a live shot of the miracle girl's building—the front door and the upstairs windows, curtains drawn. On the main screen they were interviewing a pilgrim.

Rita came out of her office. "Hey," she said.

I looked up from the TV to her back as she disappeared into the kitchen. The freezer door squeaked. "Do you want something to drink?" she shouted.

"It's a return to a more spiritual time," a woman in a Miracle Mania T-shirt told a reporter. Ice cubes clunked into one of our tall plastic cups. "Greed and materialism have had their day." The woman paused, looking blankly into the camera, bright lights on her oily face, then she turned toward the reporter, asking him, "Do you know if the pope is coming?"

"I'll just have a sip of yours," I called to Rita.

I dropped my briefcase and draped my suit coat over the couch, then I turned from the TV and stood at my puzzle. Sometimes my unconscious worked to fit a piece while I was away. I'd go days without anything, then I'd come back to the puzzle and see in an instant that I'd been looking at it wrong. I leaned over the table and tried a few combinations.

"Did you hear what that priest said?" Rita asked me, then she kissed me on the cheek.

"What priest?"

She pulled me by the waist into her soft body and kissed me on the lips, her mouth cool and fresh with ice water. "He confirmed what David Newman said about the girl's visions. He said he thinks they might be real."

"Floquet? Oh, no. Who'd he say that to?"

"I don't know. The cameras. The news."

"Frank's going to kill him." I laughed and gulped her water.

"He said he was speaking for himself. Not the Church."

"He's still a goner."

"Well, there's a lot more people coming to town. Your miracle's getting a little bit famous." She kissed me once more and pulled away, handing me her cup, then sat on the floor in the bay window—her yoga space.

"Poor Frank." And then I realized he'd want buildings opened immediately. "Shit. My days just got fuller." I glanced at the puzzle and thought I had a fit, but it didn't go.

Rita was sitting cross-legged, rolling her neck to loosen up. She took deep breaths and blew out hard. "There's fruit salad." She closed her eyes.

The bowl was shoved in the fridge at an angle, half propped on some cheese even though there was room on the shelf below. I sliced in another banana and dumped some yogurt on top. Standing at the dining room table, I looked over my puzzle as I ate. Rita extended her legs nearly to a split, and stretched her body forward.

I'd always loved jigsaw puzzles. The process was straightforward and thorough, working pieces over and over, a definite right and wrong, fit or no fit. And that rush when the last twenty or thirty pieces clicked into place was satisfying like nothing else—one hundred percent perfectly complete. It was the same part of me that loved a lawn well mowed with the minimum number of passes.

I moved around to the end of the table, considering another corner. My fork dinged on the glass bowl, and Rita said, "Do you think you could—"

"Sorry." I backed off to the overstuffed chair. The TV was showing the Greyhound station: crammed buses spilling out passengers.

I turned sideways in the chair toward Rita. I didn't mind giving her some room for yoga. I loved watching her practice. She collapsed forward and took hold of a foot with both hands. She had big sturdy feet, strong calves and thighs. If not for her fine delicate ankles, Rita probably could have been a jock. She was tall—five-eight—with broad sloped shoulders, cleavage that made me weak-kneed, a cinched waist, hips like an easy chair, strong tapering legs. I sometimes marveled that she didn't fall over. Rita's figure was old-fashioned—like Elizabeth Taylor in *Butterfield 8*. "A little *more* old-fashioned," she'd say. "Like Reubens." But it wasn't true.

She stood and slowly arched into a back bend, her hands reaching to the floor. The arch of Rita planted firmly in front of the bay window was magnificent. She seemed to radiate toward the ceiling.

I speared the last piece of fruit as Rita moved into the Warrior pose: feet planted wide, arms stretched front and back. With her breath she drove energy out her fingertips, her shoulders, the top of her head, and once again I saw it happen: Rita expanded, she stretched beyond the limits of her body. She'd told me there are seven chakras in the body, power centers drawn on in yoga. But the chakra that interests me most is outside the body, above the head. That's the one I see Rita reaching toward, expanding out to.

These were the things I loved about Rita's yoga practice—the relationship of her body to space, and to itself, the shapes she made, the secret nooks she could open up inside her. She'd used props through the years—blocks, ropes, bolsters—all designed to let her occupy the world in different ways.

I'd never mentioned this to her, but I didn't actually buy into the rest, the whole karma thing. She said when she practiced she felt connected to all living things, and since we're all connected by this life force, her good deeds enriched everyone including herself, and her bad deeds circled back to bite her on the butt. To me, karma and the life force seemed like *Star Trek*'s take on Catholic guilt.

As she finished, she curled into herself on the floor below the windowsill, a tiny ball that had taken claim to the three great windows rising to our ten-foot ceilings. And what came next was the moment I looked forward to each evening, the moment I could count on: she rose with the big cup of water, took a deep breath, and she came to me. The rest of her day—work, errands, and worries—had fallen away, and the essential Rita, open and available, settled down onto my lap.

Her skin glistened with sweat. She was warm right through, like she'd come from the bath. Pliable and fluid. She kissed me long and slow, then she polished off the water.

"Want some more?" I massaged her thigh, then her calf, and noticed a thin gold ring on her second toe. "What's that?"

She stretched out her toes and wiggled them. "Do you like it?" she said brightly. She kissed my forehead, then laid her face against mine. Sweat darkened her green T-shirt below her throat. She didn't wait for my answer. "So I've been thinking about something," she said. "I want to tell you about it."

I tried to kiss her neck, then put my lips to her ear and whispered, "How about we make love first and you tell me later?"

"Really," she said. "Listen."

I brushed my lips over her cheek.

"I'm thinking about converting," she said, pushing back.

"Rita. We haven't made love for sixteen days."

"C'mon. This is important to me."

I exhaled. "Converting what?"

"Converting *to*," she said. "Judaism."

At first I thought it was a joke, but she was deadly serious. I sighed, too dramatically. "Your foreplay's getting kinky," I said.

"Forget it."

"It's just sort of a buzz-kill."

"Then never mind."

"'The garbage disposal is clogged.' You could've said that. *That* would have been flirtatious."

"See?" she said.

"Or, 'There's a dead rat in our bed.'"

"See? You don't respect anybody's spirituality. Not even mine."

See? What did she mean, *See?* As if this was an ongoing conversation. "What do you mean, your spirituality?"

She glared at me.

I backpedaled. "That's not what I meant. I just mean you have to convert *from* something *to* Judaism. Otherwise you're not really *converting*. You're *becoming*."

"What do you think I'm converting from?"

I gave it a shot. "Episcopalian?"

"Presbyterian."

"Whatever—Rita," I called to her back as she slipped away to her office and swung the door shut. "I know they're different. I do."

But I was lying. What did I know about the Protestants? Episcopalians and Presbyterians had more money than Congregationalists and Methodists. Lutherans were frugal, Baptists had great music. Most of the rest were fundamentalists and not to be trusted. What they all had in common was that they resented the Catholics. Fair enough.

I knocked on her office door, leaning into the door frame. "Really," I said. "They're totally different. I know that." I opened her door enough to poke my head inside.

"I'm working." Her hair twisted and danced from the window fan. A rose light shone from the computer screen onto her face.

"Why are you doing this?" I asked.

She clicked her mouse and looked up. "You really are a Catholic boy," she said, calmly. "You think you're not, and that makes it worse. You work for them. You've got the hots for that nun. The bishop's your best friend, and in a few years you'll be one of those sanctimonious pasty men wearing a cheap blazer and toupee, shoving the money basket under people's noses at Mass."

I touched my very slightly receding hairline.

"And," she went on, "you think sex is all you and I need?" She shook her head. "Sex doesn't replace real meaning in a life."

I'd learned not to take Rita's caustic edge too harshly. She'd let this stuff rip without any idea what it sounded like. "*Shalom*," I said, and shut the door.

My suit pants were damp, so I hung them over a chair in the bedroom. The back of my shirt, my underwear and socks were soaked. I spread them out on the floor knowing that in this humidity they wouldn't dry. My towel had been wet for days.

I pulled on a pair of gym shorts and went out through the kitchen to the ratty back hall—washer and dryer, winter boots, Raid, a dead Power Mac. My hand tools filled the shelves, and the black walnut slats I'd shaped and dovetailed for Rita's back-bending bench were stacked in one corner. I took two slats, a scraper, and some sandpaper out the back door, and I sat on the small stoop.

I scraped the blade burns from the slats with long strokes, then sanded. This stoop was the kind of thing Buddy did. There'd been a rusted set of wrought-iron steps here until I sold Venable a former residence for nuns who had worked at the asylum. The next morning a Venable pickup pulled up at eight a.m. with three guys; by ten they were gone, and we had a new pressure-treated stoop.

Sanding dust stuck to my skin, making me hotter, but I didn't mind. I was building something for Rita. The sides were ash with cherry inlay. It would be a beautiful piece of furniture, the shape of a scroll. Rita could lie over it to stretch and open up her body. She'd do shoulder stands, the Plow pose, side stretches. All on wood I'd cut and fit to the shape of her body.

How was it possible that someone like Buddy didn't appreciate good space planning? You only had to look at Rita's back-bending bench or an ergonomic chair to understand how we shape space so that space can shape us. Everything else followed.

The night began to cool enough that I knew we'd sleep. In the bathroom I pulled off my shorts and stepped into the cool spray. The grime of the day, the patina of sawdust, the frustrations and disappointments rinsed from me and swirled gray around my feet.

I came into the bedroom naked and stood in front of the fan. There was a smell, a little harsh, and when I lifted my arm to my nose, I realized it was coming off me—mildew from my towel.

Rita was in bed, reading Jane Austen by her mother's old cut-glass lamp. She'd been burning through Austen after rereading *Portrait of a Lady* and some of the Brontës. I'd tried reading *Mansfield Park* a few weeks before—to share that part of her life—but she seemed to resent it, as if I was spying on her. I was always trying to share in Rita's life, and instead of inviting me along, as soon as I got a foothold, she leaped to something new. Now she was going to be Jewish.

The fan on my moist skin cooled me to a chill. It felt great. I lay next to Rita and touched my palm to her hip. "Cold!" she yelped and pulled away; she rolled toward her side of the bed without emerging from the English parlor where an invitation to a ball was hanging in the air.

I picked up *Fine Woodworking* and read the bar-clamp survey. Bottom line: you want tighter threads, more clamping surface, and it's worth trading light weight for more rigidity. Rita turned a page. Something we both knew but never openly acknowledged was that Rita was smarter than me. At least book smart. I could probably make more money in real estate, but when it came to seeing connections between feminism, Reagan, and Kerouac, Rita was all over it. She didn't understand, or *respect* is maybe the better word, my interest (which she called obsession) in Nixon's resignation speech. *What's the context?* she'd ask. *What are the implications?*

"So anyway," I finally said.

"Just let me finish this chapter."

After majoring in English in college, she'd planned on grad school—a Ph.D. in English Lit. She'd wanted to live in New York City, so she applied only to Columbia but didn't get in. She went to the city anyway, and through a friend got a job selling air time for WNEW. She lived in an apartment on East 5th Street with two other women. Everyone she knew was making money on Wall Street by day, and spending it in clubs by night. The next winter, grad school application deadlines slipped by, so she spent another year working and having fun. She slept with four men, as she recalled, and in the spring she had (of infinitely more interest and titillation to me) a four-month affair with a woman. She hung out in cafés, ate meals out, did a little coke, saw good movies.

The following fall she was beginning to dig back into grad school applications when her father was killed. He was on the street in West Hudson City around ten p.m. and was shot in the chest by a mugger. The gun was a Saturday night special, so weak the bullet barely penetrated his heart. But he lay on the sidewalk and bled for hours before help arrived. Rita came up from the city and sat with her mother by his hospital bed for over a month before he died. A few days after he was shot, the police told Rita's mother what her husband was doing in West Hudson City at ten o'clock at night: He was visiting a woman he'd been having an affair with for the past ten years.

The month-long vigil was terribly hard on Rita's mother. She watched her husband beneath the tubes and mask as his condition deteriorated, and she was deteriorating too, from the inside out. The greatest challenge of Rita's life was trying to summon the strength to be supportive to both her parents and to maintain herself.

Her sister and brother flew in for several days in the beginning, then returned for the funeral. So mostly it fell on Rita. Two weeks after the funeral she went back to New York and a very understanding boss. Three days later, her mother had a heart attack and died. Rita quit her job and moved back into her parents' house in Hudson City, the house she grew up in.

With her New York references, she had no trouble getting a job at WTRI. Within a month she'd sold the house and rented the apartment where we now lay in the hot breeze blowing from the window fan.

She closed the book and rolled onto her back, looking up at the ceiling. I met Rita a year after her mother died and moved in with her a year after that. I think she stayed in Hudson City because she couldn't stand the thought that her family could be erased from her hometown in six short weeks. She stayed to show—show who? I don't know, only herself, I suppose—that although her father's betrayal might have killed her parents, the shame would not force Rita's retreat.

"You know that Bible in your mother's house?" she finally said. "The one with the beautiful red leather cover and gold-edged pages, with ribbons to mark your place?"

I nodded.

"And you told me that when you were a kid, the Bible always sat in the corner of the living room on that antique reading stand with a little lamp beside it so you could read a passage while you're standing there? And there's a few programs shoved inside, weddings, funerals, your first communion. But your whole life you've never known anyone to actually read from it?"

She waited for me to nod again.

"Judaism is a way of life. It's part of every action, every thought, every day. That's what I'm looking for."

"But we *have* a way of life. You and me. Us. Watching you do yoga is all the spirituality I need."

She looked at me doubtfully. "I've always felt connected to Judaism. When I went to bat mitzvahs or shabbat with friends, I felt at home in those big noisy families."

"Is that what this is about?" I touched her arm. "Your family is gone, Rita."

"Don't say that." She shook her head. "I have my brother and sister, nieces and nephews."

"Becoming Jewish won't magically bring you all to the same *shtetl* dancing with chairs on your shoulders. And families are just another institution. Believe me, I know. Another letdown."

"If you don't have any faith, everything's a letdown."

"Put your faith in me."

"I'm talking about building a life around centuries of tradition—"

"We can start our own traditions."

But she wasn't listening. "It's more than that, Quinn. It's about being connected to beliefs older and bigger than your own existence. I think that's how life broadens and deepens. I don't know. With more possibility, I guess."

I can't say how much all this surprised me, or was news to me, but I did know that Rita meant it, or at least believed she meant it. Her eyes filled with tears as if she were finally confessing a secret, allowing us to move on.

I rolled onto my side, and she rolled into me. Her body was hot, but her skin, in the wind of the fan, was smooth and dry. My own skin was already getting sticky again from sweat. I stroked the back of her T-shirt, and up over the heart-stopping rise of her hip. She lifted her face to me and her lips were on fire. Her tongue pushed slow and easy.

She dropped her head and I kissed her hair. Her breathing deepened. She curled in tighter to me, her elbows tucked in close to her sides. My fingers moved over her butt, down her thighs, up her back. I was excited, my leg reaching over hers, but I couldn't get a handhold. Rita curled up even tighter, her face in my chest, and although I wanted to believe she was being responsive, she was mostly just there, covered up—the rope-a-dope of foreplay.

She took a deep breath at my chest then pulled back her head. She scrunched up her nose. "You're mildewing."

2. TUESDAY

At the office in the morning, Sister Rosemary was arguing with Frank. "I'm not going down there and throwing a wet blanket over their fun," she said. "With all due respect, Bishop, you're on your own."

"I'm only asking you to drive—"

"Drive yourself. Crowds make me nervous. It's too hot for this. If we have any poorly attended winter miracles, you can look me up." She headed to her office.

I gave the bishop a quick good-morning nod, then followed her, but Patsy called me back. "Quinn, you had a message from Buddy Jensen." She was watering her potted ivy. "He said he needs a c.o. to close on Immaculate Heart."

I could feel the bishop standing behind me in his office doorway. Ivy crept out from the porcelain drinking fountain set knee high in the dull green wall tiles. Patsy pinched off a brown leaf. "He said it's got to be reinspected and you better give him a buzz right away."

Head down, I took two steps toward my office, and the bishop called, "I'll need you at ten o'clock, John. We'll drive over there together."

I turned halfway around. "I've got a busy day already—"

"Indeed. Ten o'clock."

I pushed back my morning appointments then went to the workroom for coffee. Rosemary tugged on a sheet of paper rolling out of the fax machine.

"Going for the hat trick?" I said. She'd already busted two fax machines yanking the paper like that.

"Every one we buy is slower than the last."

"*Calma,*" I said, imitating the bishop's Italian expressions.

"Shut up-a." She swatted at me. "Toll booths are jammed at all the Hudson City exits. The pilgrims are on a blitz. I don't have time to wait for a fax." Her voice tweaked up a notch, cheeks flushed; a wisp of fine hair had fallen in her face.

"Sister Rosemary is losing her cool," I announced.

She scowled. The machine whined as she forced out the final inch of paper. I reached behind her for my coffee mug on the pegs. I could smell her bath powder. Or was it Secret or Caress? I lingered at her shoulder—her usual scent sharpened with excitement.

The fax was from the Chamber of Commerce, urging the bishop to keep the miracle going for at least a few more days. It went on about the potential infusion of funds. Hotels, restaurants, taxis, markets, drugstores—"every sector of the economy."

"The mayor was in Frank's office before seven this morning," Rosemary said.

"And?" I asked, pouring myself some coffee.

"And I truly dislike her clothes."

Sipping the coffee I rolled my fingers through the air, meaning *fast-forward,* so Rosemary caught me up: Last night, just in time for the late news, the miracle girl had heard the voice again. In her apartment window, Timothy Floquet stood with her for the cameras, then he came down to the street alone to report that this time she remembered what the voice had said. "Faith in our times."

And Floquet didn't show for his morning meeting with Frank. Frank had sent another priest to fetch him, but Floquet wouldn't come. Frank was irate. "I'm going to the source," he'd told Rosemary, meaning the miracle girl, "and getting the truth. Floquet will have a few years making jam in a monastery to think this over."

The mayor and her cronies welcomed the crowds, of course. The costs of corraling them were nothing compared with the money they spent. Hotels were booked; bed taxes had never poured in so fast; everybody was getting on the news. And people seemed to like that the miracle girl kept popping up in their dreams.

"The cardinal," Rosemary continued, "is of another opinion." He'd demanded that Frank bring it all to an end immediately, but cars and buses had been arriving all night. "The thing is," Rosemary stopped and looked at me, "none of us believes it's real. Most of all Frank. But it's got its own momentum now. I'm really not sure what he'll do."

"Why don't you chauffeur, and you can advise him?"

She pursed her lips. "I admire the bishop very much—he's such a rock. I don't like seeing him unsure of himself. I *won't* see it." She pinched the fax. Another wisp of hair fell in her face.

I grabbed the keys for the properties I'd be showing in the afternoon and the keys for Immaculate Heart, knowing that in the end Buddy would win out and I'd have to meet the inspector so he could walk through the old church again.

I was standing by Patsy's desk at ten o'clock when Frank came out of his office. "Bishop O'Connor!" she exclaimed. "You look very holy." He'd changed from his work clothes into one of the fancy black suits he bought on a trip to Rome. He wore his red rabat, ecclesiastical ring, and his silver filigreed crucifix inset with an amethyst.

Patsy sneaked a glimpse at the cross around her own neck, which I suspected was more about gothic fashion than Jesus Christ. But hers didn't come close. "You look awesome," she said. "It gives me goose bumps."

"Thank you, Patsy," he said. Then to me: "We'll use the back door."

We never used the back door. The poor guy. I followed him through the workroom, past the bathroom, then down a dark hallway cluttered with brooms and mop buckets, and out into the blinding sun.

Across the parking lot, my shining Land Rover dwarfed the bishop's battered Honda Civic. "Let's take your Jeep," Frank said.

I popped the locks with my remote, then stopped and looked: my Land Rover was white with safari windows up in the extended roof; as the bishop climbed in, heavy chain and crucifix clanking, and sat up tall in the seat, my truck could not have looked more like the pope-mobile.

When I hopped up behind the wheel, he was holding my clergy parking permit. Shit.

"John, you're a young man. How old are you?"

"Thirty-five."

"Not so young. In this world, you either live the good life, or you don't. There is no such thing as a little cheating, a little lying." He put the permit on the dash. "I'll leave this here and we'll use it today. Then you can decide what to do with it."

I pulled down the tight alley to the street. "Sorry," I said, but he didn't seem to hear me.

I took a right and adjusted the AC vents to blow in our faces. The Community Bank sign read 92 degrees. "Brutal," I said. No response from Frank.

Just past the Hudson City Pork Store, traffic stopped in front of the Grande Theater. Seeing "For Rent or Sale" spelled out on the great marquee always brought me down. Homeless people slept on the gold-glitter tile behind the ticket booth. Shopping carts overflowing with sleeping bags were parked in the darkness. In elementary school I'd seen all the great Disney movies here: *The World's Greatest Athlete* and *The Snowball*

Express. Willie Wonka and the Chocolate Factory played here for months. In junior high it was *Death Race 2000* and biker movies. And by the early Eighties, the Grande was a porno theater.

I rolled onto River Street, past the off-track betting parlor. As I inched the pope-mobile along, bumper to bumper, one man recognized the bishop, shoulders were tapped, faces lifted, and then there was an eruption of joyous waving that seemed to contain—and I think the bishop sensed it too—a touch of mockery.

"What is it they want, John? How do we serve these people? How do we bring them back?"

"I just handle the real estate," I said.

"People want the big show, is that it? They put all their hopes into the big win at OTB. Lotto tickets. Atlantic City. And they want their faith in the Lord rewarded with visions and miracles. But people need to understand that the Lord rewards us with thousands of miracles every day." As he spoke, he raised his hand and nodded his head to the men and women on the sidewalk. His face was serene. "My actions today might very well be the most important of my life in the clergy."

"I hope we're done by lunch," I said. At the light I turned onto Broadway, which was moving a little better, but still packed. Pedestrian traffic was picking up too. "I told DiAngio I'd show him the Resurrection High annex at twelve-thirty."

"One part of me hates to be the one to rain on all this hope. Father Timothy has worked hard to bring that parish together. The pews are packed. His first communions, confirmations, and weddings have grown in the last three years. And he's done it all himself. We've got him at one end, building a parish, and you at the other end, selling off the foundation of this diocese."

I wasn't sure how to take that. At times I felt that to the bishop I was the son he never had, and at other times I was a necessary evil, the merchant he'd expel from his temple if he wasn't so aware of the bottom line. Maybe my presence reminded him that while Christ did some really reckless things with the greater good in mind, the bishop was a little too afraid of Caesar's tax collectors. He was a practical man in a spiritual business.

"What I have to do today will run counter to all our efforts at growing this diocese. I've got to tell thousands of believing Catholics to go home. I've got to tell Father Timothy and his congregation that they haven't been singled out by God. Then I'm going to reprimand the little prick."

"What about the miracle girl?"

"Well, she . . . she's either an opportunist, a blasphemer, or psychotic. I've got to figure out which. Then, I'll decide how to handle her."

We finally reached the police barricade at the corner of Broadway and Cork—two cops, two cruisers, and a couple of blue sawhorses, beyond which it looked like a moderately attended street fair. I stopped, and when one of the cops saw the bishop beside me, he approached us. I opened my window and hot air rushed in. "Draw aside the gates, please," the bishop said. "Church business."

The cop smirked. "I don't think I can do that, sir."

I pressed back into my seat. Maybe cops make everybody nervous—but I think it's worse with someone who shoplifted a few more Blow Pops and Wacky Packages than is considered average for a third grader, stole beers too often from parents' fridges, and bought cigarettes from vending machines when I still had to reach up to the coin slot. The cop glared at me, and I shifted into Reverse.

"Young man," the bishop said. "I have neither the time nor inclination to haggle. Pull aside these gates or else one phone call to Chief Melrose will put you on parking-meter detail for the next two years." The bishop slapped my dashboard, and the cop retreated to his cruiser. I put it in Park.

The bishop wasn't a drinker as far as I knew, but he still had fine blue veins spidering his cheeks and the knob of his nose. And despite his afternoons on the golf course, his skin was Irish white. But at the moment the very young cop picked up his radio and turned his back on us, Bishop O'Connor's face turned as red as the rabat on his chest. I closed my window and turned the AC up a notch. Pilgrims were surrounding my truck: a family of blond-topped, corn-fed fire plugs, the father wearing a Pope Tour '84 T-shirt; a gray-haired woman with a rosary hanging from her crooked fingers, making the sign of the cross outside the bishop's window; a Hispanic man in his twenties, a cap reading *Jesús es mi amigo número uno,* eating falafel and nodding respectfully.

Frank lowered his window and reached out his arm with a raised palm. There was a rush at the truck, and I hit the power locks. In response to a gesture from Frank that we all understood (as if we'd learned it in confirmation class), the pilgrims moved like worker ants and carried the police barricade aside.

"Okay, John," he said calmly.

I pointed meekly at the cop. "Bishop, I—"

"*Now,* John."

I rolled ahead, and after a few feet we had escorts on each side—excited pilgrims slapping my truck, ordering people out of our path. We didn't get far before I heard the cop's PA: *"Stop immediately."*

I hit the brakes.

"Drive," the bishop ordered. I inched ahead.

"Halt your vehicle!"

I stopped.

"John!"

My window was rolled up. Through the glass, everyone froze, waiting for what I'd do. In the rearview mirror I saw the cop striding toward us. I put my hand on the shifter to push it into Park. It must be in our DNA by now that when faced with conflicting orders, we obey the guy with the gun.

The bishop was gripping my shoulder. "This is my *life,* John." He was pleading. "For the love of God—for *me*—do not let that officer stop us." He truly cared, I realized—far beyond carrying out the cardinal's orders. And I felt a little bad that I didn't. I didn't care at all.

But Frank's powerful hand clutching my shoulder aroused compassion from somewhere in me. I shifted to Drive, and as we rolled ahead, I saw the cop throwing up his arms, the crowd filling in behind us. I lowered my window and reached out; the crowd stroked me; a *Tri-City Times* photographer snapped a picture. The next day's front-page photo caption read: "As frenzied pilgrims hold back police, driver John Quinn topples barricade, ushering Bishop Frank O'Connor to the Miracle Girl."

A TV news camera was on us. Any thought the cop had of forcing me and the bishop to turn around ended right there. The dark eye of the camera peered at me, the crowds were ecstatic—reaching inside to pat me—*pet* me really—and I knew I'd done the right thing.

"Please close your window, John."

A lovely woman, maybe nineteen or twenty, with ringlets of blond hair and wide blue eyes that appeared ready to follow the next cult leader, kissed my hand.

"Please, John."

Or she was the cult's recruiter, bewitching me. Not so beautiful to be intimidating, but a woman who'd make you feel the presence of something larger than yourself.

"This is not about us," Frank said, snapping me out of my reverie. "This is the Lord's work. We're just the middle managers, responsible for the hiring and firing, budgeting, marketing, public relations. We work for Him—not for our egos. Please close the window."

I did as he asked. The TV camera pulled back, and so did the pilgrims. The girl crossed herself and blew me a kiss. We idled for a minute in front of Eddie's Lunch, where a grill on the sidewalk chuffed greasy smoke from burgers and dogs, then we crossed over Asylum Avenue onto the stretch of Broadway referred to, disparagingly I suppose, as the Ho Chi Minh Trail. It was the heart of Little Saigon. The area had been Irish Catholic until the early Sixties, when the Irish moved to the Heights and the new split-levels east of the city. For fifteen or twenty years the area was mostly black and mostly poor. After the war, a few Vietnamese moved in, and in 1987 Hudson City became a processing center for a new wave of Vietnamese immigrants, and Little Saigon rapidly grew.

People standing in the street moved aside as the bishop and I rolled ahead. Sitting on short stools in front of the dozens of soup stalls were big-boned white Americans with fanny packs hitched at their waists and video cameras slung from their shoulders. They could have just as easily been sitting at Disney World eating hot dogs, but here they were in Hudson City, propping bowls of steaming *pho* under their chins and scooping noodles from the soup with chopsticks in their fists. Latin Americans, African Americans—every kind of American sat side by side with the Vietnamese Americans slurping the endless vats of soup, all waiting for the next healing and the next message from the miracle girl. Seeing the bishop in my Land Rover, they jumped to their feet, kneeled, waved, made the sign of the cross with a combination of reverence, solemnity, and sheer thrill in the passion of the moment.

"They love you," I told the bishop.

"It's what I represent."

As the crowd in the street got thicker and I started riding the brake, my cell phone rang.

"Quinn, my friend." It was Buddy Jensen.

I switched the phone to my left ear, farther from the bishop.

"You're on live TV, Quinn. Look out your window."

I looked.

"That's it," Buddy said. "Yep."

I stared into the camera.

"It disappoints me," he said, "to hear about that property we discussed."

I decided to go on the offensive. "What's this BS about Immaculate Heart?" My voice lowered to impress the bishop. "I told you I want to close PDQ."

"I'd hate to jeopardize our pending agreement on that Lakeshore lot."

"You had time to reinspect. Good faith requires that you close immediately."

"Some free advice," Buddy said. "If you don't look out for yourself—"

"The bishop has been extremely patient, Mr. Jensen." I gave Frank a knowing nod.

"What would Rita think about you giving up a romantic house on the lake?"

"I'm afraid that's right. We'll offer the property to other buyers if Venable can't close by week's end."

"I thought we were friends."

"Oh?" I said.

"I thought friends helped each other out."

"Yes," I said. "The miracle has touched us all."

There was a pause. Buddy had relented.

"You're smiling," he said.

I glanced at the camera.

"I've helped you with so many things, Quinn. I remember helping you out with your taxes. In fact, on my desk in front of me I have a copy of your '97 return. Because I prepared this return I happen to know of twenty-seven instances of negligence, underreporting, and fraud. I'm not an expert when it comes to penalties, but I'd say you're looking at roughly twenty K in back taxes and interest, forty in fines, and somewhere between six months and five years in prison depending on . . . well, it doesn't look good, Quinn . . . greed off the back of the Church. Widows and orphans and decrepit old priests. They'll throw the book at you."

"That's impossible," my voice squeaked.

"You paid zero dollars in federal income tax. You knew it was too good to be real."

He'd said I could carry back my net operating and passive income losses from '87 and '92 to reclaim taxes I'd already paid, and forward against future income. He'd dragged his feet getting the returns done, and on the morning of April 15 when I went by his office to pick them up, they still weren't ready. I signed the return before he'd even finished. He'd had this moment planned since then.

"C'mon," Buddy said. "Where's that smile. You're on TV. Puff out the chest. This is your fifteen minutes."

I flipped the AC to max and turned another vent toward my face. "I'm glad you see it my way, Mr. Jensen. I'll let the bishop know that Venable will close on Immaculate Heart by Friday noon. Good day." I clicked off.

As if Buddy were controlling the TV camera, it moved in closer, and I blocked my face with my hand. Like a defendant.

"Everything's straightened out," I told the bishop, thinking I might vomit.

But Frank wasn't even listening. "When MacArthur tried to sort out Japan after the war, he recognized the power of the Japanese people's devotion to their emperor, an emperor who was believed by his people to be God."

Buddy wouldn't do it. He was bluffing.

"Instead of squashing that fierce devotion, he shifted its focus to economic industry and nationalism." The bishop waved absently at the well-wishers through the glass. "For fifty years the Japanese have lived and breathed that devotion to their employers and their nation. It's what made them strong. Some of the older people resent that they were misled by the emperor, and they've become cynical. But on the whole, it's been a great success."

Goddamned Buddy Jensen.

"That's precisely the sort of transformation," the bishop went on, "that I need to orchestrate. Look at these people. They've come to witness this event, their hearts and souls full of love for our Lord Jesus and his holy mother. That love, that spirit of joy for God, should not be fouled just because the catalyst is not genuine."

My first thought wasn't the audit, the fines, or even prison. My first thought was Rita. She had plenty of faults, but she never cut corners morally. "Put your faith in me," I'd told her last night. Shit. She'd never see me the same again.

Suddenly we were on the block of St. Mary's and the home of the miracle girl. From inside the cool truck, I could see the crowd packed in tighter around the miracle girl's building. Sweaty men had towels around their necks like boxers, wiping their faces. Children's skin was shiny and flushed. White women fanned themselves with magazines and folded handkerchiefs. Asian and Hispanic women used fans decorated with images of the Virgin, edged with lace.

"Take it slow," the bishop said, though I was barely rolling. "If you run someone down in the process . . ."

Two men around my age—a chunky redhead with a mustache and weightlifter's biceps, and a skinny Vietnamese who ordered people around like he was from the neighborhood—began escorting us through the crowd, point men, each resting a proprietary hand on my hood over the headlights. "Step aside!" they shouted, and the crowds parted. "The bishop has arrived." Heads turned to me behind the wheel, registering blank faces, then their eyes darted to the bishop—sudden recognition and reverence—and the crowd unzipped, opening in a wedge before us, closing in behind. Then, there it was—779 Broadway. I think I'd expected a podium in front of the building and a red velvet curtain at the door, women in veils with gaudy rings on pudgy fingers.

But it was just a concrete stoop, chipped at the edges, a wood-frame row house with asbestos siding and a beige steel door. The stoop was heaped with bouquets, cones of flowers in Shop-Rite and Grand Union wrappings, surrounded by dozens of tiny statues of saints and dashboard Virgin Marys set here with the hope, I figured, that they'd turn to gold. A cop was standing there eating a hot dog.

Until now there was nothing official about the miracles. They were reported in the press, hyped over the web, and responded to by relatively local believers. Other than Floquet, there wasn't a single acknowledgment by the Church. But now, as the bishop and I watched the growing excitement on the pilgrims' faces, children held high, cameras snapping, rosaries working, foreheads, lips, and hearts getting crossed, I understood that far from throwing a wet blanket over the proceedings, the bishop's presence was confirmation that the miracles were real, that the Virgin *had* spoken to the young woman inside this house.

I shut off the engine. Out of habit I reached for The Club, but thought better of it. When I opened my door, heat rushed in. I stood up high on the running board to see over the crowd. I was blown kisses. I was cheered for. My garments were touched. Who didn't dream about being Jim Morrison? It strikes me, even now, that there would be something wrong with someone who didn't get off on a moment of celebrity. There'd be something un-American.

As I raised my arm to wave, it was like a city-sized volume control—an explosion of cheers. A TV camera squeezed through. People looked at me, looked at the camera, then back at me. Pleased. Joyful. Ecstatic. It was another sign of the miracles' credibility. TV was here. I was sweating.

"John." It was the bishop. I leaned down to see him inside my truck. "Enough."

"I can't help it," I said.

"Don't make this more difficult."

"Enraptured," I said flatly.

"John—" He pointed a finger at me. I'm pretty sure he was about to use one of his rarely employed expletives (*Don't F with me* or *Absolute dog crap*) when a camera poked under my arm. His pointed finger transformed into the "okay" sign that Jesus makes in paintings. He forced himself to hold his gaze on me and not glance at the camera. He began to speak, but nodded instead. Then he opened his door.

I got down from the truck and waded through the pressing crowd—moist, hot bodies. A sweaty arm dragged across the back of my hand. I'd just had this suit cleaned.

Again, a path was cleared through a couple dozen people, mostly the old and infirm, propped on walkers and wooden crutches. There were two children in electric wheelchairs, their exhausted and hopeful mothers standing over them. In the midst of the heat, a dry, cool hand clutched my wrist. Shaking like nothing I'd ever seen, an old woman said, mostly air, "Bless you, son."

I led Frank up the stoop and turned around. Everyone backed away, bowing from the waist, giving him space. A few women rushed forward and kneeled beside him, kissing his hand. And he let it all happen. Frank O'Connor: the tough Irishman who followed boxing and Formula One racing, who stormed into the office on Mondays furious if he lost twenty bucks on the golf course to Monsignor Capello or Ben Hanson, the owner of seven Ace Hardware franchises. Frank O'Connor was a guy who took secret pride in cracking walnuts with his bare hands, who let it be known he could swing a hammer, snake out his own clogged pipes, put a tight spiral on a football for forty yards—he paused to let the kneeling pilgrims kiss his fingers and ecclesiastical ring.

He backed up the stoop, bestowing *Bless you*s and *God be with you*s. A baby was thrust forward and he kissed the top of its head.

"Enough, John," he said, and I looked at him like, *I'm just standing here*. Then he reached for the doorbell, and a wave of silence rolled over the crowd. I nodded in the direction of the street and turned with the bishop to face the steel door. We waited. The crowd was quiet enough that I could hear the TV camera whirring in closer behind us. I could hear babies crying, the metal creak of walkers, the strange humming of a child in a wheelchair.

We waited some more. "Why don't you ring again," I said.

"Have some faith, John."

"Maybe they didn't hear."

"I heard it myself."

We waited a minute or two, thousands of eyes looking at us hopefully.

The bishop pressed the bell again. I could sense the crowd behind us growing impatient. Then a cry rang out in Vietnamese. I turned and saw a boy, no older than eight or nine, calling toward the building. A first-floor window shot up. A head popped out, scrutinized the bishop and me. The window slammed shut, then after a moment the door swung open.

We shuffled through the tight entryway. I could see into the woman's apartment. The blinds were lowered, incense burned on a Buddhist altar, and the TV beside it was playing a commercial in Vietnamese for Venable.

She pointed to the stairs, then stepped back wordlessly and shut her door.

The hallway was dark, oily smelling. I followed the bishop, his feet pounding more heavily, more resolutely, as our eyes adjusted to the dim light on the second-floor landing.

"Do you think she can turn my car keys into gold?"

"I'll take it from here, John."

"That was intense. All those people."

"You can wait in the Jeep."

"You gotta admit it was intense."

He stopped in front of the apartment door and straightened his suit coat.

"I've never seen so many people," I said.

"I know you're curious, but it's inappropriate."

"Extremely intense."

He knocked on the door, and it opened immediately. I looked over his shoulder, past the woman who was standing with her hand on the knob. "We're pleased you've come, Bishop O'Connor. Welcome. I'm honored to meet you."

"How do you do," he said.

"I'm Kim Phong, Sue's mother. Please. Come in."

Behind her I could see the miracle girl, her back to me, at the kitchen counter. She looked tall. Lean and hipless. She wore leather flip-flops, a red skirt that wrapped tightly around her butt, a white sleeveless blouse. Her hair mushroomed out of a colorful silk scarf tied around her head. Oil-black hair in tight curls. She didn't turn around. She laid slices of tomato on bread and spread on mayonnaise.

"Thank you," the bishop said, stepping into the apartment. The woman held the door for me. On the far wall, on a shelf above the table and toaster, there were statues of the Virgin and St. Francis. A large colorful picture of Jesus holding his own heart was framed behind glass. A rosary dangled from the shelf—blue-and-rose-colored beads, silver links, and a crucifix that appeared to be gold.

The kitchen was in dire need of remodeling. The enameled steel countertops were dinged—black spots bled through like bruises. The glass doors on the cupboards didn't close right. Thick mullions separated the panes. Paint was splattered on the glass. I wondered if Venable owned the building.

Metal chairs with vinyl cushions surrounded the kitchen table. There was a warm sweet smell, like brownies baking.

"Thank you, Mr. Quinn," the bishop said, and as I turned to look at him, he closed the door in my face.

I stood alone in the dim hallway. Muffled through the asbestos siding, mildewed sheathing, and brittle tar paper came the din of the crowd waiting in the street for the next words from the woman standing in this depressing kitchen making a sandwich. For a moment I sat on the top stair, but that seemed equally depressing. My phone was in the car. Nothing to read in my pockets. Inefficiency defined. What prison must feel like.

I went out the front door. The sun hit me directly and I felt immensely hotter. The wave of silence spread again and the faces of thousands looked to me for the latest word. I stood on the stoop, my hand clutching the two-by-four rail peeling with paint and deep cracked splinters.

Victory parades in World War Two documentaries always filled my eyes with tears—Allied troops kissed by French girls on the Champs-Élysées, ticker tape floating twenty stories in the air over crowded streets in New York. And people are jubilant, packed together, singular in their purpose, the same spark of hopefulness in their hearts.

And that's what these people seemed to be feeling here. Kids on shoulders, families in windows, signs held aloft sending blessings to the miracle girl, warning of doom, praising God.

"What did she say?" someone yelled to me. Then someone else. "What's her message?" My first impulse was to make a joke: *Chew your food* or *I blame society*. But I glanced at the woman closest to me—her child's wheelchair looked like a mini-gurney, his head supported with black vinyl pads. She was hot and tired, her hair pulled back, no makeup.

She was no older than I was. And as she fanned her child, she was smiling. What was she doing smiling?

As deluded as the girl upstairs might be, there were too many hopes in these streets to treat recklessly. Jerry Garcia never said anything from stage for fear someone would interpret it to mean *Blow up a federal building* or *Commit mass suicide*. I felt for that moment that my words would have the punch of Jerry's, the ripple effect of Alan Greenspan's.

And then I wondered what I *could* say, what I *would* say. What message did *I* have for the crowd? Nixon would have looked straight at the cameras and lied: "The miracle girl has asked you all, along with the IRS, to forgive me . . . for my thoughts and my words, for what I have done and what I'm about to do."

Had Buddy forced my hand? Was driving Lilian out and selling him the building my only option?

Suddenly I noticed a commotion surrounding my truck. Then, as if it were a note on a silver tray sealed with the king's wax, my phone, ringing "Feelin' Groovy," was passed to me. The TV cameras, thousands of faces, waited for me to answer. I clicked it on. "What are you thinking about, Quinn?" Buddy. Of course.

I turned toward the building, covering my ear, pretending it was so I could hear, but really it was so no one could hear me. I tried to go back inside, but the steel door was locked. "Nixon," I hissed into the phone. "You asshole. The resignation speech. Humiliation. Justification."

"It's not polite to turn your back on a crowd."

"I watched it on a dying TV when I was eleven, drinking chocolate milk that tasted too sweet. It's my first political memory."

"Like where were you when JFK . . . et cetera?"

"I got sick. Turned out it was sour."

"November twenty-second, 'sixty-three," he said. "I was in a civics class at the old Hudson City High. Sophomore year. Big deal."

Did he remember that November 22 was my birthday? "This thing about the IRS, Buddy. Let's not do that."

"Congress can override a presidential veto with a two-thirds vote.

So I remember that day's topic. So what? It's nothing to make myths about."

"We can work something out," I said.

"I remember a banging radiator in the classroom and the medicinal smell of steam, like the taste of iron."

"Something amenable."

"I remember the hollowed-out shock in the hallways, like a punch in the stomach. Nobody knew what to do—the la-la-la life-is-a-picnic generation. I remember we reacted like we thought we were supposed to react. We were just kids, acting like adults. But very soon the acting becomes genuine."

"Okay. So it's settled?"

"And I remember distinctly when everyone started crying. The salty smell of snot on your tongue in a poorly ventilated building packed with people all crying over the same thing. Slippery on the tongue, like okra. Do you eat enough okra, Quinn? Delicious and overlooked by us Yanks. Loaded with . . ." I could hear him sucking his tongue as if he were tasting it. "Loaded. But all this is meaningless. My memory of that day. I remember lots of days. I remember the day my mother weaned me from a bottle. I remember the day I finally fucked Dina Perkins. Easter Sunday, nineteen sixty-five. Sunny and the grass was so wet it made slurping noises under her butt. Big deal. We remember things. It's not anything to explain history about."

"We'll talk."

"Just do it," he said. "It's win-win." Then he hung up.

I turned around. The camera was poking at me. The first notes of "Feelin' Groovy" dinged from my phone and I switched the power off.

The crowd was staring. What did they expect? Did they think the call was from God? I mean, really. They didn't even know who I was, and they were looking to me for the words that would change their lives. These were people who proclaimed the depth of their spirituality on

T-shirts, bumper stickers, placards, some of them with tattoos for God's sake, yet they were standing in heat that would give a camel a stroke waiting for the next word from . . . from *me*. A tax cheat. Absolute dog crap.

I went down the steps. With nods and smiles that were losing sincerity, I made my way through the old people, the cripples, and the front-row zealots to the leather interior of my Land Rover. I was exhausted by the heat. I dialed Rita at home and left a message. "I'm on TV, sweet cheeks. Check me out." How would I ever tell her?

After forty days and nights the bishop emerged. The crowd roared then cut silent. But he didn't pause at the stoop to make a statement as they'd hoped. He got in, and I started the engine. He said nothing, so I just drove. People peered in the windows disappointed, miffed even, that the bishop hadn't relayed the latest wire from heaven.

"You're letting down your fans," I said, but he didn't reply.

Another moment passed. "Nice chat?" I tried.

He just waved through the glass, nodding, his lips moving soundlessly.

"They gave you some of those brownies, I bet. Iced lemonade. I'm broiling in the streets and you're having come-up-for-a-frosty-one." I said it in an elbow-in-the-ribs way trying to break through, but the placidity remained on his face, the hand kept rising, head dipping. He looked more and more like a healthy John Paul.

Back at Eddie's Lunch, WHCR, the rock-and-roll station, was setting up a remote broadcast booth—banners, satellite dishes, speakers. Rita had an offer from HCR when WTRI went right-wing, but she believed in striking out solo, grabbing her own piece of the pie. Probably a mistake.

"So is she a real basket case?" Suddenly everyone I saw was sucking on green and orange water bottles—every man, woman, child, every grandma in a wheelchair, every nun, every baby in a stroller—identical green and orange plastic bottles with thick bendy straws poking through the lids. Then I saw the Gatorade truck, a refrigerated tractor trailer, and chilled drinks being tossed out to the pilgrims as fast as they could catch them.

At the barricade I had a moment of panic, but the cop never even looked at us. Sucking on his Gatorade bottle, he dragged the sawhorse aside.

"Drive up through Rockefeller Park, John," the bishop finally said. His voice was butter in the sun.

I took a left and started up the hill. Traffic was moving. Frank relaxed back into the seat. "Is there something specific? I have a million things to do today . . ."

He loosened his collar.

"Bishop?"

"Rockefeller Park. Specifically."

"I've got quite a few appointments. Our Lady of—"

He scowled.

Huge stone gates stood at the entrance to Rockefeller Park, carved with a coat of arms and a nearly Soviet realist celebration of industry—smokestacks, locomotives, and bridges.

"Let me paint you a picture," Frank began. "A simple tidy kitchen. The smell of fresh baked brownies. An old dish drainer stacked with aluminum pots, mismatched plates and utensils. The enameled steel counters we had when I was a boy. My grandmother swore by them. There's a lip all the way around," he was gesturing, smoothing his hands over an imaginary counter, "so you could rinse them down with bleach and boiling water. When Formica came in, she never believed counters were clean. She'd always lay out a paper towel before she'd set down an apple or even the knife to cut it. Around the kitchen, a few icons, St. Catherine of Siena, the Virgin Mother, Our Lady of La Vang. The fridge is an old Westinghouse with a rounded top. Open shelves are stacked with boxes and cans, bright Asian labels.

"She turns around, and there's a young woman the likes of no one I've ever seen. At first I think it's all in her eyes. And I can't keep from staring at her left eyebrow. It's true. The shape of the sound hole in a violin. Elegant and lovely.

"She wipes her hands on a tea towel and takes a few strides toward me, one arm extended, and I expect a weak little submissive handshake"—the bishop looked at his knobby knuckles—"but her long fingers reach right up around my wrist, and she shakes like we have some business to do. I say, 'Good morning,' and she smiles. Then she lays her left hand over the top of mine. My hands are an embarrassment," he said, still gazing at them.

"Her mother says to please sit, and iced tea is poured and we all get comfortable. I'm letting the silence build a little, letting some trust and ease settle in, letting the importance of this meeting pressurize a bit before I'm going to open with something that I now realize is completely patronizing—*Tell me a little about what you've been going through*—and then Sue starts signing to her mother. 'Sue welcomes you, and she has some concerns. She says, "I don't know what's going on. Over the last weeks I've feared I was losing my mind. I don't feel that way right now, and it's not as important as these thousands of people in the streets. What can be done? We've had no success with the police. I'd thought Father Timothy was trying to help, but he's made things worse. It's not right. These people are out there waiting for me to speak, waiting to be healed. I don't know what's happening to me. I don't know why people are dreaming about me. And all those old people and children in wheelchairs."' Then she pauses, resting her hands one on top of the other on the table."

Frank paused too, as I parked in a turnout—a stone parapet tagged with spray paint. We overlooked the dry lawns sloping with Olmsted's initial vision—the sparse mature trees, the wading pool and fountain, and the vast development of the Tri-Cities below. I was always amazed when I saw this view that it didn't look much different from photos taken from hilltops over the Tri-Cities one hundred years ago—the dour Hudson River flanked by hunkered-down brick and stone, spiked with steeples and the soaring double bell towers of the cathedral. I thought of my lunch meetings, then I thought of Buddy and the IRS, and a feeling like urban blight spread through me.

"I asked her about herself, her own history, what has led her to this place at this time. Her work, her lapsed faith. For quite a while she shaped her hands into speech, tapped her lips and chest. She told me about the visions, about the physical experience. It's astounding. It's . . ." Frank drifted off, silent for a few moments before clearing his throat and speaking again. "I told her I'd already taken steps with the Red Cross and the city. I told her I'd take care of things." He fiddled with the seat controls until he managed to recline a few inches.

When he was silent for a full minute, I jumped in, hoping to get on with my day. "We'd better get back to the grind. Floquet still needs that paddling."

He gazed out the windshield. "You know, my grandmother lost her faith when she lost her husband," he said, "and she never got either one back. When I told her I was going to the seminary, she slapped my face. If you called her a Christian, she'd spit on the ground. Still, in her dignity, conviction, and compassion, in her humanity, she was one of the most spiritual people I've known. And this girl today . . . everything about her was like my grandmother. I mention this, John, because your faith is lapsed for foolish reasons. You'll rediscover it one day. But with my grandmother, and I sense with this girl, too . . . it's as if they found something else. Another way to God."

Driving against the stream I made it to Li'l Tykes by five-thirty and parked on Hoosick Street just a block away. As I walked by a storefront, my reflection in the glass looked thinner and more gangly than I imagined myself. I dropped my shoulders and gripped my briefcase more firmly, compressing into a beefier man. Filling the space I occupied. Owning it.

Inside, the air smelled sweet, an insidious sweetness—smell of overactive bodies, runny noses, and damp pants. Lilian waved to me across the carpeted room. She looked older than she had a few months ago. She'd been divorced for eight years, twice as long as she'd been married, and she was getting thinner, her kinky red hair going frizzy. She was an attractive woman for sure, but she seemed so much older than I was.

"How goes it?" I said, switching my briefcase to my left hand, her long cool fingers squeezing my right.

"Insane as always," she said. "End of the day. They're ready to go home. How are . . . Zach, let's not do that," she said calmly over my shoulder. "We don't bite the piano." She flipped hair off her face. There was still no ring on her finger. The hair fell back where it had been.

Two children appeared at my feet. One tapped a yellow plastic hammer on the toe of my shoe, the other worked a green screwdriver on my laces. "Owen, Charlie," Lilian said. "Leave Mr. Quinn's shoes alone."

"We're fixing them," one of the boys insisted.

"They're all fixed," she said. "Good job. Why don't you go fix the play table?"

They pulled themselves up by fistfuls of my suit pants and stumbled away like apes with tools.

"Have a seat," she told me and dropped down to a tiny molded plastic chair. Her knees angled up as high as her shoulders.

I laid my briefcase flat on the low table and squeezed myself into a chair. My suit jacket rode up my back like football pads. My shirt collar cut into my throat.

I clicked open my briefcase and Lilian asked about Rita.

"Fine," I told her. "Her work's going well."

"Getting married one of these days?" I'd forgotten how Lilian would pin me down with personal questions. And she was genuinely interested in the responses. Which seemed admirable.

I looked away. "Or something," I said.

"Something?"

I looked back at her and she was staring at me expectantly. In my fingers, I held the lease, the rent line blank. I looked away again. "I hope so," I said, then added quickly, "How's your daughter?"

"She loves junior high. Now she wants a skateboard. I can't believe it. Her boyfriend taught her to ride one."

"Boyfriend?"

"Incredible, isn't it?"

It *was* incredible. A skater daughter with a boyfriend. I thought about spin the bottle and wondered if Lilian might be thinking the same.

"I always liked Rita," she said. "In that yoga class we were in . . . she seemed real solid. Like her spirit . . ." Lilian moved her hands over an imaginary shape in front of her. "Her spirit was right there."

"How about your own life?"

She laughed. "No time for that. The day care and Jasmine are all I can manage. I *was* seeing this . . ." She slowly twirled her arms around each other. ". . . you know . . . *guy* for a while in the spring . . ." She turned her head, pressed a cheek into her shoulder. "But it fizzled." Her contorted posture and the light around her eyes—she suddenly looked ten years younger.

I thought of my college girlfriend and the two others who followed her. I might have married any of them and had my own kids in junior high.

"Listen," I tried to start in. "There's been some movement in the market—"

"But the big question," Lilian continued. "What's up with the miracle girl?"

"She's Amerasian. She's thirty," I said, relieved to change the subject.

"But what are they saying in the Church? The priests and the bishop."

"Just that there's plenty of things doctors can't explain that aren't necessarily miracles."

She touched my knee across the table. "But is it real?"

I couldn't hold her gaze. I clicked my pen and held it over the rent line.

"Has this truly happened?" She really meant it. "Here in Hudson City?"

"I'll have to get back to you on that." But it sounded flip, so I added, "I'll let you know whatever I hear. I will." Then I wrote, "$1500/month." A fifty-percent increase.

She was silent. She'd twisted her legs around each other. She looked into my eyes and finally I looked back. My breath caught: it was as if her face was inches from mine, sweat from her lips salty on my tongue, and in her eyes the same look from that summer day under the water tower. Like she knew something.

Across the tiny table she hugged her knees. "I just hope the miracles are real." She laughed. "That's my main emotion these days."

"That they're real?"

"Hope," she said.

I looked across the room at the kids. One boy was sorting blocks by color: three neat stacks of red, blue, and green. The favors from Buddy had seemed so innocent, what everybody did. But here was the real me: a tax cheat, forcing Lilian out to save my ass. "I can't do it."

"Can't do what?" she said.

I hadn't realized I'd said it aloud. "Nothing." I covered. "I messed up this lease. I'll drop by with another." I had to think it through.

But she wasn't concerned with the lease. "Maybe it's because I'm in here with these kids all day, but when I look out at the rest of the world there seems to be a lack of . . ." She rose slowly, her attention already shifted back to the children. "I don't know," she said. "There's a lack."

Rita had a dinner with one of her accounts—Tri-City Mattress, *the soundest thing in sleep*—so I'd planned to stop by my mother's. She and my stepfather, Charles, lived in Belleview on the north side. The houses were built in the Fifties and Sixties. *Leave It to Beaver* houses, brick-face colonials, and early contemporaries. With cramped bedrooms, wall-to-wall, ostentatious and unusable front doors, they were much easier to sell if the kitchen was remodeled. I counted four "Offered by Venable" signs on my mother's street.

There was nothing more to think about. I took a fresh lease from my briefcase and filled it out for Lilian. $1000/month. Her rent wouldn't change. I would not turn into Buddy.

My mother was waiting at the front door. "So what? What's the word? We saw you on TV. What did she say?"

The central air was cranked and she was dressed without regard for the blistering weather—her white apron with pink frills over a tropical wool blue suit, white blouse with ruffles at the collar. I'd never known my mother not to look put together. She'd gone to the hairdresser every Thursday at ten ever since she'd married Charles. She bought her clothes at Saks. She was always pressed and spotless.

"I didn't talk to her," I said. "The bishop wanted a private audience."

"So what did *he* say she said?"

"She really didn't say much, Mom. It was more like a business meeting."

"Charles," she called, pulling me by the wrist into the living room. "He's here. A *business meeting*, he says."

"Hi, Charles. How goes it in the trenches?"

He set his book on his lap. "Battle of Cambrai. Ninety-five thousand lost on the two sides. Many froze to death at their posts." He sipped a glass of beer.

"I want it verbatim," my mother said. A muted corsage was pinned to her blazer—pink and yellow somethings. (I've never known the names of flowers.) She was always going to luncheon banquets honoring decrepit Republicans who were about to die with their money.

"Get you a drink?" Charles asked.

"Beer'd be nice."

"We saw you go in there on TV," my mother said. "Don't tell me you didn't go in there."

Charles tucked a leather bookmark between his pages and rose.

"G and T, dearest," my mother requested with a tap to his arm.

He wore a seersucker jacket, white shirt, bow tie, and khakis with a crease. Whether or not he was leaving the house, he put on a coat and tie every morning. My mother married Charles the year I began high school, 1977, and since that day I'm not sure I've seen him in anything other than the Brooks Brothers suits and blazers he owned when he worked in the Nixon administration.

This jacket I always noticed in particular because of the video I own of Nixon's final press conference. The camera moves around the audience packed into the East Room of the White House, and about halfway back near the side, there's Charles in the seersucker jacket, laughing as people laugh at anecdotes in eulogies, then he's weeping, then he's holding his face in his hands.

"So she opens the door," my mother prompted me, "invites you in. A lot of people are milling around. There's a strange glow, a golden light. And . . . ?"

"She didn't open the door. Her mother did."

"She's an orphan," my mother countered, as if she'd caught me lying to sabotage her story.

"Her adoptive mother opened the door. The miracle girl was making a sandwich. Then the bishop slammed the door in my face."

"No."

I nodded.

"Was there a smell of any sort? I've heard there's often a smell."

"Brownies."

"Intriguing."

"Then I went outside."

"I saw you talking in front on the phone. Then when *I* called, you didn't answer."

"I was busy, Mom."

"You were just standing there."

"I didn't know it was you."

"You could have at least answered."

"I didn't hear it ring."

"Sit, you two." Charles barreled into the room to deliver the drinks. I backed down to the couch and my mother sat in her chair. He handed her a drink and me a beer in a tall glass—Schaefer, which he bought in cans by the case. He drank his beer warm, poured into a glass and left to sit on the counter, draped with a Kleenex for half a day to let out the fizz. Charles had an ulcer. His ulcer was a living thing, a fully developed animal with demands, needs, personality quirks, living in his stomach. He'd also had cancer in his small intestine and colon. He'd had an impressive amount of intestine removed. I can't remember how much except that at the time it seemed like a *distance* of intestine rather than a *length*, something you could time yourself running.

He sat back down and reopened his book.

"The bishop told you in confidence what she said. He told you not to breathe a word. But it's fine to tell us. Nothing leaves this room. Not a peep."

"Mainly she's worried about the crowds. She wants them to go home."

"Did he tell you she said that?"

"Does it surprise you?" I said.

"Does it surprise me? I don't know. Does it surprise you, Charles? I suppose it does. I'd think she'd want to share this event. That is, if it's for real. And if it's *not* for real, I'd think she'd be doing it for the crowds, for the attention. How did the bishop interpret this?"

"He's worried about the crowds, too."

"Intriguing."

My mother had worked for the Republican party in the Tri-Cities in the heady Rockefeller days, when everything seemed possible. She met Charles in Nixon's final year. Every few weeks she'd leave me with my father and travel to D.C., ostensibly on business, but I knew better. Even at age eleven.

"Then," my mother went on, "the bishop describes a revelation coming to her. The inexplicable light at her heart, she seems to float, her voice like an angel's."

"It was mostly about the crowds. And she doesn't talk. She signs."

"And the bishop—?"

"Her mother," I said. "She interpreted for him."

"The mother reads the sign language in Latin and the bishop translates."

"He was only there for half an hour," I said. "She didn't have a vision."

"Or is it in English? Do the revelations come in English?"

"Vietnamese, I would imagine."

"Don't be ridiculous."

"Don't you think it would be like dreaming—you'd do it in your mother tongue?"

"I've never heard anything so absurd. Have you, Charles? Anything so absurd? The Virgin speaking Vietnamese? Italian maybe. Or English. Possibly Spanish. But Vietnamese?"

"The pope is Polish," Charles offered. He never seemed to be listening but always was.

"You two are pulling my leg. And how does she hear the Virgin at all if she's deaf? Did the bishop ask her that?" She pointed at me as she stood. "What sort of Catholics are they anyway? Catholics in orange robes? I don't think so. Charles, you're the one who said the Philippines was filthy, and they claim to be Catholics too." And she left Charles and me alone, seemingly in protest, for the kitchen.

Charles kept on reading. He took a sip of his beer and set down the glass. I picked up a copy of *House Beautiful* from the glass coffee table and thumbed through the pictures of rooftop terraces overlooking skylines I didn't recognize, adobe houses in Cincinnati with Southwestern burnt-sun décors, classic bathrooms with pedestal sinks and rolled white towels stacked in wicker cubbies.

Charles turned a page. He sighed. His life, it always seemed to me, shut down after the resignation. He stayed on in the Ford administration, but with a sense of defeat, a sense that whatever excitement he'd been a part of had died. I'd never heard him defend Nixon, but he'd never said a bad word about him either. He talked mostly about the first term, about

Nixon's political cunning, his deep love for the nation that no one, not even Charles, could fully appreciate, and his role as a visionary. When Carter came in, Rockefeller helped Charles get a job at the State University of New York, lecturing on the economy and international relations. He married my mother, and ten years later he retired.

His wife had left him just after Nixon's reelection. I've seen her in photographs looking extremely sexy, a drink in one hand, a cigarette in the other, miniskirt, false eyelashes. In the famous *Life* magazine photo of a boozed-up Kissinger looking down a woman's blouse, she's *that* woman. She left Charles for a draft dodger and still lives in Canada. Charles heard about her through his children, but he only heard from them occasionally. His son was a dancer in the Portuguese National Ballet. His daughter was a missionary in Ghana. Neither ever married or had children. "*My* suspicion?" my mother often confided. "Homosexuals. Both of them."

Dinner was meat. Cold chicken marinated in brandy and wrapped in prosciutto to start. Filet mignon in port wine sauce next, and about five string beans soaked in so much Cointreau they made me shudder. String beans that needed a beer chaser.

At home, I parked on the sidewalk. A strange laser-show light flashed in the air: from every apartment around the square—what seemed like every window, including our own—the same TV channel was playing, bluish light flickering in sync.

In our apartment, the lights weren't on—only the TV. Channel 6 had gone to twenty-four-hour miracle coverage. Old people were lined up in the hall at the emergency room, each with an IV. The heat was taking its toll. They were staking their health, maybe their lives, on something they believed.

In the bedroom, in the dark, with the fan blowing over her, Rita slept.

3. WEDNESDAY

At dawn the next day, a second student in the computer class, a seventeen-year-old boy, deaf since a car accident at age five, regained his hearing. The miracle girl had appeared to him in his sleep and touched his shoulders, exactly as she had the evening she visited their class. By noon, the mayor was on TV with Floquet at her side, inviting Christians and non-Christians alike to join them in Little Saigon to keep vigil over these blessed events. That afternoon, the city council met to change our official slogan from "Hudson City: We're Rebuilding!" to "Hudson City: Where Miracles Happen!"

By the time the six o'clock news came on, over three thousand pilgrims were packed into our streets. The heat wave showed no signs of breaking.

There was talk of putting large fans on flatbeds at either end of Broadway to move some air. There was talk of stringing up a canvas shade cover three blocks long. Fire hydrants were opened, and the mayor pledged to pay the water bills for all of Little Saigon to encourage distribution. Firemen worked with the Red Cross to bring in water, cots, food and medical stations. "Help Wanted" signs appeared in shop windows. Grocery stores were selling straight from the cartons without bothering to shelve. Restaurants added tables. Hotels edged up rates.

There had been three deaths, all elderly people who succumbed to the heat and, in a lovely symmetry that inspired poetry in Hudson City news reporters desperate to fill air time, three healthy births. In front of cameras at Good Samaritan Hospital, all three babies were baptized into the Catholic faith by Father Floquet, whom the press had dubbed "The Miracle Girl's pastor, spokesperson, and confidant."

I canceled my Wednesday appointments and spent the day working up models for all our vacant properties to determine the number of cots that could be delivered per building and per room. We didn't need more than the armory and St. Mary's Middle School for now, but Frank wanted to be ready just in case. I emptied our key cabinet into a cardboard box and drove around the city with a cop in his cruiser. Lights flashing, we snaked through traffic and mobs of pedestrians, opening buildings for the Red Cross, Con Ed and the water department, security guards, fire inspectors, and cleaning companies. Everyone wanted to be ready.

Buddy called me on my cell. "It's all staticky," I said too loudly into the phone. "Can you hear me?" even though our connection was clear. "Maybe there's interference because I'm in a police car." He didn't call again.

Around midday, Frank issued a one-line press release: "Although the Church does not in any way endorse the suggestion that recent events in Hudson City are of a miraculous nature, we recognize, particularly given the extreme heat, a civic and humanitarian duty to temporarily house these visitors to our city."

That evening, I walked into the apartment to the sound of Rita laughing with pure delight. She and her friend Trisch were facing each other across the length of the couch, the two fans blowing on them from the middle of the living room. Rita seemed to laugh more freely with Trisch than with me.

"*Buenas noches*," Rita said in the way I knew meant sangria.

"Hey," Trisch said, and I leaned down to kiss her warm cheek.

The cut-crystal punch bowl and silver ladle—gifts to Rita's parents for their wedding—sat out on the coffee table. Slices of lemon and orange floated in the blood-red sangria. Rita and Trisch drank from the matching punch cups, and scooped up guacamole with blue corn chips.

"How's the vision quest?" Trisch asked.

"How's the sangria?" I asked back. Rita made the most amazing sangria.

"Exquisite," said Rita, "if I do say so."

I reached for her cup, but she pulled back and pointed toward the kitchen. I could taste it already.

The punch cups were up on the top shelf. I took one down and rinsed out the dust. We only ever used them for sangria, and this was Rita's first batch of the summer.

When I came back into the living room, Rita and Trisch were talking softly and hurriedly, their cheeks red and moist. Both of them were in T-shirts with the sleeves rolled up to the shoulders. Trisch had on gym shorts. Rita was wearing a pair of my boxers. In the middle of the couch their toes were touching.

I stirred with the ladle, ice cubes chiming against the thick crystal. I chugged a glass then filled another.

"Yum, sweets," I said to Rita.

"So what about the miracle girl?" Trisch asked.

I shook my head. "Can't these freaks go home?"

"Official Church statement or your personal view?" Trisch said.

"It's killing me. The bishop, yeah, yeah, it's a thorn in his side, but the extra work is all mine. I spent my day with a cop."

"So it's safe to say you're not caught up in the rapture?" Trisch said.

"You have to feel sorry for those people, standing out there in the heat, thinking faith'll cure their athlete's foot, or that she'll say something that'll finally straighten out their lives."

"You stink," Rita said. "You should take a shower."

Trisch swallowed a gulp. "But the miracle girl hasn't said anything. Herself, I mean."

"Exactly," I said. "These pilgrims should clean scabs with Mother Teresa instead of waiting around Hudson City for a glimpse of God."

"God is in the scabs," Rita said, and she clinked my glass with hers.

"Lilian," I said to Rita. "You remember her?"

Rita nodded.

"She desperately wants this to be real. I'd never say this to her, but it's like, 'get a life.'"

"Do you know her, Trisch?" Rita said. "A very sensual woman. Very grounded."

"That's what the bishop thought about the miracle girl," I said.

Rita swallowed. "So he *does* think there's something to it?"

"I don't know what he thinks. He's got a job to do mostly."

"Anyway," Trisch said. "That's not what I meant." Condensation from her cup dripped down the inside of her thigh. "Everything we've heard comes from that priest."

"She's deaf," I said. "She doesn't talk."

"Obviously, but she doesn't even stand next to him when he's supposedly speaking for her. I don't trust him. I think he's using her."

"For?"

"The usual. Power, influence. Some sort of Catholic rejuvenation." She dipped a chip in guacamole and crunched it. I refilled my cup, then Rita's. "Hudson City's been a Vatican outpost for a century, and they're losing their grip. I think she's the native queen the Church wants to co-opt to get the locals in line. She's beautiful, exotic, and they can be her voice. It's perfect."

I slapped her knee. "You sound like Buddy Jensen."

"Who's that?"

"Quinn's sleazy pal," Rita said. "From Venable."

Trisch smiled. "Even better. The sun never sets on Venable. They just bought my building, and they made everybody put up the same blinds so the building looks uniform from the outside."

"Those batik curtains?" Rita asked.

"Gonzo."

"The problem with your theory—"

"I love those curtains," Rita said.

"—is the bishop wants to call the miracle off."

Trisch shook her head. "It's all over Shakespeare. The king pretends to be reluctant about assuming his new power."

"You're wrong," I said. "He wants to retire."

"Will you please go take a shower?" Rita said.

I downed my sangria and refilled.

Rita admired Trisch because Trisch had done everything Rita hadn't. She'd gone to grad school and finished her Ph.D. in comp lit; she'd had a post doc at Columbia and was now teaching two courses on postcolonial literature at SUNY Albany. She remained close to her large family, all living in the Tri-Cities. She'd gone on three yoga retreats in India. And she shunned long-term partners, moving through a series of men all characterized by Rita as "interesting," even "fascinating." Stepping into the rush of cool water, I set my punch cup on the edge of the tub.

I turned my face into the stream, closing my eyes, and a sway that I'd normally have caught became a stumble, and I groped out with one arm, falling backward. Miraculously, my fingers hooked the curtain rod. More miraculously—the rod held. I didn't fall, but the sangria had hit me like a tequila bottle to the back of the head.

The punch cup was still sitting on the edge of the tub. I reached for it with great care and took a sip. Then I jiggled the curtain rod. A little shaky but still hanging. Music came on in the living room. I heard Rita's laughter.

The two of them sweaty on the couch, basically in their underwear, whispering, twiddling each other's toes—it was all very sexy. I lathered up and rinsed. Toweling off, I broke a sweat. I thought it must be getting hotter. Plus the sangria.

"It's the same with yoga," Trisch was saying when I got back out there. Rita was stretching on the floor in front of the couch. "The good and bad of America. We absorb and steal. Both the miracle girl and yoga are commodified. Consumed for our own regeneration."

"I believe it about that priest and the bishop," Rita said, her head at her ankles, "but I'm not sure about the pilgrims. I'd like to think their belief is more pure. I envy them. I wish I could believe it, too. It would be comforting, I think."

"You *can* believe it," I said, slipping onto Rita's spot at the end of the couch.

"Look at Calvin Klein," Trisch said. I'd put on boxers and a T-shirt and left it at that.

"It's easy," I said. "Just forget what you know is true, and bring on the blissful ignorance. Because that's all it is: the act of washing away what you know. Plenty of people take comfort in superstition."

"It's hard to reconcile," Trisch agreed, "how otherwise intelligent people seem to be Christians."

"Does she know you converted?" I asked Rita.

"Weren't you going to take a shower?" she said flatly.

"She's Jewish now."

"That's not so bad," Trisch said, mussing Rita's hair. "I thought you were going to say Catholic."

Rita rose out of her stretch and rested her hands and chin on Trisch's leg. "For a while," Rita said, "I've wanted to have my everyday life more infused with the spiritual." With two fingertips, Rita rubbed condensation and sweat into Trisch's thigh. "A little recognition that my spirit is alive in my work, while I'm eating a meal, riding a bus, doing the dishes . . . I don't know . . . making love."

Trisch's nipples were poking through her thin T-shirt more robustly than usual. Definitely hard. She lightly scratched the back of Rita's neck. Rita's fingers wandered over Trisch's skin, inching up her thigh. "Judaism is a way of life," Rita said, the same words she'd used with me two days ago.

I topped off everyone's sangria, and settled back on the couch with my leg touching Trisch's and my hand on Rita's shoulder, the two of them caressing each other. We were listening to the Indigo Girls. Too much.

"From what I heard, the miracle girl's visions are sort of sexual," I said. "The bishop and Floquet were too embarrassed to talk about it."

"And?" Rita said.

Trisch nodded. "I read that somewhere, too."

"I'm just saying she's infused it all pretty successfully." I scooched closer. "Erotic in the spiritual. Spiritual in the erotic. Very Catholic." I laid my hand on Trisch's calf. "Once you have a Catholic boy, Trisch, you never go back."

"I thought it was all guilt and virgin-whore dichotomy and abstinence as birth control." She hadn't flinched at my hand so I gently massaged her calf. I brushed the fingers of my other hand along the inside of Rita's arm.

"Long before birth control, Catholics were popping out more kids than everybody else," I said.

"Is that true?"

"The girls are hot, and the boys know how to satisfy. Tell her, Rita."

She scowled at me like I was being an ass. Which I already knew.

"In fact, the Catholics and Jews have a lot in common. Since she decided to convert," I said, "Rita's body has been electric, her breasts are swelling, tender with desire, overflowing—"

"Wait," Trisch said, a smile growing on her face. "You're not pregnant?"

Rita tipped her punch cup. "I hope not."

"Are you trying?"

"Huh," I grunted. "Hardly."

Rita shoved my hand away.

"You've got to believe me," I said to Trisch, smoothing my hand higher up her calf. "She's much sexier as a Jew. She's wearing me out."

"Shut up, Quinn," Rita said.

"You should convert to something too, Trisch, and we could be a household of three sexy religious people. Sixties free love meets Nineties family values."

"For God's sake," Rita said. "Give it a rest, Quinn."

But I was desperate. The shift in space required was minute: a few scraps of clothing removed and the slight rearrangement of our bodies. I ached for the slip of loins and bellies, bodies intertwined, lips sliding over breasts. Slow kisses and the taste of sweat. A bite on my shoulder.

My fingertips nuzzled Rita's breast, and my other hand moved up over Trisch's knee. Trisch took a long drink, and when Rita noticed my hand creeping up Trisch's leg, she craned around looking at me a little surprised and a little drunk and, I hoped, secretly pleased. Her face was flushed, sweat beaded on her upper lip. "All Catholic joking aside," I forged ahead, "for me, the Sixties and Seventies gave me the freedom to reject Catholic authority about sex, gave me the freedom to enjoy sex without the layers of guilt, gave me a sexual identity that I wouldn't have had otherwise. I wouldn't be such a sexy bastard. None of us would. It gave me—"

"Herpes," Rita said.

Blood had never surged from one part of my body to another as it surged from my groin to my face in that moment. Trisch suddenly realized my hand was on her thigh, and she curled up her legs. Rita turned away. She folded her arms across her chest and seemed to feel bad already for saying it. The song ended, and in the silence I could hear my eyelid throbbing with my pulse. And then there was a crash—steel clattering on porcelain and tile. The shower curtain rod had let go.

I folded my arms over my stomach.

"I was just kidding around," Rita said, but I couldn't read her tone.

I could *always* read her tone. The whole *point* of Rita was that I could read her tone. Generous. Honest. Caustic. Good-naturedly humorous. These were Rita's tones.

And then I was jealous. "You two are doing it, aren't you?"

"Are you drunk?" Rita asked me. "You sound drunk."

"Doing what?" Trisch said.

"Because *I* feel spinny," Rita said.

"I want to know," I said.

"Wait." Rita took a few deep breaths, her head bobbing. "You really thought . . ." She started laughing. "You wanted . . ." She was laughing so hard she couldn't speak. ". . . the three of us . . . ?" She started to choke.

Trisch was laughing too, but didn't know why. "Doing what?" she said, waiting for the joke.

Rita laughed and gasped, rolled onto her knees, then struggled to her feet. She wobbled to the bathroom, choking. And in one long heave, then a second, and a third, she vomited into the sink.

When Trisch left, I put Rita to bed with a cold washcloth on her forehead, a fan blowing over her, and a plastic wastebasket ready for the next round. I flopped on the couch and redosed myself with sangria. It was dark out, but if the night had brought cooler air, it was reheated by the wine in my blood. I was sweating and drank for relief.

With the remote I switched on the miracle. At least twenty men—all Vietnamese from what I could see, mostly shirtless and sweating with the strain—were carrying a white statue the size of a large car on their shoulders. You'd have thought it was a Buddhist parade in Asia. I remembered seeing a Tet festival in Vietnam on TV. The women danced in the streets, there were drums and music, and the men carried a huge statue of their village holy guardian away from the temple. They washed and bathed the statue, then returned it to its home renewed.

Rita groaned and I muted the TV. I took a drink. I hadn't even gotten herpes from sleeping around. That was the most pathetic part. I got it from Carolyn. Three years of average but regular sex.

Rita and I used condoms for the first year or so, but we eventually let that slip, and it was another few years before she had an outbreak. It had been in the winter, late February, and she hadn't been able to shake the flu for weeks. When she was finally better, we went out to dinner to welcome her back to the living. She was uncomfortable in the restaurant, squirming in her chair. And before bed, putting in her diaphragm, she noticed those first pinhead blisters. She knew what it was in an instant, like she'd been waiting.

From our bed I heard her crying, and when I rushed to the bathroom, she was sitting on the toilet in her robe with her face in her hands. Her diaphragm, smeared with jelly, lay on the counter looking deflated. And *I* knew too. I touched her shoulder. Her body was tense, bracing against the virus, and bracing against me. "I'm sorry," I said.

While she cried, I sat on the cracked linoleum floor, counting slivers of toenails and curls of hair along the baseboard. I rinsed her diaphragm. Our feet got cold.

We moved to the bed and warmed up under the blankets. I'd never wanted her to bring her body to mine more than at that moment. Then she rolled up against me. And when I speak of Rita's generosity, it is times like those I'm speaking of, because I know that she rolled against my body not for her, but for me.

"I knew," she said, "eventually . . ." and she choked on the words. The lights were out. Her breathing was rough. "I just wanted to have kids first."

She was too embarrassed to go to her regular doctor, so she got the diagnosis from Planned Parenthood. They gave her a prescription, some pamphlets, and a T-shirt.

Only a few months later, in the spring, she had another outbreak. "I didn't think they'd come this often," she said, discouraged.

And then that summer, in the middle of a hot, humid week, I came home from work and she was squatting over a mirror in the bathroom, sobbing. It was much worse than the first two times.

"Oh, no," I said, and she looked up at me with such virulence that I took a step back. Without rising she reached for the door and swung it shut. I leaned my forehead against the wood. Her sobs were wrenching. "Can't I come in?"

She didn't say anything, so I opened the door and poked my head inside. She was still squatting, arms crossed on her thighs, her head dropped.

"Rita?"

She lifted her head, and when I saw her face, I backed out and silently pulled the door closed. My hands started to shake, my heart pounded. I paced around the apartment, working into a panic. I stood in the living room at the bay window gazing at the buildings around Burden Park, waiting for what I knew was coming: We were through. Every scrap of hatred and anger in Rita rose to her face in that look—as if she were stabbing out a cigarette in my eyes. I'd never known she was capable of it.

Later that night I took her hand, and I started to cry.

"Don't," she said.

I stopped so easily I wondered if I'd forced the tears.

"I love you," she said. "Let's just get over it."

And for that I felt I owed Rita everything. But still, between us, there was a presence as real as if I'd had an affair and brought the woman home. I'd hurt her, infected her, and like the betrayal of an affair, even after it was forgiven, it lived with us like a ghost. When I had an outbreak, I informed her, and the ghost moved among us. When she had an outbreak, the ghost turned malicious, there at every turn to stick us in the ribs.

I tried to learn from the generosity of Rita's forgiveness, not just for the herpes but everything. When she forgave me, she tried as hard as she could to erase it from our lives; when I forgave her, no matter how much I wanted to make it complete, I seemed to let her live with a little guilt that I could draw on later.

Rita was right: except for a lot of heavy petting and hickeys in junior high, the only thing I got from the Sixties was a virus they germinated with free love. Now the hippies are investment bankers who make their own granola and drive Ford Excursions with Sierra Club bumper stickers, and we're left with the plateful of diseases they passed on.

The men carrying the statue on TV reached the miracle girl's front stoop. I recognized two of the women with their children in wheelchairs, still there, nearly ten at night. The men set one end of the statue on the sidewalk, and in a formation reminiscent of the flag-raising on Iwo Jima, they got under the other end and raised the statue upright—the photo ran the next morning on the front page. It was as tall as the miracle girl's second-story window—the veiled Virgin, arms outstretched. I recognized the statue and suddenly realized it had come from the courtyard down the block between St. Mary's and the rectory where Father Floquet lived. People immediately started setting votive candles around her along with handfuls of incense sticks, vases of flowers, and old framed photos.

The cameras pulled back to let an old woman with a walker come forward, then a man with his bent-over wife in a wheelchair, and then the two mothers with their children. The mothers kneeled side by side on the curb. I still had the sound muted, but I could see the reporter slide in among them with his microphone. "Shrine to the Miracle Girl" flashed on the screen. "Live." He touched the shoulder of a boy who stared straight ahead, face expressionless, a clear tube running into his mouth. The reporter put his microphone in front of the mother, and the camera zoomed in on mother and son, her eyes closed, lips moving in prayer.

4. THURSDAY

The pilgrims kept coming. Reporters interviewed municipal employees about the stressed infrastructure. There were doomsday predictions about sewers erupting into the streets, reservoirs drying up. The word "pestilence" was used.

Thursday afternoon I had an angry call from Chip, the building inspector, waiting for me at Immaculate Heart. It was one of the many buildings I wasn't considering for pilgrims because of its location, the single toilet in the basement, and the lack of usable square footage. "We have a situation in this city," I told Chip from the passenger seat of a police cruiser on my way to check if the rats had moved out of the old St. Bernard's Boys' School so pilgrims could move in.

My contract of sale with Buddy for Immaculate Heart allowed him to bring in a city inspector to stipulate which code noncompliances they'd sign off on and which ones would have to be upgraded. On principle, the city went easy on the diocese. And since they wanted to keep Venable happy, they went easy on Buddy. Venable agreed to pay for the Immaculate Heart improvements—railings, banisters, fire extinguishers, and exit signs—and all that remained was a reinspection and certificate of occupancy. So Buddy requested Chip, a famous prick among building inspectors. Buddy was taking potshots.

"It took me an hour to get here," Chip said. "At considerable sacrifice. Five miles. I could have walked."

"You should have," I told him.

"Go to hell," he said.

"May the Lord accept the sacrifice at your hands and praise the glory of—" He hung up on me.

We rounded the corner and a billboard appeared. "Hudson City: Where Miracles Happen!" printed in gold over a city skyline floating on a cloud. Across the bottom in the same gold lettering it read, "Generously paid for by Venable."

I got home at midnight and flipped on the TV. My day had gone like this: I opened a building, knocked down cobwebs, decided how many volunteer cleaners to request and what special equipment they'd need, and arranged for security guards. In fourteen hours I'd ordered 658 cots. On the news they estimated that a thousand new pilgrims had arrived during the day. I'd called Rita at six-thirty to tell her I'd be late and again at ten so she wouldn't wait up.

There was a story on the news about the appearance in a municipal motor pool of two refrigerated trucks—rented from a meat packer—for bodies overflowing the morgue. Down the Hudson at West Point, brush fires were sweeping through the hot open fields; fire crews' efforts were hampered by the hundreds of rounds of unexploded ordnance that kept blowing. Military helicopters were filling their bellies in the Hudson and trying to douse the fire from a safe distance in the air. Father Floquet married two couples on the stoop of 779 Broadway.

Then there was a story about the miracle girl's life. She was born near Quang Ngai seven weeks premature, less than four pounds, and her mother had carried her, curled up like a nut, in an American army helmet lined with cloth. She'd returned to her mother's village a few years ago with a group of Tri-City vets. One of them told the Channel 6 reporter that Sue had met people who remembered her as the war baby not much bigger than a papaya. The story went that anytime Sue's mother heard gunfire, helicopters, explosions, she would quickly roll her baby from the helmet to the ground, flip the helmet over her and sit on top. But the one that killed came from below, not above. The old people who saw it showed Sue the place on the road and said that her mother was walking, as she always did, with a basket of GI laundry on top of her head. The helmet sat cradled in the laundry with the baby curled inside, a light cloth over her to keep off the sun. When her mother stepped on the mine, she was killed in an instant. But the baby was launched in the helmet across the road and splashed gently among soft stalks of rice in two feet of water.

When the villagers came to her, blood trickled from her ears, but she wasn't crying. She was awake and hungry. A water buffalo had been hit with shrapnel and had to be killed. But before the farmer slit its throat, he milked it dry, and fed the baby. She passed through many hands before she landed in an orphanage in Saigon, then a few years later a home in Hudson City.

I showered and stepped softly into the bedroom. Rita's reading lamp was on. My skin still moist, I stood naked in front of the fan. *Tenets of Judaism* lay open on her chest. I closed the book and set it aside, turned off her light, and crawled in beside her. I kissed her behind the ear. Still sleeping, she rolled away from me onto her side. Her freshly showered skin smelled like her cucumber-melon soap. I kissed her again, at the nape of her neck, and smoothed my hand over her T-shirt down the soft valley between her ribs and hip, then down to the skin of her thigh. I tugged up her T-shirt and pressed myself on the warm cushion of a butt cheek. "Rita," I whispered.

She made sleep noises, a long contented sigh. Then she said, hopeful, clear, and bright: "My dear Josh."

I lurched back, and Rita startled. I could sense her shoulders and hips tightening.

In full voice I said, “What?” but she pretended to be asleep. “Who's Josh?”

She was silent. Too silent to be sleeping. No sounds of breath. No rise and fall in her chest. She was a knot, tense. “Rita,” I said in the darkness.

Silence. I rolled onto my back and listened to my heart pounding. The heat caught up with me, and I smelled something like panic unleashed though my pores, and something much quieter—cornered, calculating—rising off Rita.

5. FRIDAY

I might have fallen asleep around dawn. I'd spent the darkest hours of the night working on the cloud puzzle. About forty pieces, not bad. I didn't remember getting into bed. Then suddenly the phone was ringing, and I was counting the rings. Flaming light from the low sun shone through the window fan and flickered on the wall. When the voice mail picked up, I looked at the clock: 6:45. A moment later my cell started ringing, then the house phone again. I dragged out of bed naked to the living room.

". . . right away, John. Seven-o'clock meeting in my office." It was the bishop.

I looked in at Rita, lying on her side at the edge of the bed.

"I mean it, John. Fifteen minutes."

I dressed quickly, making plenty of noise, but miraculously, Rita didn't stir. After I'd knotted my tie, I slammed my sock drawer and she jumped. "Rita," I demanded. "Who's Josh?" Buttoning down my collar I'd broken a sweat.

"What time is it?" she said.

"Who is he?"

"Why are you up so early?"

"Rita."

"What?"

I tied a shoe. Then the other. The fan was already blowing warm air. I turned it off and the room got much quieter.

She stretched and said in a yawning voice, "There's lots of Joshes." Then she curled into a ball, her face turned away. "There's Josh Maxwell who one of my roommates in New York was dating. There's a Josh at WTRI, the one with the wife with cancer and two kids in the Navy. My first boyfriend in sixth grade was Josh Levine. There's the Josh in London at WorldMedia. I knew at least two Joshes in college." Then she took *Tenets of Judaism* from her nightstand and held it up for me to see. Rabbi Joshua Feingold was the author.

"Which Josh did you dream about last night?"

"I've told you," she said. "I don't remember my dreams anymore."

I blasted the AC in my truck and rolled along the sidewalk into the street. Doubling back in front of the apartment, I could see the top of Rita's head already at her computer.

Twice at intersections I had to blow my horn when cars nudged into my path. Along Congress Street, the sidewalks were bustling—families, groups of men, nuns—looking for breakfast. It was like August in Provincetown or Vineyard Haven, vacationers out searching for blueberry pancakes before the heat of the day. There was way too much relaxation, expectancy, even joy in their strides. This was Hudson City, for God's sake, at seven a.m. in a heat wave.

I pushed through the front doors. Patsy wasn't in yet, her desk still neat, chair tucked underneath. But the bishop's voice bellowed into the front hall, and I hooked into his office. He stopped talking and glanced at me. I glanced at my watch, lamely. Then, from the chair across the desk—cool as a cucumber in a white polo shirt with the collar turned up, legs crossed, sipping coffee from my *Fine Woodworking* mug—Buddy Jensen nodded.

The bishop waved me in, took a slug of Diet Coke, and said, swallowing, "Everybody's got to keep the IRS in mind."

"Taxes, taxes," Buddy said, smiling at me.

"The relationship between the diocese and Venable is special indeed." The bishop's eyes met mine in a look that suggested the complete collapse of my world: an audit, an investigation into kickbacks from Buddy, my firing and the humiliation to follow. A series of disappointed faces flashed before my eyes: Rita, vindicated for her affair; the bishop, lips trembling with fury when I admitted every detail; Rosemary, cutting me down to nothing with a sharp remark; my mother, embarrassed, calculating her public explanation; Charles, flashing back to Nixon's resignation. I saw Buddy Jensen laughing, drinking from my coffee mug, and an IRS auditor retracting his mechanical pencil and closing an oversized black binder as the handcuffs snapped closed on my wrists.

The bishop furrowed his brow. "We've been talking about the asylum," he said to me.

That was the trip to Jamaica. DiAngio had offered more money and better terms, but Buddy had mentioned sun and beaches. It was the beginning of February. I'd told Buddy that Rita was getting depressed about the cold and gray. She'd loved the trip, but I never revealed how it was paid for. We smoked pot every night on a balcony overlooking the surf and then made love. And now the bishop knew it all.

"A dollar a day," Frank said to me.

"Just for tax reasons," Buddy said. "You understand, don't you, Quinn?"

"Venable and Mr. Jensen have offered . . ." The bishop stopped. "What's wrong with you, John?"

Buddy leaned close to me. "You look terrible." He was beaming. I heard something behind me and jerked my head around, half-expecting the IRS or the police.

"I'm fine." My voice squeaked.

"Well, get a glass of water. Dehydration's a concern in this weather. But we'll need some number crunching by nine o'clock. I want upwards of two thousand cots in there."

They both looked at me. Buddy uncrossed and recrossed his legs. The bishop tapped the eraser end of a wooden pencil on his desk.

I wiped sweat from my forehead with the sleeve of my suit coat. "What?" All air.

"The asylum," the bishop repeated. "Mr. Jensen is offering to open it up. We'll rent it for a dollar a day."

"Tax reasons is all," Buddy said. "And liability."

"I'm hopeful we won't need the building, but if we do, I want it ready to go."

"Plan for the worst, hope for the best." Buddy smiled broadly.

"Get some water," the bishop said, "and do your magic with the numbers."

I backed though the doorway.

"The key is to lower your core temperature," Buddy said. "What you need is a cold bath."

My legs were still wobbly when I closed my office door and turned on the air-conditioner. I took off my suit coat and loosened my tie. I had sweat through my shirt.

From the wall of file cabinets I pulled what I'd need on the asylum. Before I sat down, there was a rap at the door. I knew it was Buddy, and I didn't reply. He walked in anyway, still drinking from my mug.

"You suck," I said and looked down at my work.

"That's no way to talk to a colleague."

I wished I'd taken the time to shower. God, I felt like crap.

"How's the audit going?" Buddy said.

I didn't look up. "Nice bluff." I was sure he wouldn't do it.

"I'm getting a finder's fee, fifteen percent of whatever the IRS collects from you."

"Listen. Buddy. You've done some nice things for me, and I've done some things for you. We've been friends. I didn't feel good about forcing out the day care. It would have been the wrong thing. So let's move on. Okay?" The air blowing in my face tasted like an icy glass of swamp water.

Out of the corner of my eye I saw him turn my coffee mug in his hand, grimly assessing the chisels and dovetails glazed into the ceramic, as if he were about to bargain for it. "I *will* get my fifteen percent. And unlike you, I'd never lie to the IRS. But I did make a certain implication when I ratted you out." He set my mug on top of the file cabinet. "They think I'm an old boyfriend you jilted."

"Go away."

"You brute," he said.

My stomach turned sour.

"Too late to do anything about the audit," Buddy said, "but if you sell me Eighteen-Ten Hoosick, I'll have one of our best Venable tax men defend you. You're gonna pay something, but he could minimize prison time—with luck just get you parole."

Frank's hand dropped on Buddy's shoulder, then his face appeared in the door. "Get Mr. Jensen whatever files he needs, John, to move things along."

"Quinn's a real help," Buddy said. "We'd love to snatch him up at Venable."

Frank gave me a complicated nod—his genuine pride edged with a rebuke for any pride I might have felt myself. "We'll all work this weekend, John," he said, to cut me down to size.

Buddy waited until Frank had gone then pointed at me. "By noon today. You take care of it." He turned and walked away, leaving the door open.

I got up and closed it. My coffee mug stood on the file cabinet. Half full. Schmuck.

I called Rita. *I'm unavailable right now . . .* My stomach burned. I hadn't eaten anything, but I wasn't hungry. I spread the asylum stats on my desk. A year of inventorying organized in neat tables, rows, and columns of numbers. Five buildings minus two—the powerhouse and maintenance shed. I felt sleepy. Dizzy. I dialed Rita again. I smelled a sharp nervous sweat rising out of my shirt. It wasn't even eight a.m. Thirty-two square feet per cot. Corridors eighteen feet wide. I dialed one more time. *I'm unavailable* . . . I crossed my arms on top of my inventories and laid down my head. Rita sighed as the hands of another man moved over her hips.

At ten-thirty I was in the back room of the downtown Hudson City post office, a cavernous old building with plywood tables and sorting bins, ill-placed dividers—a poster child for inefficient utilization of space. From a cheap tinny boom box in a far-off corner, Bob Seeger longed for a woman and the open road. The air was frosty.

Cradling a stack of mail in one arm, my father flipped envelopes and magazines into boxes, each one a leg of his route. He was biting his lower lip as I talked.

"It was just a sandwich," I said. I was sitting on a stool, my heels hooked over the rungs. "I'd show him a property, he'd say, 'Let's get a sandwich,' then he'd grab the check. Next it was Claude's Bistro and the Lobster Pound. We got into a thing where he's the mentor. A little fatherly advice over lunch." My father's smooth mail sorting—flicking to the rhythm of Bob Seeger's guitar—missed a beat. "Meanwhile he's asking favors on the properties. More time to close, better closing terms." My father had figured out by this time that he hadn't been much of a father. However, he was pretty happy with himself, so a reminder of his failings was like a stubbed toe, reverberating through his body and soon forgotten.

"He took an interest in my woodworking," I continued, "so then for my birthday he got me a full set of Marples chisels. And then a few months later some carbide-tipped router bits to make a back-bending bench for Rita. He's always asking me about Rita, and now I know why. 'She needs to get away,' I'd say, and, boom, next thing I know there's a Venable ski chalet at Killington. He knew I wouldn't turn it down. He talked up Land Rovers for months before his pal at the dealership gave me a deal. *I* was the one who went to Buddy for help. I didn't want to cheat on my taxes. I wanted to do the right thing. But I didn't want to pay more than I had to, either. You know, I work my ass off in that job. For salary. Nobody works for salary. Commissions. Stock options. IPO." I had huddled up on the stool, my arms wrapped around myself. "It's freezing in here."

"You know, Quinn," my father started in. "The reason I got out of academia was because I found myself surrounded by the worst kind of competitive cutthroat people with petty politics and backstabbing friendships." I had heard this warm-up before, although sometimes it was "petty people with backstabbing politics and cutthroat friendships." "After eight years of grad school and six years of teaching, I felt dirty. I felt myself getting sucked in. I did some backstabbing myself—in the *Philosophical Review*, trashing a colleague's book, a good friend, your godfather." My guess is that anyone my father delivered mail to, anyone he met in a coffee shop or tavern had heard this story. His personal mythology.

As I added up all of Buddy's gifts in my head, I tried to remember the last present my father had given me. I think it was a back issue of the *Dallas Morning News* from the day I was born. He gave it to me in his apartment, still wrapped up in the postal tube, watching over my shoulder, a little excited, as I opened it. The headline read: "Oil Companies Optimistic."

"Huh," he grunted, and wandered off toward the kitchen.

"That's great," I said. "Thanks." He'd obviously thought it would be about Kennedy's assassination, but of course that didn't happen until later in the morning. I think I put the paper in the back room with my tools. Rita might have recycled it.

He hefted a stack of junk mail. "The point being, you step in dog doo, you're gonna stink." With this nugget of wisdom, he went back to sorting.

I'm not sure what I'd expected. I knew that he wasn't much good for advice, but we'd developed a sort of friendship over the last few years. I spent low-key time with him and his girlfriend, Luna. They'd lecture me on the most recent Noam Chomsky or Helen Caldicott tape they'd gotten in the mail from their network of friends around the country living "off the grid" and "in deep with the real people." I got high with them occasionally. Most of my friends—*all* of my friends—had moved away from Hudson City after college. I didn't keep up with anyone from Monticello Furniture. I counted the bishop as a friend. Buddy had been one. Rita. And my father. Since he was the only one I could tell about my predicament, it seemed like the closest a disgruntled and lapsed Catholic could come to confession.

"Fact is," he paused in his sorting, "you never want to get involved with corruption. It can only damage yourself and the social fabric."

Of course in his mind, we'd always been pals. And pals was all we could be. A father who doesn't believe in patriarchy is limited as a father. He doesn't believe in capitalism, a meddling government, or any formal institution with more than a dozen members. When I asked about his seemingly hypocritical decision to work for the U.S. Postal Service, he said, "Mailmen always seem happy. They're outside, whistling, walking, meeting new people, providing a humble service. They also have a good pension and health plan, which you have to consider"—he pointed at me—"living in a country that doesn't respect its old people."

And he *was* getting older. He'd turned sixty this past year. He'd always been thin, but in the last few years he seemed to be shrinking down. His legs had gotten bonier in his mailman shorts, his shoulders narrower. His beard was gray and dry. Dandruff flecked the front of his Hawaiian shirt. He was bald up top where his scalp was eerily white, since he always wore a hat. The hair that he had—around the sides—was pulled into a ponytail that reached almost to his waist.

"Fact is, though," he said, "there are three institutions you can justify ripping off: insurance companies, the IRS, and the Catholic Church. So, morally you're in the clear. As far as what you should do? You got a copy of this tax return?"

I nodded.

"Give the thing to an accountant, have him figure what you owe. Pay it off. I've got friends in the steel chateau. It ain't disco to fool with the man, Quinn."

He was right, I decided, so I headed home for my tax records through the hot stew of Hudson City traffic. I didn't even try to find a parking space. It was the usual routine: drive up on the sidewalk and toss the clergy permit on the dash.

Rita wasn't there. I went straight to her office. Her briefcase and laptop were gone. She was at a meeting.

The screen saver on her computer caught my eye—something new she must have downloaded in the last few days. The face of the miracle girl floated angelically across the monitor, her body draped in billowing robes. Images of the Virgin Mary, a rosary, and Christ's face from the Shroud of Turin materialized then faded. The miracle girl was definitely stunning. I could see how Frank was a little disarmed. She seemed to know things. Her eyes were big and dark. Her eyebrow was extraordinary.

I scanned the stickies posted around the edge of Rita's monitor, looking for "Josh" or "J," but there was nothing. I gazed at the postcard on the bulletin board over her desk—a sexy painting of two lovers embracing that I'd bought for her a few years ago. Then I tapped the mouse to bring back her desktop. Her icons were scattered around the screen in no apparent arrangement over a photo of a little English cottage, flowers, a brick path.

I poked around the office, flipped through a stack of mail. I opened a drawer: staring up was a photo of me in the small hot tub on the deck of the condo at Killington. After Rita took the picture and set the camera back inside, she stepped naked over the snow. I remember her feet spearing into the tub, then her legs and hips and body displacing steamy water that rose up my chest around my lungs and my throat, taking my breath away. Soft and hot, she floated to me—*around* me in a sort of floating squat—and squeezed my chest with her knees, covering my mouth with her lips. I stopped breathing, as if I'd submerged. Rita—the brimming excess of her—was my air.

Rita overflowed herself, gushing laughter. When she cooked for me, I tasted her in the food. This was true. If someone else made the identical recipe, I'd know it wasn't Rita's. The sweet taste of Rita's neck and the peppery smell behind her ears seasoned her cream sauce and asparagus soup. In bed at night I'd taste a splatter of pesto inside her arm; the burned sugar smell of rice pudding filled her hair. If I had chopped the garlic, I'd smell it on my fingers, fresh and strong, as I parted her labia and tasted her. And when she was on top of me—her face against mine, her hair spread wildly in my eyes and mouth, sweat rising from the dip of her spine—the weight of her took my breath.

I held a corner of the photo. Sex wasn't all that was missing with Rita. Sex wouldn't fix it. Something had gone wrong. Rita's generous heaping of plenty was going somewhere else.

I pulled my files for '97 and '98. I knew some accountants but all of them through Venable or the diocese, so I drove to my mother's house in Belleview, rang the bell, and let myself in.

Charles was in the kitchen with a paring knife in one hand, a tube of pepperoni in the other. He cut a slice against his thumb and offered it to me balanced on the blade of the knife. I shook my head, and he flipped the disc of meat into his mouth. He was wearing my mother's apron over his seersucker suit, white shirt, and red tie. His book on the Battle of Cambrai lay open on the counter in front of him. I set the files beside it.

"Your mother's at a luncheon," he said. "She'll be sorry she missed you."

"It's you I wanted to talk to, actually. I was hoping you might glance through my tax returns from the last couple years."

He looked at the files, cut the corner off a block of cheese, and popped it in his mouth.

"Someone prepared them for me, and I'm suddenly concerned about errors."

"Why's that?" he said, reaching for the files.

"No reason in particular," I said too quickly, and he withdrew his hand, flashing me a look. I already knew this was a mistake.

He chewed a cracker then swallowed hard and dry. I was dying to offer him a glass of water, but he was already back to the beginning of the cycle—slicing a chip of pepperoni and lipping it from the knife. "As you know, I prepared Nixon's taxes, seventy-one through seventy-three. It's all confidential, of course. A confidentiality I'd never violate. But let me say this. I'll be happy to look over these returns. In doing so, I'd be acting as your accountant. And what I've learned over the years, punctuated in the White House, is you never withhold information from your accountant. I believe in the sanctity of that relationship. It's a two-way street. I believe in it as firmly as I believe in honest government and dignity through honest work. These men in the trenches," he said, pointing at his book with the knife, "they understood dignity in a way that people don't anymore. They understood right and wrong, good and bad, in a way that's been blurred beyond distinction. They believed in universal truth, *real* truth." He offered me a cracker.

I shook my head. At this very moment Rita was fucking some guy named Josh and I was getting lectured on dignity. "I just thought you could look for any glaring irregularities that they could catch me on."

"Exactly my point." He emphasized this with a wave of the knife. "Taxes are a privilege and obligation. A responsibility to community and nation. Those without moral structure have no reason not to cheat and steal. Unless they're afraid of being caught. But living right only for fear of punishment is not a moral life. It's a childish life, a small life."

"Let's forget it," I said. "I just thought you could do me a favor—"

"I'll tell you something about favors. In the spring of seventy-two I spoke to Nixon on behalf of an old friend regarding a favor. Nixon looked at me for a long moment, those eyes like skewers, and he said, 'Charlie—'"

"You talk about Nixon like he was the last decent man in America."

"He was a complicated man. Misunderstood. He recognized we were at a crossroads. We could turn back to a time before the so-called counterculture, which was giving this great nation such a beating. We could go back to a time when men would leave their families to sail across the ocean and wipe out evil. He believed it was simple. Right and wrong. What else *is* there when you think about it?" He speared a hunk of cheese and held it in my direction. "What do you believe?" he asked.

"No, thanks," I said, about the cheese.

"In your heart." He chewed. "Never mind the op-ed page."

"My heart?"

He swallowed.

I believed in the feeling of Rita—hot water rising, submerging my chest. We went bowling once: we laughed at each other's gutter balls and bouncing balls followed by explosive strikes. Rita fell cackling to her knees, and the bowlers in the next lane complained that she was shaking the floor. So she sat with her feet propped on the scorer's table, but my next ball crashed into the resetting gate and started rolling back. Erupting with laughter, she clutched her gut, snapped the chair off its base, and went flying: Rita couldn't be contained. She'd gotten an inch taller doing yoga. In a general way, that's what I believed.

But that wasn't what Charles meant. He stopped eating.

"Look," I said. "Are you surprised to see a generation of cynics who have a hard time taking the government seriously? Playing by the rules seems a little naïve after Nixon and Reagan."

"So an honest tax return is naïve?"

"I didn't *do* my taxes. That's the point."

"But you knew they were prepared with questionable methods?"

"I never saw them."

"But you knew?"

"How could I?"

"I don't know. How?"

I opened my mouth to defend myself, but nothing came out.

He ate a piece of pepperoni.

"You loved a crook," I said. "Don't try and tell me." I grabbed up my files and slammed the door on the way out.

The dank office air was a disappointing eighty degrees at best. "He hasn't called back," Patsy was saying, standing in the bishop's office door. Her clothes were a cross between a stooped Polish widow at a funeral Mass and a New York City Goth at an after-hours club: a black dress made of a resilient-looking industrial synthetic and a belt made from metal rings linked with short pieces of leather and rivets. Thank God priests started laying communion in the hand before the arrival of pierced tongues.

"Hey," Patsy said as I passed.

"Get him in here," Frank said.

Patsy backed away from the door. "Hey," she said again, this time more quietly.

"About Mr. Jensen." Frank was looking through several bank and investment statements. He made a mark on one, checked a figure on another, entered it into an adding machine. "Mr. Jensen," he repeated, then he hit the Equal key; the machine printed and the paper tape curled onto his desk. "He's a straight-talker. He's saving our fannies."

"The asylum's got lots of space," I said. I noticed my file for the cathedral on his desk.

"He's offered to help us out for a few days, give us the benefit of his connections at Public Works and the permit office. He's even got pull with the National Guard. He's a go-getter. He'll use the desk in the workroom."

I didn't respond.

"And a genuine *joie de vivre.* You get the feeling he truly loves his work. Recognizes a need and fills it. Is he a family man, do you know?"

"Wife plus two."

"Lots of ways to serve the Lord. Providing shelter. Is he a Christian?"

"Some sort of Protestant."

"Well, you could learn from him, John." He wagged a finger at me. "You're always so morose."

How could Rita do this? I could've tried harder. If she'd just told me. If she'd given me the chance.

"What is it, my lad?"

"I'm glad you like him, Frank."

"Depressed? Is that it?"

"Happy as a lark," I said.

Frank glared at me. "Leave your attitude at the door."

"I really don't feel like being preached to right now. Can I just go do my work?"

"You could use a little more spiritual guidance in your life. You wouldn't be such a malcontent. What is it, John? Living in sin with a Protestant isn't as fulfilling as you'd hoped?"

"It might loosen you up."

His face went red. "Just because she's the one no doubt taking the pill, it doesn't get you off the hook."

"It's worse than you think. Now she's Jewish. She converted."

"Good Lord," he said.

"She's joining those who killed Jesus."

"You're very childish, John."

"But without them we wouldn't have much of a religion, would we?"

"How about you go to your office and cool off?"

"How about if I . . ." But I didn't know what I was going to say.

I looked away. Then I pushed out his office door, pounded down the hall, and flew into my own office. The air was nauseating—microscopic mold spores glommed onto the plaster, fuzzy and oozing and reproducing. I smacked the air-conditioner, and cloudy water streamed from a corner, splashing the toe of my shoe.

I dialed Rita but hung up before it rang. I couldn't bear to hear the recording. I put my head down on the desk. In seconds, I was asleep.

I woke to Sister Rosemary floating on a cloud above my desk. But when I rubbed my eyes, she was merely standing in front of me.

"May I sit down?"

I was still groggy and imagined curling up against her.

"Hel-lo," she said, like a high school girl on a sitcom.

I touched a fingertip to the dent on my cheek. It was the size of my shirt-cuff button. What I'd thought before was true: sex with Rita wouldn't solve everything. But I sure could use a quick fix.

Rosemary sat in the chair facing me. "You look terrible," she said with too much cheer.

"And you look smart as always." I rubbed my eyes. She'd have to wonder a little—a man's chest pressing down on her tiny nun breasts.

She was quiet, giving me a chance to say more. But when I didn't, I felt foolish for what I'd said, even more foolish for what I was thinking. And I was sure she knew it all.

"Quinn." She laid her hands flat on my desk, which seemed to mean we were putting the jokes aside. "The bishop asked me to find out what's wrong with you, and set you straight."

"I can't take this."

"Can't take what?"

"Everything." I swept my hand through the air above my desk. "All of this."

"This telephone? This lamp and these paper clips?"

I rolled my eyes.

"This file cabinet? This map of Hudson City? *Moi?*"

"Not you." Surely she had enough carnal knowledge to be curious. "I just can't take it. Frank's righteousness. I'm sick of being scolded, sick of the moral superiority."

"You feel morally inferior?"

Doing it on the washing machine? Climaxing with the spin cycle? Was it in her realm of consciousness? "Rosemary," I said. "Tell me the truth. Honestly, now. Truly. How much of this Catholic stuff do you really buy?"

She straightened up in her chair, which seemed impossible. To sit even straighter. "That's a very big question, and I'd be happy to discuss it with you if we could block out a couple hours one day."

"How about just a few of the biggest stretches? How about transubstantiation? How about immaculate conception? Was it like in the paintings? Golden sun rays of God's sperm shining into Mary's belly? And did she stay a virgin? You'd think after the fact she might want to try the whole thing in the down-and-dirty un-immaculate way. You'd think Joseph might get a little randy once in a while. Do you believe that God and my dead grandmother watch me masturbate from heaven and put a black mark in my logbook, then erase it if I go into a dark closet and describe it to a priest? Do you find the similarities between confessionals and peep shows troubling?"

"Most people are more reluctant to flaunt their ignorance, but you—"

"Me? Don't you see how naïve it is to believe this nonsense? It's myth. It's old stories told for thousands of years for comfort. Superstition."

"I always find it curious, Quinn, that people like you think that those who believe, those who have faith, are naïve, and those who don't believe are enlightened. Enlightened to what? To nothing? You've got it backward. Those with the knowledge are the enlightened ones. They *know* something. That's what knowledge is. That's what enlightenment is. It's the opposite of naïveté. The naïve ones are those who believe in nothing. It's sad really. It makes you—them—feel empty, purposeless. It causes them to lash out at people who care about them."

Carpet burns on the knees. "Thanks for coming in and cheering me up," I said.

"Why do you work for the Church, Quinn?"

"Somebody's got to do it."

"There are other jobs. Jobs that pay more."

"But in other jobs I wouldn't have you."

"Sarcasm doesn't suit a pretty face."

"Believe me," I said. "I'll parlay my experience here into something more lucrative."

"I think you're searching," she pressed on. She was fifty-five tops, and well preserved. Skin as smooth and milky as a white marble statue of the Virgin. Sleeping with Rosemary would be like going to bed with whole milk, macaroni and cheese, pot roast, my first communion.

"You're searching for your faith," she said.

Butt cheeks chirping across a hardwood floor.

"You're starving, Quinn. You're looking everywhere except where you know you'll find it." And with that, she smiled knowingly and walked out. Despite her good points she was still a nun.

It was past nine when I got home that night. There was a note from Rita saying she was out with Trisch. Nothing about when she'd be back. I marched into her office without turning on the light: her computer was switched off, laptop and briefcase were leaning on the leg of the desk, a T-shirt was tossed on the floor. The fans were motionless in the stifling room. Standing there I felt far from the miracle, far from Buddy's threats, the bishop's righteousness, my job. I picked up Rita's shirt and pressed it to my nose. A bead of sweat ran down my back, and a sense of vacancy settled inside me.

I turned on the fans to draw some cooler night air through the apartment, and decided to go to my father's. I drove around the south side of the university to avoid the congestion that Tri-City traffic reporters had dubbed "miracle jam."

Luna answered the door, crying.

"What is it?" I asked.

"Same old." She wiped her eyes with her palms. "How are you?"

"You know." I shrugged. My father was on his knees with a butter knife turning on the stereo. Several buttons were missing—metal prongs and springs remained. Static and scratches came through the speakers.

"I will *not* bring a bastard child into this world!" my father proclaimed as he stood. He was wearing nothing but a pair of silk pajama bottoms.

"Oh, that," I said to Luna. "I'll see you another time."

"No, come in." Luna sniffed. "It's hopeless."

"That's precisely my point," my father said, the opening chords of Buffalo Springfield's first album playing over the stereo. "The kid's not even conceived and my only son already feels displaced." He was shameless. Like Nixon. "Come in here, Quinn. Come on. I've let Luna in on your tax troubles, I hope you don't mind. No secrets in our relationship. The foundation of trust."

"Don't give me 'trust,'" Luna said. Her sandy-colored hair was fastened on top of her head with a clip. She was wearing one of my father's Hawaiian shirts, which hung midthigh. We were standing just inside the door. The apartment smelled a little dank from the air-conditioner, but mostly the sweet herb smell of incense imbedded in their carpets and upholstery was a greeting, like bread in the oven. "His idea of trust," Luna said, "is that he runs into his ex a few times at the tavern after work. Gets the hots. Wants me to write her a letter saying he's got my permission to sleep with her."

She was referring to his second wife, not my mother.

"Total honesty," my father said to me. "Trust is 'You know your lover wouldn't do it without asking, even if he wanted to.'"

"Trust is 'Why would he want to?'"

"Trust is 'You don't trick him into fathering a bastard child.'" They were both appealing to me, which is how they always argued in my presence, and it made me wonder if they were able to discuss anything without a third person there.

"Listen to him. 'Bastard child.' All sanctimonious. Like he's saying 'first amendment' or 'sanctity of life.' He's probably got more bastard children than Thomas Jefferson."

"She loves saying that, Quinn. I don't. You know I don't."

"And he won't marry me."

"I told you . . ." he said to Luna, then turned back to me. "I told her I would."

"Get him to tell you the conditions," she said.

"They weren't *conditions.*"

"Tell him."

My father pulled on his beard and scratched his chest. Luna's hands were on her hips. "Can you stay awhile?" he asked me.

"Whatever," I said.

"I'm taking a dip and then I'm going to meditate."

"The negative energy." Luna rolled her eyes. "It's bringing him down."

"Afterward I'd like to hear about your predicament," he said.

She went to the kitchen. He went to the bedroom. I had backed against my father's hat rack and could smell the oily scent of his scalp coming off his baseball caps, sun hats, and white safari helmet arranged on the homemade peg board. I picked up his Uncle Sam's Hot Dogs cap—my Little League team. My father hadn't been a coach, but he'd gotten a team cap and rooted from the stands. The visor was floppy, the band streaked yellow with sweat.

The hat rack was probably the only thing you'd call "arranged" in the apartment. The posters on the walls—Hobbit scenes, Mars-scapes, and Native American women with long braids sitting cross-legged beside pottery in misty encampments—seemed randomly tacked up, some high on the walls, some low, some at angles, one on the ceiling. In the far corner, the love seat and coffee table were placed diagonally. It wasn't a big apartment, and this wasted space drove me wild. I'd think the first time you banged your shin on the coffee table, you'd wish you were using those three or four square feet behind the love seat. To confuse matters, a tapestry was draped over the couch and another smaller one over the coffee table; they were turned forty-five degrees, so the squares of cloth were actually square to the room. A mind fuck, for sure.

Cloth was draped over everything, in fact—the TV, end tables, stereo speakers, milk crates full of books. Luna and my father threw famous impromptu parties—it was an apartment where you could set a sweating beer bottle anywhere, knock over a glass of wine without a care, find a pillow to sit on, a piece of wall to lean against. They were always ready: a bottle of Bombay Sapphire in the freezer, my father's spaceship-inspired blue martini glasses, jugs of wine, frozen mini-eggrolls you could nuke, plenty of towels and swimsuits no matter how many friends showed up.

My father came out of the bedroom in his regal robe, royal blue and, I think you'd call it, vermilion. He went out the door, and I listened as he unlocked the pool gate across the parking lot and clicked it shut. With his splash, I sat on the love seat and picked up a copy of *Mother Jones*.

"I want to ask you about the miracle," Luna called from the kitchen, then she came in and handed me a cold Rolling Rock. As she bent down to set a bowl of beer nuts on the table, I looked at the tattoo on her breast—"Sturgis ~ 1988." I always looked at it. Luna was only six months older than I was, so I thought of myself at twenty-four that summer after Black Monday, back to square one financially, living with Carolyn. Then I thought of Luna straddling a Harley with her arms around her boyfriend rumbling into Sturgis for the biker rally. I imagined her whipping off her T-shirt, boobs exposed to the street, the needle and ink stinging her soft flesh. In the next ten years she owned a bar in Wyoming, cooked on a ranch, was a checker at Safeway, clipped the feet off chickens coming forty-five a minute down a conveyer belt, owned two horses, changed her name from Christine to Luna, and worked at a hot springs in Montana, which was where she met my father when he went to escape the woman he was living with before her. The tattoo was slightly blurred now because the skin there had roughened up and puckered a little. Luna had done a lot of living in those ten years. Drugs, booze, and lots of men: bikers and truckers, cowboys, and married salesmen. She talked about it openly to me, to my father, to anyone. "Kicks," she'd say. "Damn, did I have kicks." But now she was looking for what she called "spiritual grounding," the firm footing that she hoped my father, with his Buddhism and self-proclaimed good sense, could help her achieve.

She also wanted a baby, and I suddenly noticed, along with the tattoo, a hint of white fur trim across her cleavage. As she shifted her weight, more fur bulged beneath the Hawaiian shirt along her hip. I realized she was wearing a teddy.

"Sorry if I interrupted something," I said.

"Jack shit."

I swigged my beer. "You ever say a man's name in your sleep?"

"That's not a name. It's an expression."

I smiled.

"An expression meaning your father figured out I went off the pill so he's holding back the seed."

"He didn't know?"

"Am I supposed to find someone else to get me pregnant?"

"Don't you think he should be willing?"

"For the last two months, in the morning, I get up to put on the kettle, then hop back under the covers. I've got until the whistle blows to cowboy up. Mid-month I'd snag him every morning and night. But today he snoops around my side of the medicine chest. And I'm not pregnant yet."

"How about getting married?"

"He wants to know it'd still be okay for him to go to Bangkok and have sex with prostitutes." As she said this, my father came in the door in his robe, drying his beard with a towel. "I'm twenty-four years younger than he is," she said, "and he wants teenage prostitutes who scrub you in a bubble bath before they screw you."

My father pulled the needle off the record. "I've never done it," he told me, "and probably never will. But I need to know that I *could*. I need the freedom." He took a deep conscious breath. "Voices down, please," he said and closed the bedroom door.

"What if I'm too old?" Luna said. "What if I can't get pregnant?"

"People are adopting Chinese babies," I suggested. "And Russian."

"They used to be the enemies and now we're raising their children."

"I'm pretty sure they're still the enemies. Technically."

Luna rubbed a hand over her belly and turned her head to the side, striking a pose. She never sat. At parties or visits like this one, she stood in the middle of the floor, talking with dramatic gesticulations, turning out a thigh, pointing a toe like a dancer. At mealtime, my father sat on a pillow on the floor and Luna stood, picking at saucers of vegetarian sushi, hummus and pita, stuffed grape leaves, and sliced tomato.

"He's not going to change," I said.

Luna looked at the ceiling, touched her forehead. "I know."

I started to say "Why don't you move on?" but stopped myself. She already knew that was the smartest thing for her, but something kept her with my father for these three or four years. What, though? Love?

I was feeling like I had to say something, but she saved me by asking, "So Rita moaned some guy's name in her sleep?"

"Josh. She didn't moan it. She just said it. Spoke it."

"Josh who?"

"No idea."

"I hate that name." She wrinkled up her nose. "It's squishy and indecisive. Makes me think of suede shoes with gum soles. Skinny legs."

"Sounds like my father."

"No," she said. "Josh would knock me up *tout suite,* thank me for the sex, and weep when the stick turned blue. He'd want to snuggle. Josh loves women for their affection and breasts, and he willingly surrenders. But your father is basically a misogynist. He needs to make a woman come, make a woman love him, need him really, to feel good about himself, and he hates women for the control they have over his self-image. Sure, they both look in your eyes all empathic, bring you ice cream in bed, hold the door, and wash your back in the shower. But your father is sort of a prick. Josh is a pansy."

She did a plié. "So what's up with this miracle chick?" she asked.

"I'm sick of the whole thing."

"Just getting revved up is what I heard."

"So you think it means something if Rita says 'Josh' in her sleep?"

"Everything means something." She turned the TV on to the miracle. "Do you want to toke up?"

"Nah," I said.

The cameras were in St. Mary's School as pilgrims got ready for bed. My stomach twitched when I saw how poorly the cots were arranged.

My father appeared at the bedroom door. "Luna," he said. "A word."

"Hashin' and rehashin'." She rolled her eyes at me.

"Quinn," he said. "I still want to hear about the tax situation. Give us a few minutes." Luna stepped in the bedroom and shut the door.

The news showed pilgrims lining up at the showers. At a first-aid station a nurse looked in a baby's ear. The reporter warned about the lack of emergency lighting if the power went out.

Pot smoke seeped under the bedroom door. My father coughed high up in his nose, trying to hold an expanding hit in his lungs. This seemed to be how he and Luna worked out their disagreements.

They had cable, and I switched to a documentary I'd seen before on the Battle of the Bulge. Eisenhower was partying in Paris while the Germans regrouped, and when they started to push, the American soldiers were totally unprepared. In the fierce cold, they fought with all they had left. Men slept standing, they slept marching, and at a bend in the road a soldier would march into the ditch and wake when his face hit the frozen ground.

I heard Luna's deep raspy laugh—a smoker's laugh although she'd quit cigarettes before she met my father. A German tank festooned with pine boughs toppled a stone wall beside a farmhouse. The narrator's voice—who was this guy?—projected great authority. And certainty. There were no gray zones when it came to Hitler.

I was surprisingly comforted by this fatherly voice documenting World War Two. And I still remembered the absence of that voice when I sat in this room, eleven years old, watching Nixon resign.

. . .

My mother had dropped me here on the day of the resignation so she could fly down to Washington to be with Charles. She waited until she saw me unlock the apartment door and step inside, as she always did, then tooted as she pulled away.

The shades were drawn. The TV was on, volume low. The alluring smell of pot was in the air. At that time there was another couch on the far wall in what was intended to be the dining area. Slowly, my eyes adjusted to the dim light, and I could see my father lying on his back on the big brown couch. Bonnie lay on top of him. They were both nude from the waist down, both sleeping. The bare white moon of Bonnie's butt reflected light from the TV. My father's arm jutted like a dead man's toward the floor where one pair of jeans lay tangled and strewn, and one pair stood like a cartoon character who'd had an anvil drop on his head, making an accordion of his legs.

My father was married to his second wife at this time, but she'd left him and they were getting divorced; Bonnie was on her way in. Still carrying my duffel and trombone, I tiptoed over to get a better look at Bonnie's bare ass. She was quietly snoring. *Am I ready?* I asked myself in an earnest voice that would have had short hair and polished shoes. I had hair hanging in my eyes and down past my shoulders, a leather thong around my neck. My biggest dream was to cruise the country on a chopper. I shoplifted, vandalized, chugged beers, and smoked pot. But this voice within me, as sensible and careful as an altar boy's, was always there to disapprove, put on the brakes, and spoil the fun.

I looked closer between her legs but could only see darkness, and the voice in me said, *Be thankful for the ass.* I reached out as if I were touching her, rounding my hand through the air inches from her skin. I'd tuned up an erection. Standing at the bathroom sink I jerked off, then snagged a slice of pepperoni pizza and a carton of chocolate milk from the fridge.

There was a game show on. I rolled the TV stand around so I could sit on the floor to watch the show and still keep an eye on Bonnie's ass. The cheese on the pizza was cold and chewy. The chocolate milk was sweeter than usual, a sharp sweet smell. Bonnie coughed and shifted her hips. One cheek rose higher than the other. The game show cut to a commercial for Breck shampoo, then a dark shot of the White House, then there was the president, sitting at his desk. I thought of Charles, whom I always imagined in a meeting with the president, gathered around a conference table late at night with cups and saucers, maps and graphs. I thought of my mother sitting primly on the plane so she wouldn't wrinkle her dress.

Bonnie moved, and I froze. She reached for the ashtray, then flipped open a lighter, no idea I was watching. I stayed quiet as she arched her back to lift her face away from my father's. She took a long hit off the roach and held still—skin stretched tightly up her neck—then blew the smoke slowly into the air. President Nixon talked about the good of the country, and about needing a full-time president, as I willed Bonnie to take off her shirt. More than her ass, more than anything, I wanted to see her breasts. The president boasted about bringing an end to our longest war, and Bonnie settled back down on my father's chest.

When I looked back to the TV, the president pulled aside a page from the stack of papers he was reading. Then Bonnie rose up again. Her movements were more clumsy and labored than I imagined the intimacies of sex—she turned herself around on her knees, rocking my father on the cushions of the couch, like someone moving around in a canoe. And even after she'd turned fully and was straddling my father's chest she kept shifting, working her hips and knees into the cushions.

There were jokes about 69, but I hadn't fully understood the mechanics until this moment. Bonnie settled over my father's sleeping face, then with quick birdlike tugs of her head brought him to life.

My father's leg jerked, then he reached up a hand and sank his fingers into Bonnie's soft thigh. The president said the words everyone was waiting for: "I shall resign." I looked at the TV, aware of the moment's historic importance. My stomach didn't feel right. The president looked like he might cry. None of this was really his fault, he said. He felt bad that it had gotten out of hand. But no one was supporting him anymore, so he had no choice.

Bonnie and my father got into a rhythm, like a wave sloshing end to end on the couch. Lots of slurping and sighing. I rubbed myself through my pants. On my bike I had a decal of the American flag, like the one pinned to the president's lapel. Bonnie's ass started to shake and my father gripped her thigh tighter. I unzipped and sprang out. The president said, "I've never been a quitter." Bonnie cooed. My father's hips were bucking. I stroked faster. Bonnie groaned, then gasped. My father released a muted howl like he'd burned his mouth on food. A silent snap ricocheted through me and a thick white drop squeezed out—no more than the end of a Q-tip. The president fought back tears.

None of us moved.

Long after they were asleep again, I went into my bedroom. I woke in the night to the sounds of them making a meal, listening to music. I was sweating, my heart racing. I puked in the toilet and went back to bed. With the music playing, they didn't hear me. The chocolate milk had been sour.

In the morning, they were asleep in his room. Eating a bowl of Chex, I stood by the big brown couch—the heaped-up ashtrays, the dirty plates, the half-empty gallon of Hearty Burgundy.

I took two more slices of pizza and a chocolate Snack Pack for my lunch, and hefted my trombone and duffel to the day camp bus stop—Camp Tekewitha. I was supposed to play two songs that day for the all-camp variety show, accompanied by the music counselor on guitar. But when I got to the corner of Hoosick, no one was there. I sat down on the sidewalk for a while and watched the cars speed up the long hill even though I knew I'd missed the bus.

Sitting on the sidewalk, I couldn't see drivers, just cars—tires smacking the pavement, engines howling, sun reflecting off the paint. I counted one hundred red cars, then one hundred blue. I ate a slice of pizza and rolled the Snack Pack can across the four-lane street watching until a car tire flattened it—a disappointing little explosion of pudding—then walked back to the apartment.

I pulled on the TV and the president was on again, now crying openly. He was leaning into a podium, reminiscing about his father, "a common man," then his mother, "a saint." The camera turned to his wife and his daughter, Tricia, no doubt uncool, but blond. Then the camera panned the audience packed into the East Room. I recognized Kissinger, arms and legs crossed, head pulled into his shoulders like a leery snapping turtle.

I kept listening as I fished a couple roaches out of the ashtray and torched them with Bonnie's lighter. I sucked in the smoke and felt immediately high, those quick serious highs that pot no longer produced for me by the time I got to high school.

As the president chided himself for barely passing the bar, the camera zoomed in slowly on the far side of the room, on Charles, in his seersucker suit, white shirt and burgundy tie. His chin was lifted, face beaming, laughing with the president, hanging on his every word, tears streaming down his flushed cheeks. I took another hit. My mother sat beside Charles in her white dress with black dots and a ruffle at the neck, a white patent-leather purse on her lap. She held Charles's upper arm in two gloved hands as if to keep him from floating out of his chair. As I burned my fingers on the roach, she looked directly into the camera, directly at me, then realized the camera was on her and turned her face away.

Then the president left the White House, parading past his friends and staff, boarding his helicopter with one final wave. I looked for my mother and Charles on the White House lawn, but they were lost in the crowd. When the helicopter had lifted off, I remember a silence catching the TV by surprise—no voice-over told us what to make of all this. The helicopter just disappeared into the hot summer sky, and no one on the lawn knew what to say or where to go. They looked around for direction that didn't come. And the cameras did the same—focusing on a woman with a 1950s hairdo patting her eyes with a hankie, then on a bush still quivering from the helicopter blades, then a red theater rope, a Marine at attention guarding nothing, a man wandering across the lawn. The camera jiggled, for a moment showing nothing but trampled grass, then cut to a commercial for air freshener.

I hadn't heard a peep from my father and Bonnie. It was nearly noon. I fired up the last little roach in the ashtray, then opened the fridge and leaned inside. I grabbed the jar of maraschino cherries, and fished a few into my mouth, so sweet and cold they made me shiver. They tasted red. Then I drank down the juice.

Where my trombone lay in its case, the lining was packed down smooth like a dog's fur under his collar. I attached the slide to the bell and popped in the mouthpiece. I opened my father's bedroom door. Sunlight burned around the white curtain. They were asleep under the covers.

I began with "The Night the Lights Went Out in Georgia," bellowing out the four-bar intro. They shot up in bed, my father getting one foot to the floor, Bonnie covering her ears. She was naked, small beaklike breasts on her thick torso. Disappointing. I closed my eyes and blasted the entire song, then played my second song for the show at camp, "Speak Softly, Love: Theme from *The Godfather.*" When I finally opened my eyes, the sheets and blanket were twisted in knots and the bed was empty.

Luna and my father were still hashing out the baby question in his room, so I left, back into the night simmering with heat and miracle mania. It was nearly one a.m. when I got home, and Rita was in bed. I looked around for evidence that she hadn't been with Trisch. But what? A cocktail napkin? A poker chip? A Magnum condom?

I stood next to her side of the bed. The first time we'd slept together, she'd reached into her nightstand and passed me a Trojan's Magnum—a black package with silver lettering. I forced a laugh. She said it was left behind by her last boyfriend. *Big shoes to fill,* I thought, and went limp. It took me nearly an hour to spring back.

I got myself a cold drink of water and picked up the phone to check the voice mail. As I was entering the access code—dim yellow street light creeping in the kitchen window with the hot sticky air—I saw a note from Rita on the pad beside the phone: "Q. 4:45. Homer Wilcox from IRS. Audit. Yikes!"

I shook Rita's shoulder too hard, and she woke frightened—her elbows shot up, hands in front of her face. "You talked to him? What did he say? You talked to him?"

She reeled back.

"Tell me exactly what he said!"

"Said about what?"

"Are you crazy? Is he coming here?" I was shouting now.

"No." Her face turned defensive.

"This could really mess me up." My hands were fists.

"He wouldn't come here. You're overreacting."

"You don't get it. There's evasion, cheating." I was listing them off on my fingers. "Bad faith—"

"It's not!"

I was hardly listening to her.

"And I'd never let him come here." She broke into a sob. "This is something for me."

"Fraud—" I said, then cut myself off. We both froze. We stared like two wary wrestlers, each waiting for the other to make a move. It dawned over her face in the instant it dawned over mine.

I sat on the edge of the bed. We were quiet for a minute. Finally, Rita said, "The IRS guy said he'd call again tomorrow. I'm sure you don't have to worry. He was very nice."

This is something for me? I'd never let him come here?

"I've heard about people getting audited." Her voice was much too soothing. "Even if you screwed up, you just pay the extra and maybe some interest. As long as you didn't cheat on purpose. And they'll know you didn't cheat on purpose."

My breathing speeded up.

"Did you?" she persisted.

I couldn't look at her. "What's 'something for you'?" I said.

"You didn't cheat on your taxes, did you?"

"Buddy Jensen did them."

"That sleaze?"

"He works things out."

She shook her head, looking away.

"He's been good to me." Why was I defending Buddy?

"I can't believe you'd cheat on your taxes. It's so . . . so . . ." Whatever she was thinking—pathetic, moronic, repulsive—she couldn't bring herself to say it in our bedroom, the two of us, at one a.m. "I can't believe it."

"You'd never let *who* come here?" I said.

She rolled over, her back to me.

"You only fuck him at his place? Is that it? How decent."

She reeled around. "How dare you accuse me of infidelity after what my father did? I'd never cheat on anyone. Get out of here!" She was crying again. "I couldn't fall asleep for two hours my legs ache so much. I'm having the worst outbreak I've ever had. It's everywhere. It hurts to sit. It hurts to walk. It stings when I pee. And you always want me to leave a note for you, but I had no idea where *you* were tonight. And when I finally fall asleep, you bust in here screaming!"

I touched her ankle through the sheet, my head dropped, then I stepped out, leaving the bedroom door cracked for air. Rita's outbreak trumped everything.

The night never cooled. All the fans were in the bedroom, so my penance was to sit on the couch and sweat, staring at Rita's note, hoping I was dreaming, hoping I'd look down and the note would really say, "You never had herpes and you never gave it to Rita, and you never took kickbacks, and your tax returns sparkle." But it kept saying the same thing: "Homer Wilcox . . . Audit."

I turned on the miracle. Three nuns in black habits—the night shift—were kneeling in the street in front of a row of flickering votive candles. Rosaries dripped from their twitching fingers, their lips trembling. I wondered if they wore knee pads under their robes. How would anyone know? The reporter held a desultory interview with a personal trainer from Tri-City Health and Fitness about heat prostration.

Maybe there'd be only a cursory audit, and I'd just seem sloppy, not fraudulent. "Off the backs of widows, orphans, and decrepit priests," Buddy had said. Maybe Homer Wilcox would fall for Nixon's line: "If some of my judgments were wrong, and some *were wrong*"—the magnanimous admission—"they were all made with the nation's best interest at heart."

During the night I caught up on the miracle. A diocese spokesperson, which I knew meant the bishop, had demanded that the statue of the Virgin be returned to St. Mary's courtyard. A group of vocal pilgrims then threatened to prevent any attempts at removing the statue from its "proper" place.

A doctor was interviewed about the many medical explanations for spontaneous recovery of hearing.

The miracle girl still hadn't appeared, but Father Floquet said in a press conference replayed throughout the night that she was healthy, in fine spirits, and awaiting her next revelation.

The press conference had been held late that afternoon in St. Mary's Church. Cameramen and reporters huddled around Floquet and the mayor, standing at a podium in front of the altar.

There were questions about crowd control and sanitation, questions about the miracle girl's ethnicity, rumors that her father was not killed but MIA. There were questions about proof and her ability to bilocate—appearing to people in crisis and in dreams—about a response from the pope, about Catholic precedence in these matters. Father Floquet was asked if it was true he was negotiating with Benetton and Absolut on behalf of the miracle girl, a question he shrugged off as unworthy of an answer. The mayor was asked how long the city could sustain the crowds. "As long as it takes a camel to pass through the eye of a needle. There's a reason why people the world over say, 'Hudson City is where miracles happen.' The Lord will provide. Come, I say to believers. Hudson City opens its arms to you." Then she opened her arms.

I worked on the puzzle, placing a dozen pieces. When I slept in the early morning, it was just long enough to wake in a fright, sweating, hardly able to get a breath. Every twenty minutes or so I switched ends of the couch to let the cushions dry and cool. I calculated how many times I'd have to switch ends before the sun came up. I calculated how many times I'd watch the news conference before the sun came up. I tried to calculate how many ounces of fluid I sweat per hour. I calculated that if Rita had four or five outbreaks a year, she might have two hundred more before we died. Two hundred times she'd suffer the sting and ache and silent humiliation. Two hundred times she'd glare at me with broiling anger. Although I know she'd tried, I realized she'd never forgiven me. And I didn't see how she could.

6. SATURDAY

The sun did finally rise. After a cold shower I stood in the kitchen watching coffee trickle from the filter to the pot. I had that hyped-up feeling that comes from no sleep: a symphony of musicians on psychedelic mushrooms tuning up inside my head.

I took my mug through the back hall to the stoop in the alley and leaned on the rail. Although the air was still muggy, it was bearably cool, cooler than inside the house. Over in Little Saigon, the pilgrims were setting stakes for another day's vigil despite the heat. In their apartment, Luna was lying in bed beside my father, planning to seduce him while he was half-asleep even though he was too self-involved to help her raise a child. Buddy was dreaming about Hudson City's implausible comeback, and Frank was doing toe touches, praying the Church's backslide might be reversed. We hang on tight to our lifelines. We *have* to. I couldn't let Rita slip away.

A little after seven, the fan in our bedroom window stopped spinning, and I heard Rita's bare feet padding across our floors. Her computer booted up. She walked room to room looking for me but didn't see me on the stoop and returned to her office. I heard her modem dialing.

In the kitchen I filled Rita a mug of coffee and refilled my own; I went to her office doorway. She'd taken off her T-shirt and was wearing just a robe—fully open—the belt hanging down the sides of her chair. Her chin was lifted to the screen, and rose-colored computer light shone on her throat. Then, without turning to me, a warm smile spread over her face that seemed to say, *You brought me coffee. I love you.*

I began, "D'you want—"

She jumped in her chair, and I jerked, coffee splatting on my feet. Her one hand reached toward the screen and the other seemed to shiver on her mouse. "What are you . . . ?!" she blurted. "Sneaking around . . ." Her face was red. But in a moment she'd composed herself. "Sorry," she said. "I thought you were gone."

Swiveling in her chair to face me, she pulled her robe closed.

"Want some coffee?" I asked, pretending, for both of us, not to understand what was happening.

When I parked in the small lot behind the diocese offices, the clock in my dash read 7:46 so I sat for a minute with the AC blowing, listening to music. I must have fallen asleep, deeply asleep. I dreamed I was running through cold and wet black tunnels beneath a city, running from a figure whose shoes snapped against the stone, gaining on me, the snapping louder and louder . . . I burst awake in a panic to see Buddy Jensen's face through the side window, laughing, clicking his keys on the glass. The clock read 7:49.

I lowered my window. Part of me was still in the tunnel—the chill of slimy moss against my face. "Tell me this is a joke, asshole."

Buddy's face collapsed. He looked genuinely hurt. He shook his head slowly. "You know, I consider you a friend."

"So it *is* a joke," I said hopefully. "You didn't call the IRS."

"Oh, that. That's business, Quinn. Yes. Of course I did. But it doesn't have to affect our friendship." He turned and headed into the office.

When I got inside, Buddy was already at the desk in the copier room examining my property files under the pretense of housing pilgrims. "Hey, pal," he called as I stepped into my office. "I'll need more info on Nineteen-Ten River Street."

I stopped in the doorway and thought for a moment. The building was a massive brick warehouse on the riverfront, upwards of 200,000 square feet, built last century when this was the biggest port on the Hudson River north of New York City. The diocese owned it as part of its investments in a long-defunct shipping company. Now we rented the first floor to a moving company for storage. The upper three floors were vacant.

"It's a warehouse," I said. "There's no sanitation facilities. There's probably rats. We can't put people in there."

"Whatever he needs, John." The bishop had come in. "We've got to cooperate."

Buddy slouched in his chair, crossing his legs. "That's right." He grinned. "Now that Venable and the diocese are in merger talks." He gently smacked the bishop's back. "Eh, Frank?"

The bishop took a step away from Buddy and scowled.

Buddy forced a laugh. "I was just joking around."

"Jokes are meant to be humorous, Mr. Jensen, and there's never humor in irreverence."

The grin on Buddy's face took too long to disappear. Finally he uncrossed his legs and lowered his head.

I got Buddy the River Street warehouse file. Exposed twelve-by-twelve handhewn timbers, wide-plank floors, old brick, floor to ceiling windows—perfect for condos. Buddy was positioning himself between Venable and the diocese, using the miracle to broker an empire.

My head was pounding. Tomorrow was Sunday and despite what the bishop said about working, I would sleep late, get my sanity back, then talk with Rita. In fact, I wouldn't wait. I dialed her and, thank God, it rang. "Hi," I said when she picked up.

"Hi."

I took a deep breath, comforted for a moment just to have her at the other end of the phone, at home. But the silence spiraled downward, pulling us with it, and I blurted, "Let's have lunch. Noon at Joey's?"

There was a pause before she said, "Okay." Joey's had served us blackened catfish on our first date.

I spent a couple hours on leases, then called a mortgage broker at home to stick my nose into a buyer's financing, then I set up some appointments to show properties. My hands were shaking from too much coffee.

Around ten, Patsy buzzed me for the bishop, and I slunk toward his office.

"Oh, yeah," Patsy remembered in the foyer. "The building inspector, Chip, called about Immaculate Heart. He said if it has to be tomorrow, make it seven a.m."

"Call him back," I said. "Tell him Monday at ten."

"Be there." Frank was standing behind me with a Diet Coke. He bilocated more than the miracle girl. "Then you can close Monday morning."

I shook my head. "I—"

"You'll be there," Frank said. "Come to the cathedral afterward. I'll be saying the nine-thirty Mass."

"That's no good," Patsy said. "Father Floquet is saying Mass outside St. Mary's at nine-thirty."

Frank's face burned.

"I know, Bishop O'Connor. I know." Patsy looked like she might burst into tears. "I tried calling him a hundred times, but he never came to the phone. I left messages. I told him you were ordering him not to have the Mass. But look." She held up a half-page announcement for the "Mass of the Miracle" in today's *Tri-City Times.*

Frank scowled. "That little b. Call him again," he said calmly, then turned to me. "As I said, I'll see you both at the cathedral Mass, then we'll get to work here at the office by eleven. You look terrible, Quinn."

"Thanks, I—"

"No time for that. I need you to drive me to Little Saigon."

"I've got a meeting," I said. Rita and I would get a table overlooking the river.

"Push it back, John. Floquet might think he can refuse my phone calls, but what'll he do when I pound on his door? It's time to remove him from his position as pastor of St. Mary's." He drained his can of Diet Coke and retucked his black shirt.

The miracle jam seemed lighter than usual. If I was speedy, I'd make it to Joey's on time. But then I turned a corner, ten blocks from St. Mary's, and traffic stopped. Sitting high in my Land Rover, we could see a few blocks ahead. Police barricades were set up along the curb. I shifted to Park and leaned back in the seat. It was 10:22. "You might have to hoof it," I suggested. Rita would reach across the table for my hand and ask forgiveness.

The bishop adjusted the AC to blow in his face and relaxed into the seat. "Where are all these people on a rainy Sunday morning in November?" he mused. "Where are they when politicians are bragging about men they've put to death, abortions they've sanctioned, countries they've bombed?" Until now, as far as I knew, Frank's life had been a series of practical decisions. The Tri-Cities diocese had been in shambles when he took over in the late Eighties. The churches had been empty, cold, and dilapidated. The schools, poorly enrolled, were run by inept administrators and embittered teachers. The seminary had closed its doors. Catholic Family Services was nearly bankrupt; their one thriving facility offered family counseling out of an old fish market because their own building had been contaminated by a cut-rate exterminator whose poison collected in foundation cracks, causing patients and staff to vomit uncontrollably. Frank haggled with OSHA, the state, and the exterminator for five years before tearing the building down and settling out of court. He'd turned the diocese around. And now, if he could get through this miracle and get the cathedral renovated, he'd be satisfied that he'd done his job. I respected him for keeping the cathedral for last. To his ego, it was the most important symbol of his resurrection of the diocese, but he recognized that for the everyday lives of Catholics in the Tri-Cities, it was one of the least.

"Floquet's been a good priest," the bishop said. "I know he thinks he's working for the good of the diocese by celebrating the miracle. But can't he recognize that he's cheapening the mysteries of faith? He's very misguided." Frank's voice rose. "Never mind the insubordination."

I'd listen to Rita, let her explain. "I could just drop you here," I said. But maybe I'd already lost her. She'd closed her robe, covered herself—from me.

"And this Buddy Jensen," the bishop said. "Do you really like him as much as you say?"

I didn't think I'd said a kind word about Buddy to the bishop. *He* was the one who liked Buddy so much. I thought of warning Frank that Buddy was dying to get his hands on any commercially viable Church properties, that he was a backstabber and conniver. But instead I said, "Buddy's just the man to be helping us now." There'd been enough betrayal.

"He holds you in very high regard," Frank said. "Fact is, I don't trust him. We need him, though. I think it's a compromise I have to make." He looked ahead, seeming to have come to a moment of clarity. We were sitting in traffic at the mouth of an alley. "Where's your clergy permit?" Frank asked, then he fished it from between the seats. "Park in the alley here and we'll walk."

"Frank, I'll get towed. You go on ahead and I'll go back to the office."

"Like heck," he said. "Park the Jeep."

"It's a Land Rover."

"Park it, John."

"Why don't you walk, and I'll pick you up after lunch at the police barricade on Asylum?"

"This is *not* a debate. Just park." And he tossed the permit on the dash.

I inched through the river of pedestrians into the alley and pulled in tight to a Dumpster overflowing with take-out food containers, Burger King cups, chopsticks. I dialed Rita on my cell phone to tell her I might be late. It rang but she didn't pick up. She was already out. Damn.

"These Jeeps," Frank said, "are deadly for the environment. Dominion involves caretaking, you know. Show some respect. If not for God, then for your children. Anyway, if you can afford this thing, we must be paying you too much."

Children, money, how I paid for the Land Rover. How did Frank squeeze so many stomach-churners into one sentence? "Can we just call it a *truck*?" I said.

The heat was crushing. As we got out, I felt weak and sleepy. Hot bodies pressed in on me. I remembered tripping at an Allman Brothers concert in high school at Shady Grove—a sun-baked pasture, manure gases rising from the ground. It was so hot that when the crowd started writhing, I hallucinated that I was in hell.

I followed Frank for a few blocks before asking why I was tagging along. "I've got so much to do. These people need a place to sleep tonight." I wanted to go back to my truck, turn up the AC, and nap.

He didn't answer.

When we crossed Asylum Avenue, Broadway was closed to traffic and the crowd expanded into the street. People recognized Frank, waving, nodding, staring. Frank walked along saying, "Nice to see you," "Bless you," "It's a scorcher, all right."

The miracle had brought out the festival crowd too—slackers in knit rasta hats playing Hacky Sack, a clown on a unicycle wearing pants as a shirt, a crooner for Jesus. The air smelled of hot sugar and Coppertone.

Half a block down, a panel truck was surrounded by people waving white fans at their chins, like little drone bees buzzing, hot, expressionless. We waded into them—hundreds of white fans flickering in the crowd. I zeroed in on one and saw the crest and gold lettering: "Compliments of Venable." As we passed the truck, someone held one out for the bishop. He refused, so I snatched it up and fanned my face.

Deeper into Little Saigon, the smell of grilled sausage from Eddie's Lunch gave way to the smells of incense, cloves, chilies, fried meat rolls, and barbecued shrimp paste. We passed an alley that led to a Buddhist temple, and a monk in orange robes reached out to the bishop, who stopped to shake his hand. A flash ignited and I turned to see a photographer following us. Small boys raced down the alley from the temple and gathered around Frank and the monk.

We continued with a small entourage, mostly children. There was a TV camera on us now, the cameraman walking backward, with a partner shoving people out of the way.

We passed a video store with Vietnamese movie bills in the windows and Vietnamese music blaring into the street. We passed prayer groups, some of five or six people, some of fifty or sixty, staking out a piece of the pavement. We passed vendors with rosaries, paintings of the Virgin and Child on wooden plaques, crucifixes, miracle buttons, bumper stickers, calendars, sun hats, and spritzer bottles with propeller blades on the nozzle.

It was almost eleven. I dialed Rita again and left a message. I could still make it to Joey's if we kept things rolling.

People were standing, waiting, sitting on lawn chairs. There were beach umbrellas, strollers, playpens. Around the hydrants fanning out water, kids screeched and adults got serious about cooling off.

We moved more slowly now, the crowd thickening, nearly shoulder to shoulder. We could hear a voice ahead, amplified, calm and desultory. A woman fainted. She was caught and fanned, and water was put to her lips. We could see the stone wall surrounding St. Mary's courtyard, mostly young men sitting eight feet off the ground along its top. Some held signs for Jesus.

As we got closer, I recognized the voice. I turned to tell Frank. His eyes were narrowed, the rough skin around his mouth was clenched. He already knew.

We elbowed our way through the gates and saw Floquet. He was standing on the pedestal where the statue of the Virgin had stood in the middle of an island of flowers. Dressed in black with an embroidered stole around his neck that hung to his knees, he had a microphone in one hand and a Gatorade bottle in the other. "And the statue of our Virgin stood on this pedestal," he was saying, "as a monument *from* Christians *to* God. But it now stands at the same threshold over which God has stepped—a monument from *God* to *Christians*. To *us*, my brothers and sisters. Those of us who have witnessed the seed being planted and who will protect the tree until it bears fruit."

His preaching was measured, calm. The bishop and I threaded and stumbled our way to the front and stood at the edge of the flowers among people who were mostly seated. A TV camera bobbed between Floquet and us. The bishop raised a hand, not to ask a question as it might have appeared, but to indicate to Floquet that he wanted a word.

Floquet ignored him.

By now there were more eyes on us than on Floquet. I looked around for a path through the flowers, but since it was not a podium but a pedestal, there was none.

"Excuse me, Father Floquet," the bishop called out, but Floquet continued with only a glance at Frank.

"Christ tells us," Floquet said, "that a sower went out to sow his seed and some of the seed fell by the side of the road and it was trodden on and eaten by birds. Some of the seed fell on rock and as soon as it sprang up it withered from lack of water. Some fell on thorns and the thorns grew over the new sprouts and choked them. But some of that seed fell on good ground, and sprang up and bore fruit a hundredfold. And he proclaimed, 'He that hath ears to hear, let him hear.'"

"Floquet," the bishop said louder, and "shushes" came sharply from the crowd.

"And Jesus tells us that the seed is the word of the Lord, and those who are on the side of the road hear it"—Floquet put his finger to his ear—"but it is snatched from their hearts by the devil, and they are not saved. Those on the rock have no root so God's message cannot grow. Those in the thorns hear the word but are led astray by temptation, pleasure, riches, luxury. Has the Virgin announced herself to a rich man in this city this week? Has the Virgin announced herself to a politician? Has the Virgin announced herself to a leader of the Church? No, she has not. She has announced herself upon the good fertile ground of a simple girl, not a rich girl, not a privileged girl, but a deaf girl, one of God's great and beautiful gifts to us, in whom His word will bear fruit."

The bishop called to Floquet again, sternly, and I suddenly wondered if the miracle girl was pregnant. I wondered if Floquet and all these people could be right. Looking at the crowd—children on crutches to our left, twenty or so people in matching pink T-shirts from a church in Colonie, rapt faces of every color listening and waiting—it seemed the tide was against us.

I waited for Floquet's preaching to combust into fire and brimstone, but it never strayed from an easy conversational tone. He wasn't sweating. He didn't appear pressured or anxious. Occasionally, there were long pauses as he considered the right word, sipped his drink, rested his voice. During these silences the crowd edged forward, open-mouthed. Floquet slid his glasses up his sun-reddened nose. He had a baby face, soft in the cheeks despite his thin frame and narrow shoulders. His teeth were small and crooked. He could have passed for an extremely confident college sophomore.

In his entire world, Floquet's only irritant seemed to be the bishop. But even that—he held up an annoyed hand or shot a quick glance as a grandparent forestalls a child who is interrupting—was not worth getting upset about.

However, Frank was not a man who took well to being ignored. He didn't make suggestions, he gave instructions and admonitions. His authority was conveyed by sternness. He felt there was decadence in tentative speech, walking slowly, picking at food, going unshaven or barefoot, taking long showers, sitting on the floor. I imagined Frank rising in the morning at six, wearing slippers and a robe into the bathroom, returning to his bedroom to dress and lace up his shoes before he'd even consider going downstairs. Frank in his kitchen reading the paper in slippers and robe was as absurd as Frank getting his nipple pierced.

"Nobody lights a candle," Floquet went on, "then covers the candle with a vessel or puts the candle under his bed. Of course not. He sets it in a candlestick high up on a table so everyone who enters can see." Floquet paused, smiled easily, and looked directly at Frank with great serenity. "Anything else would be foolish."

Frank jerked so severely I thought he'd dislocated his shoulder. "Floquet!" he shouted. His voice, as loud and deep as a beast's, was amplified by the microphone on the pedestal. The crowd stirred, gasping. Auto-advance cameras whined. Heat and fear rushed through my body and burst in my face. All of a sudden I was terribly thirsty.

"So why is it *we,*" Floquet asked gently, "who are blessed with this miracle?"

Frank reared up, shouting slow and strong: "I want you off Church property this instant!" He led with his shoulders, stomping one foot into the flowers, charging up the small mound toward Floquet.

A bar-fight instinct came over me, and I lurched to hold him back, but several men reached him before I did, tackling him into the flowers. Floquet just kept talking. I wasn't sure it was happening. Sparkles glittered at the sides of my eyes.

In seconds the men had hoisted Frank, one under each limb and one holding his waist. They could have been the same men who'd carried the statue of the Virgin to the miracle girl's stoop, the men who Frank had indirectly threatened if they didn't return the statue to this spot.

I remember lunging at the man who was holding Frank's leg, grabbing him by the waist and flinging him quite easily with a jolt of strength to the ground. Then the sparkles spread across my vision. I'd never felt so thirsty. I remember seeing Floquet's face oddly upside down, then

St. Mary's stone steeple, then the sky . . . and I remember the feeling of flower petals on my cheek, the moist smell of mulch. . . . A cold pressure pinched my forearm, and a pillow crinkled beneath my head. A child cried. A metal cart rattled by. I was cold, lying on a cot, an IV stuck in my arm. Off to my side I could see an old TV with no sound. On the screen, Timothy Floquet was standing on the pedestal, preaching. The picture jerked, and I watched five Vietnamese men getting Frank off the ground. In the corner of the screen, in the foreground, I saw myself. As the men began to carry Frank away, my head tipped strangely back, and my hands made a feeble grabbing gesture at the air. Then my knees buckled, and I dropped straight down as if a hole had opened up in the earth. I collapsed into the flowers.

"You fainted." A man's voice startled me. I turned and saw a brown mustache hanging from his nose. He was a nurse from the American Red Cross and I was in a St. Andrew's Elementary School classroom outfitted with air-conditioners and medical supplies.

"What time is it?" I asked.

He pressed two fingers inside my wrist and looked at his watch. He said I'd been there an hour, and he'd watched me faint on TV every five minutes. "What have you eaten today?" he asked.

I twisted my arm away from him to see my own watch. "Twelve-thirty," I said. "Is that right?"

"What have you eaten?"

"Shit." Rita had probably given up on me already.

"Can you be more specific?"

I watched the men carry Frank over the heads of the crowd and out the gate again. "I've had coffee."

"Eaten," he repeated. "Like food."

The picture was jumbly as the cameraman tripped over the crowd to follow. "Just coffee," I said.

"And to drink?"

On the street it seemed there'd been an argument about Frank—some pilgrims insisting that the men put him down. The men had refused, tightening their clutch on his limbs. Two Vietnamese nuns intervened.

"To drink?" the nurse repeated impatiently, tapping his pen on a clipboard.

"Just coffee, okay?"

"Apparently it's not okay," he snipped and walked away from my cot.

My cell phone was still hooked on my belt, so I called information, then called Joey's. I heard the phone rattle on the bar and Rita's name shouted out a few times. "Sorry," the waiter said and hung up. I tried home. Nothing.

Frank was eventually set back on his feet. He had a word with the nuns then reached out papally to the men who'd carried him off, obviously aware of the TV camera. Everything seemed okay until Frank tried to return to the courtyard. The men accompanied him to the gates then blocked his path. Frank made several attempts, gesturing for the men to part, then wedging his large body between them. But they didn't give him an inch, and as the camera nudged closer, Frank finally laid his hand on the head of a small boy beside him, moved his lips in prayer, and turned away. The camera watched him go, but didn't follow. The bishop was no longer the story.

There was a commercial for Venable, and I drank the glass of water that the nurse had put beside me. I ate some strawberry Jell-O, surprisingly good. Miracle coverage returned: a live shot of two local commentators superimposed over WHCR's remote studio in the street.

I called the office. "Is the bishop okay?" I asked Patsy.

"He's fine," she said. "The mayor and police chief are in his office. What's up with *you*, Quinn?"

"Eating Jell-O," I said, spooning up the last red cube. It tasted like the smell of Rita's shampoo.

"The fainting was awesome. Is it true what they're saying?"

I was on the TV again, Frank lifted on high, the whites of my eyes gleaming, my mouth slack as if from a minor stroke—

"Boom," the nurse said in my ear, startling me as my image on the silent TV collapsed, suddenly boneless.

"Tell Frank I'll see him when I get there. Or he can call me." I clicked off.

I lay back on the cot. "Wait five minutes," the nurse said. "And you can witness the rapture again."

"Can you turn on the sound?"

"It's broken."

I could get a blanket, I realized happily, kick off my shoes and snooze for a while, then go home and talk to Rita refreshed. I curled onto my side and my phone rang. I clicked it right on. "Hi, Bishop," I said. "They've hooked me to an IV so it might be a while." I brought my knees up to my chest.

"Pardon me?" the caller said.

"Who's this?"

"Mr. Quinn?"

I didn't say anything.

"This is Homer Wilcox with the IRS." My heart launched a bubble of blood the size of a water balloon. "I'd like to make an appointment with you for an audit."

"I'm losing you," I said. "Hello? You're fading in and out."

"An appointment for an audit," he said. "It's nothing to be concerned about—"

"Hello?" I said.

"Homer Wilcox with the IRS for a routine audit."

"If you can hear me," I shouted, "try calling back." My heart was pounding so fiercely the IV needle quivered. I turned off the phone and threw it as hard as I could at the wall. The IV stand crashed to the floor. There was blood on my arm where the needle had been.

I felt like I'd been thrown out of a bar—an orderly shoving me back out into the heat, then holding me there as the nurse taped a chilly cotton ball to my arm and forced a bottle of Gatorade and two Fig Newtons into my hands. This, I thought in a light moment, was how nurses played hardball.

I started up the hill from St. Andrew's and the light mood left me. I was getting audited, I was getting fucked. And so was Rita. Getting fired and losing Rosemary's and Frank's respect were the least of my worries. Everything was crashing down. At the top of the hill, I wiped my sweaty face with a sleeve and decided to take things one at a time.

It was ten or twelve blocks to the alley where I'd parked. If my truck was towed, I'd take it like a champ and move on. Along the way children began to point at me. "What did she say?"

I shook them off, but they pressed closer as I waded through the crowds. I had a single-minded focus and nothing was going to slow me down. As I made my way up the street, I saw myself fainting on TVs in shop windows. "Tell us," a woman implored and grabbed a handful of my shirtsleeve.

"Get off me!" I yanked my arm away. She looked like she'd seen the devil. I started running, knocking into people, knocking one down. There were shouts at my back, shouts to stop me. I ducked in the alley and my Land Rover was there, blessedly waiting. As I opened the door a man grabbed my shoulders from behind. His wide face was red and pockmarked, madly overheated, a few days' stubble. But he spoke softly. "We're dying out here."

"I never even talked to her," I said, and he let me back away into the truck. "She was making a sandwich, okay? You know more than I do."

I started the engine and fired down the alley, my right side mirror catching on a Dumpster but springing back in place. I shot out on Division Street. My heart was pounding.

I headed home. "We need to have an honest talk," I rehearsed the conversation with Rita. "I'm willing to forgive," but was I? If she was balling this Josh, I'd go crazy. What else could it be? "We need to talk through this so we can put it behind us," but what the hell was there to talk about? It's not like I didn't have opportunities to sleep around. That chick at the State Street Deli who remembered me from grammar school and always piled on the capocello. "We should hang out," she'd say, slipping extra pickle spears in my bag. But I remained faithful. "We have to talk about our relationship and what you're not getting." Ha! She seemed to be getting plenty.

I waited at a red light, squeezing the steering wheel, and I suddenly realized he was there with her, I felt sure, in our apartment. He was telling her a joke, and as she laughed, she stroked his face and he kneaded the soft flesh of her upper arm. I'd stood her up for lunch, and she was pissed and decided that today was the day to break it off with me. She'd brought him over to hurt me so bad there'd be no going back. I'd call first, I decided, and if he was there I wouldn't go. But when I reached for my phone, there was only the flaccid leather case strapped to my belt.

I double-parked at a phone booth. The receiver was so hot it burned my ear. *I'm unavail*— I'd go anyway. I dialed the office to tell Patsy I'd be held up a few hours. On the shelf beneath the pay phone, a popsicle stick floated in a puddle of vanilla ice cream. On the fourth ring a voice said, "Tri-Cities Diocese." It was Buddy Jensen.

"What the fuck?"

"Miracle boy!" he said.

"Put Patsy on."

"I'm afraid she's away from her desk. Is there something I can help you with?"

"God, you suck. Tell Patsy to cancel my appointments, and tell the bishop the Red Cross sent me home to bed." I tapped the end of the popsicle stick with a finger, but it didn't move. The ice cream had congealed. The sour vanilla smell turned my stomach.

Twenty minutes later, when I got to the apartment, she didn't appear to be there. I headed straight for the bedroom. The door was closed. I stood in front of it for a moment before I burst in.

But the room was empty, bed made, window closed tight and locked.

I looked in the kitchen, the back hall, the bathroom, her office. The

English cottage shone from her computer, not the screen saver, so she hadn't been gone long. And she hadn't moved out.

Until I saw that radiance in her face this morning, I hadn't realized how long it'd been. I remembered a night in Jamaica, moonlight and a warm breeze in her face. I remembered one afternoon driving to Lake George singing (embarrassingly) "The Piano Man" along with the radio at the top of our lungs. I remembered sitting here on the living room floor feeding each other gnocchi with a walnut cream sauce that she made after her sister gave her a Cuisinart. And until this morning I'd believed that I was the only one who could produce that radiance in her.

But I saw it myself: as she looked at her screen, Rita's breasts rose with anticipation, then when I spoke, they dropped. She pulled her robe closed.

Standing in front of her desk, I toyed with the mouse for a minute then pulled down "Recent Applications": all work stuff. Then I dialed into her e-mail. I couldn't help myself. My thinking was this: I'd make only one attempt at her password. If it worked, then no one could say I was violating Rita's trust because my guess was "Josh," and if I was right, her violations were much greater than mine. I typed it in and hit Return. "Invalid password" flashed on the screen. I exhaled slowly and considered my options: "Cancel" or "Try again." I typed quickly: "MyDearJosh." A red-and-green "Welcome" burst on the screen.

Motherfucker.

I went straight for the inbox. The dizzying reek of sour vanilla and cream came back. Most of her e-mail was from Josh Katz. I scrolled up and down reading his name, over and over, like a mistake. Patterns raced up the screen, every fourth or fifth message from someone else, then another block of Josh Katz, Josh Katz, Josh Katz. There were six, eight, sometimes ten per day. I opened one from January. "My dear Rita." I was reeling. "I'm just back from lunch at that Indian place on Tottenham Court Road. Chicken Vindaloo exciting my taste buds nearly as much as the thought of you. The day's still dreary. Hoped the sun might sneak through during lunch but no such luck. Good morning. And what a dream. Was the tiger wearing black shoes too?! I've got a meeting that could go long, so I won't be able to write for a couple hours. Loves."

A couple hours?! I opened one from May. More chitchat. I clicked to the outbox, and the same eerie Warhol-Rorschach flew up the screen: "Josh Katz," like a computer virus.

I opened message after message. He was in London, and every morning he wrote Rita four or five e-mails by the time we woke up. *Her* first e-mail each morning began with her dreams. The e-mails went back and forth until he left his office. Then Rita would send a few long ones at the end of the day for him to read the next morning. He worked for World-Media, which owned Rita's radio station. He was married with two small children. It was sick. I was sick.

"I have a vision of you," he wrote, "moving room to room in an apartment, always sunny, never needing to brush your hair or get dressed. You rise from bed a goddess kept from me and kept *for* me in the sunlight, then lie down to dream in the darkness. Loves." *Give me a fucking break.* I searched for "Jolly good time balling you last week" or "Your tits are smashing," but there seemed to be no actual references to sex.

I clicked on one headed, "Re: Judaism." He wrote about his close-knit family all together at the holidays, his son memorizing the same bar mitzvah prayers that he memorized as a boy, and his father and grandfather and back for thousands of years. The rootedness. The bonds of culture and family. What crap. He ended with "Judaism is more than a religion. It's a way of life." Rita's exact words to me.

I read her most recent notes—bullshit about her day, walks she took, career and life goals. Life goals? They were upbeat. Fun. Fun!

She mentioned my sensing something. *Sensing?* How about *I'm gonna kill the cocksucker?* This wasn't right, she said. They had to e-mail each other less. She referred to times she'd tried to cut it off but then they started right up again. She referred to "the years." I zipped to the top of the outbox—their correspondence went back a year and a half, which was how old this computer was. I read the first and second—they were already in full swing by then.

I found the e-mails where she tried to cut it off. "We mustn't continue," she wrote. "It's not right for your family, your wife. It's not fair to Quinn." I did a search of my name. Seventeen instances in a year and a half—approximately 550 days, times 8 per day—4400 e-mails—she mentioned me something a little better than one-third of one percent of the time.

There'd be a break of a day or two when Rita made these threats, then Josh would come back with, "I know I'm being bad—:)—but I just had that cheesecake again and wanted to tell you how yummy it was." She responded, "You won't believe this—I had a craving for cheesecake today," and they were right back into it.

"I dreamed," she wrote two days ago, "that you and I were sheep farmers, our pastures set high on bluffs along the coast of Scotland. We wore Wellingtons and heavy sweaters stretched out at the neck. I was sitting on the edge of the bluff looking out to sea feeling terribly empty, the weight of the sea draining through me. I was listening to you in the barn, helping a sheep in labor that was dying—oh, the bleating was horrid. Then I felt a tickle on my cheek, and when I turned, you were there holding a baby lamb and I felt suddenly filled up. I looked in your eyes, held the lamb to my face, and said, 'A miracle. My dear Josh.' I said it out loud, unfortunately, which has caused some trouble here."

I read obsessively for over an hour, not close to everything, not five percent. Despite my quest for proof of sex, as if I were browsing a porn site for the one hardcore photo that would put me over the edge, I finally couldn't go on. I wasn't even devastated, I was bored. The e-mails were all the same. They were the smoochy talk of a mildly romantic late-middle-aged marriage.

I composed a reply to Josh: "My dear Josh, you bland dickless Brit, I dreamed last night that you were a castrated sheep and I was a wolf ripping out your heart with my fangs. Your blood and flesh tasted like chicken Vindaloo. Loves." I read it over, deleted, and began again. "My dear Josh, I hope you had a nice lunch, and on the way back to your office a double-decker bus ran over you, crushing your skull, and the rear tires got stuck on your neck and the driver kept his foot on the gas spinning your organs and yummy crumpets on the mud flaps and into the street. Loves." I deleted again and went on in this vein for several more messages before some sense came over me and I wrote:

"My dear Josh, This time I mean it. It's destroying me and my relationship with Quinn. I'm falling apart. I'm in love with Quinn. I realize Quinn is everything to me. I want nothing but Quinn, and my shame over our correspondence is . . . is . . . It must stop this instant. If you e-mail me again I swear I'll kill myself. I swear." I sat back for a minute, then clicked Send.

I went to the kitchen. I felt somehow okay. I'd taken a positive step toward dealing with the crisis.

A big pitcher of leftover sangria was in the fridge. I poured a tall glass and brought the pitcher with me to the living room where I sat on the couch to wait for Rita.

Two gulps in, I wanted to read more, to discover Rita's true feelings about me, and about Josh. Find the smoking gun of their sexual romps. But I was too tired. The bishop was right: "Not so young." I was thirty-five and complacent in a relationship with a woman who was cheating on me. Ten years ago I'd thought I'd be rich and happy by now. Ten years ago I'd thought that when you found yourself prefacing statements with "Ten years ago," you were already old. But when I heard myself say it, it didn't seem old anymore. I still thought of the Seventies as ten years ago. I thought of high school as ten years ago. I had to shake my head and correct myself: *Twenty* years. I was twice the age I'd been when I started college, three times my age when Nixon resigned. I was halfway dead.

Anyway, I was too old and too tired to read any more. So I waited, the sangria helping me through the heat. I flipped on the TV and there I was, fainting. Jesus Christ. Then they showed an older Latina woman dressed in church clothes fainting on the same spot. And then a hefty white woman with a cane. Then a Vietnamese woman holding a fan. A bald man with a Navy tattoo. It turned out that since I'd fainted this morning,

there'd been a rash of faintings on the mound of flowers at Timothy Floquet's feet. It looked like a promo for Stupidest Home Videos—one after another dropping on the same spot. They came to with remarkably similar stories: they'd seen the miracle girl dressed as a Renaissance Virgin receive a revelation and whisper it into the ear of the first fainter, "the man in the tie." Me. What could I do but laugh and pour myself another glass?

The buzzer sounded, and I went to the door. A man with thick gray hair and a handlebar mustache stood on the stoop holding his briefcase. "Mr. Quinn?" His glasses were slightly tinted.

I knew the voice.

"Homer Wilcox. We spoke earlier." He held his open wallet—a plastic window with documentation—IRS. "I tried calling you back, but the cell phones must be down." He shifted back and forth on his feet.

I opened my mouth to speak but it was all air.

"We don't have to do this now," he said, "but I was having so much trouble phoning, and I was in the neighborhood."

If I lived another thirty-five years and I spent five of those in prison, it would be nearly fifteen percent of the rest of my life. Crucial years for working things out with Rita. Would she get on the bus at dawn with the other inmate wives and visit me? Why wasn't she home yet? Was she coming back at all?

I intended to say "another time would be better," but instead I said, "Want some cold punch?" and next thing I knew, Homer Wilcox was standing in the living room holding one of Rita's parents' crystal punch cups. I think I really needed someone to talk to.

He took a sip and shook his head.

"Don't worry," I said. "It's nonalcoholic."

"Well, cheers." He smiled from behind the cup.

"It's a mix. A powder. You just add water and fruit." He looked suspicious but downed it and I poured him another. "They have it at Wal-Mart."

He smacked his lips. "What'll they come up with next?" We stood together for a moment, silent, then he said, "Hey. You're the one who had the vision. The one who fainted. You're the man in the tie."

I shook my head.

"Did you see the miracle girl?" he asked.

Probably it was over with Rita. Why wouldn't it be?

"I love this part," he said, pointing at the TV. The men were carrying the bishop out the gates. "Are you sure there's no alcohol in this?"

Frank was helpless. A beetle on his back. I truly felt bad for him. "Nah," I said.

We looked at each other for a moment. Then, looking back at the TV, I said, "Well, I guess we should do this thing."

"It's your call." He resumed shifting side to side.

"I'll get my records. Help yourself to more punch."

I took my glass, nearly full, out through the kitchen to the back hall. I rattled open the file cabinet. The dead bolts on the back door were greased and silent; I covered one quick squeak in the hinges with a cough; Venable's new pressure-treated deck was rock solid.

I ran, careful not to spill my sangria, hopped in my truck and rolled it off the sidewalk. In minutes I was five blocks away, stopped dead in traffic nosing toward the miracle, a prayer in Spanish on the radio: the hollow sound of a massive stone church was broadcast through the microphones, faith and hope echoed between the soaring arches and stained glass, high above the heads of believers in that vast empty space.

Luna worked in a store selling candles, crystals, incense, Tarot cards, Wiccan paraphernalia. Although there were no customers when I walked in, the store was next to the university campus and usually did a brisk business. For the job, she dressed as a leather witch—black leather halter top with laces straining at her cleavage. The Sturgis tattoo looked especially splotchy. Wind chimes that I'd brushed with my shoulder were

tinkling. She nodded at me, smiling. She was missing a molar, only noticeable when she smiled broadly. "Very cool," she said.

"Didn't happen."

"I saw it on TV at lunch."

"I guess I fainted, but that's all it was."

"I could see it in your face. Something passed through you."

"I don't even remember keeling over."

"But you will. Later today or in your sleep. It's in you and you haven't seen it yet."

I shook my head.

"When you're open to it, it'll appear."

"Sorry to disappoint."

"Very cool," she said again.

I sat on the stool by the counter, where *she* would be sitting if she ever sat. "So listen—" As I began to tell her about the e-mails, I shuddered. She hugged me, cradled my head as a mother would on her bare shoulder. Until I laid it out for Luna, it hadn't struck me that every morning when I was making tender ministrations toward lovemaking, and Rita bolted from bed, it was to rush off and read his e-mails. With him on London time the overlap of their working day was only a few hours and she couldn't bear missing a minute. Luna pushed a tissue into my hand.

"Okay," she said. "You don't think Rita's lying to you about sex with this guy, right?"

I nodded.

"I don't either. If they were having sex, a pansy like Josh would be waxing poetic about her nipples. It would be unbearable. He's serious about the wife and kids, but he loves the idea of a young hotty who'll play the other woman. It's a safe and sanitized affair. Another woman's attentions without any of the guilt.

"As for Rita, she's in love with him. She's in love with you too, because I've seen it in her face, but there was always something she held back. And now we know what it is. You'll never really have her while she's giving so much to him. She betrays you every morning." Luna smoothed her hands down her hips. "God, I love sex in the morning," she said mostly to herself.

"You told me. The tea kettle."

"I love it anyway. For its own sake. It's like hatching at dawn. The rooster's crowing and I'm busting off the shell for a new day."

The bell attached to the door jingled and I jumped. I fully expected to see Homer Wilcox walk in, curling the handlebar of his gray mustache with a forefinger and thumb. But it was just a customer.

"So," Luna said, moving in closer. "Do you believe in sexual healing?"

It had been twenty-one days. My heart missed a beat as I realized I'd never lay my cheek on Rita's bare chest again.

The customer held a crystal up to the front window, shooting blue and yellow lasers around the store.

"When I saw you have that vision—"

I held up my hand. "Oh, for God's sake."

She bowed her head then raised it, lowering her voice. "When I saw the spirit, that you haven't yet recognized, visit you this morning, it was a great convergence because I'd been thinking of you that very instant. And here's what I was thinking. I'm not saying that this is what your visitation was about or this is your mission or anything like that. You've been blessed for some reason, maybe random luck, maybe not, but on this day that something special moves within you, how about we conceive a child?"

Green and red light danced across Luna's forehead and on the hand-dipped rainbow candles hanging on a wooden rack behind her. I'd stopped listening for a moment, but when I caught up with her, I almost laughed. She and my father were a perfect pair. He'd probably want to negotiate a trade: a night with Rita for him.

"For all your father would have to know, it'll be his. For all any of us would know. Babies look like their grandparents anyway. I wouldn't expect any responsibility from you. I could get anyone to do the job, obviously, but I want to have a child with your father, and you're the next best thing. I think today's my last shot this month, and with you being blessed today . . . I know it could happen."

Rita held another man's head to her chest: she breathed in deeply, filled with the scent of his scalp.

"I know it seems weird, but those hang-ups are all in the head. Think of the positives. We're two people who dig each other, right?"

I didn't nod.

"Right. The *negative* vibe is this connection to your father. Don't let that bum you out. Love the one you're with. And let's face it, you could use a little skin to skin."

All I wanted was to curl up in our bed with Rita, make slow gentle love, then sleep wrapped up tight for a day.

"You're thinking about Rita," Luna said. "Of course you're thinking about her. And that's cool. It'll help get you going."

Rita's head thrown back, giggling uncontrollably as he kisses her neck.

"Your father plays darts tonight so why don't you come over around nine?" Luna leaned in very close, her breath at my ear. For all her vegetarianism, I swear a meaty smell came off her, sandwich meat, roast beef or ham, not unpleasant, but definitely protein. "We'll put some candles in the spare room, I'll treat you right, then you can sleep like a baby for a solid twelve. You could use it. You look like shit."

I shook my head. I was so tired.

"So, you game?" she asked.

"I really don't think so."

She winked. "I know a couple neat tricks."

I got up to leave.

"You think about it," she said. "I'll be waiting. Nine o'clock."

Beneath the old Royal Crown Cola sign—"the fresher refresher"—hanging from B&L Cash Market, an air-conditioner in the transom rattled so loudly I covered my head as I stepped under it to go inside.

I grabbed a pint of milk and a bag of pretzels, and had to practically fight my way out. The old woman who ran the store had seen me faint on TV. Women and children and a German shepherd appeared from behind the curtain leading to the back room. They surrounded me as I paid, wanting a piece of me, a piece of the truth.

So I drove around. I didn't want to go anywhere. Everyone suddenly knew who I was. I figured that Homer Wilcox had an APB out on me. Police had probably staked out the apartment. Was it against the law to leave the scene of an audit? I didn't know where to go. I thought of hitting the road and getting out of Hudson City for good. I'd tried once and went as far as my imagination reached at the time—Key West. In my entire life I don't remember such shimmering expectation as I felt on that drive to Florida.

But I couldn't come up with a destination that revived that excitement. Maybe Luna was right: a good screw would get me back on my feet. But what was I thinking? Fucking my father's girlfriend? That was more than a Catholic prohibition. Sort of generally frowned on.

I slammed on the brakes. My tires screeched. Standing in the crosswalk a fat man with a patch over one eye raised a white cane to whack my hood.

It was nearly six, and if the air had cooled at all, the heat radiating off the sidewalk cranked it back up—hot through the soles of my shoes. I stood at a pay phone looking for Lilian's home number in the book. She answered on the second ring. "It's the man in the tie," I said.

"Pardon me?"

"The man in the tie."

"Wrong number," she said.

"Lilian, it's Quinn," I blurted. "John Quinn. Don't tell me you haven't seen the news today."

"No, I haven't."

"Well, you need a miracle mania update."

"You know," she said a little apologetically, "I don't really care about it anymore. It's turned into such a circus."

At first I thought I'd misheard. But I hadn't, and somehow this was a blow to me. It *was* a circus, she was right. But I guess I'd counted on Lilian to keep up the hope.

"Hello?" she said after a long silence.

"I can't believe the week went by and I never got you a lease. I'm really sorry."

"Don't worry about it. We'll do it Monday."

"Well, it expires Monday. I really hate to wait, and I'm in the Heights right now. Why don't I swing by."

"It's really not necessary," she said.

Cars were backed up in the street. Faces behind the windows of a chartered bus seemed to recognize me, so I huddled into the phone. "Maybe we could grab some dinner too—?"

"Is everything all right, Quinn?"

"It's just important we get this signed."

There was a pause, and I could tell she was thinking. "If you don't mind spaghetti with Jasmine and me, you could come over here."

I felt a rush of relief. "I'll pick up some wine," I said. "I'll be right over."

In front of Lilian's bungalow a lazy sprinkler waved back and forth over stalks of corn, bulbous yellow squash, and fat tomatoes. A picnic table on her glassed-in porch was covered with pots of thyme, parsley, a few kinds of basil, and other herbs I didn't know the names of. The front door was ajar, and when I peeked inside, I nearly stuck my face into a bowl heaped up with peaches and plums. Above the bowl a postcard was thumbtacked to the wall—a stone statue of a powerful man with forearms and hands rivaling Michelangelo's Moses, dressed in light armor, sitting in a simple armchair, napping. And I knew the statue was Holger Danske.

Standing there with my hand on the knob, I remembered the hot smell of grasses in a meadow along a deserted Highway 33 in Phoenix County, Georgia. The sun had broken through after a brief but intense rain. Ripe peaches hung heavy on their branches in the orchard down the road. I sat in my car, August 1986, broken down. The car had just quit, no bucking or choking, leaning itself toward the shoulder and coasting to a stop. I waited for hours. The car was a bust, twenty-two hundred dollars to get it rolling again, so I traded the tow for the parts and took a Greyhound the rest of the way to Key West.

I'd wanted to get to the end of something, to the edge. I thought I'd work on a fishing boat for a year or two. But all I saw in Key West were T-shirt shops, Planet Hollywood, and mocked up cabañas selling "Cubans" rolled in Guatemala and souvenir cigar cutters from China. The "edge" was lined with Holiday Inns and umbrella-drink huts. The fishing boats took Houston and Salt Lake City executives out for marlin at five hundred dollars per half day. I stayed less than a week, drinking too much rum in bars packed with cocky overdressed people in sales and marketing who reminded me a little too much of myself.

The morning I left, I was sitting at a sidewalk table eating scrambled eggs and bacon. A small middle-aged man with thinning hair and bright eyes sat with a coffee at the next table and asked if I knew of any good deals on hotels. "Clean," he'd said. "Nothing with luxury. Quiet. And you can walk."

At first I thought he was a hustler after my money. Then I thought he was gay and after me. Then I thought he was just who he said he was: a Danish computer consultant and a Hemingway buff, who sneaked down from a convention in Miami for a couple days. I told him where I'd stayed was overpriced and noisy.

"Five nights?" he asked.

"Yep."

He looked right at me. "Why didn't you move someplace better?"

"I know," I said. "I just thought if I switched hotels, it might be even worse."

He was about to get up when a waitress refilled his coffee. With a broad smile he told her, "I love this part of America."

"It's nicer in the winter," the waitress said, but I think he was talking about free refills.

She topped off my cup too, and soon he was telling me with great pride about Denmark—how everyone bikes and walks; they love beer, socialism, and Hans Christian Andersen. And after we'd talked awhile, he told me about Holger Danske, a great Viking, a giant really, who, as a baby, had required five nursemaids to satiate him. Holger drove the Swedes from Denmark in battle after battle, and when Denmark was finally safe, he sat down to sleep, telling the people that if Denmark ever needed him, he'd rise and defend her again.

All the way home my lower back was sore from the Greyhound seats, and from disappointment, and a feeling of dread about returning to Hudson City that has never fully passed. I thought about the comfort of Holger—his strength and bravery. Always there if he's needed. I wondered if that was how Nixon felt sitting in Upper Saddle River, New Jersey. *When this country realizes it needs me, I'll be here.*

Lilian met me at the door. "Holger," I said, pointing at the postcard.

Surprise and delight lit her face. "Right. How do you know about Holger?"

"I've actually never seen a picture of him before. But I knew right away."

She liked that. I'd pleased her.

I followed her to the kitchen to meet a shy, polite, and suspicious Jasmine. But in no time the three of us were working together at a massive cutting board chopping carrots, celery, and mushrooms. The music was poppy and loud, a teen band I think, and somehow the kitchen was comfortably cool. Jasmine explained the technique for launching off stairs on a skateboard and, more importantly, landing.

"You don't *seem* glum," Jasmine said to me, and Lilian shushed her. Jasmine threw a carrot slice to the dog and he caught it with a snap. The low sun sparked on Lilian's wineglass as she touched it to her lips, and I suddenly thought I could stay here with Lilian and Jasmine and Holger at the door for the rest of my life.

We ate tri-colored corkscrew pasta, red sauce with chunks of turkey, salad with creamy Italian dressing and herb croutons with lots of crunch. Jasmine talked with her mother—gradually speaking more to me—about the lunch she'd had with her girlfriends at Dairy Queen, a boy who broke both his wrists, and disaster rumors she'd heard about miracle mania. Lilian seemed happy to listen: a relaxing day, the occasion for a glass of wine, a proud mother. She ate very little, then slipped down low in the high-backed armchair with the wineglass propped up in her hands. I gorged myself. When the platters were empty, the salad gone, Lilian urged me to go to the kitchen for thirds and fourths. I opened the second bottle of Chianti. When I sat back down with a full plate, I refilled Lilian's glass and told Jasmine about standing at the miracle girl's apartment door. "What was she wearing?" Jasmine wanted to know, especially the shoes. Was I "positive" there wasn't a halo? I felt like the man of the house. I felt larger than normal, useful, thoughtful, generous. I sat straighter. I felt as I imagined Frank felt every day of his life, a feeling I'd never known in our own household—Rita's and mine. Or with my parents. Or my mother and Charles.

"She's beautiful," Jasmine said of the miracle girl. "She's partly an angel." Jasmine had her mother's hair—blond and kinky, making her face look tiny and smooth. "And today a man in a tie had a miracle too, but no one can find him now."

"Another miracle," Lilian said facetiously.

"It wasn't a miracle," I said. "The miracle girl supposedly relayed a message from God to the man in the tie. The spirit entered him."

"So what about it, Quinn? It seems your boss doesn't buy any of it."

"Poor guy," I said.

"I wanted to believe in this girl," she said. "I *want* to. But it's gotten so tawdry. And you say she's got a partner now? Are they going on the talk shows?" She picked a single slice of mushroom from the bottom of the salad bowl. "The miracle girl has gone commercial." She snickered, tired and a little tipsy.

"Don't laugh," I said. "I'm the man in the tie. I'm the one God spoke to."

Lilian choked a quick laugh, like a cold car trying to start.

"I'm serious. I'm on the run from the pilgrims."

She laughed harder, putting down her wineglass and holding her ribs.

I kept it going. "Turn on the TV if you don't believe me."

"Stop," Lilian forced out, doubled over at the head of the table. And I couldn't help laughing with her. "You?" she said, tears streaming down her cheeks. "The holy spirit . . . ?" She was gasping for air. ". . . in you?"

"Ridiculous, I know."

Jasmine was slumped back in her chair. Her laugh sounded just like her mother's. "People who don't have faith in anything don't have miracles," she announced.

"Shush!" Lilian said, frowning at her daughter. Clearly, she'd given Jasmine the score on me.

To look at Lilian it was hard to know whether she'd been laughing or sobbing. Her face was flushed, her eyes red. She wiped her cheeks with a paper napkin.

"No," I said, looking at my hands in my lap. My shoulders narrowed. "You're right. It's absurd."

"No more absurd than the spirit entering that woman," Lilian said, trying to cover. "It's nothing but media hype. She's probably cutting a CD with Ricky Martin."

"Hey," Jasmine objected. "I love Ricky Martin." And as she raved about the singer, Lilian focused back on her daughter, relieved that the topic had changed. She sat up in her chair, took a deep breath, and composed herself.

When Jasmine exhausted the subject, we were quiet for some time. The music had ended. I looked at a speck of food on the lip of my wineglass.

Lilian's head rested on the back of her chair again. "I'd really hoped," she said to no one.

Jasmine looked suddenly bored.

From the kitchen the dog sighed.

Lilian lifted her head. "Sorbet?"

At eight-thirty we were all three standing around the kitchen, clean dishes drying in the rack, the dog asleep, light through the windows softening. I poured wine for Lilian and me then drifted to the living room. As I smoothed my hand over the woodwork around the fireplace, negotiations went on behind my back; then Jasmine said, "Good night," and Lilian joined me. I gazed at a framed poster of a Copenhagen canal over the couch. "Are you Danish?" I asked.

"*Ja,*" she said. "Half."

"Been there?" I sat down.

"Just once." She rolled her eyes. "For my honeymoon." Then she sat at the other end of the couch, facing me. "You?"

"I haven't been anywhere."

"So really," she said. "Did you have a religious experience?" She felt bad.

"What?"

"Did you have a vision?"

"What?"

"Did you—"

"Oh, my God," I said. "I can hear!" She smiled, and I was glad I'd made her feel better. Lilian was honest and compassionate. Her honesty had made her laugh at the suggestion that an angel might choose me as its messenger. Her compassion had moved her to invite me here to dinner. I couldn't expect one without the other. "So how was Denmark?" I asked. "Other than the marriage not working out, I mean."

"They drink huge beers. You have to pee all the time."

"Did you trace your roots and all that?"

"Some twelfth cousin who's an attorney for Lego."

"Seriously?"

"Ninth, maybe. He gave me Legos that weren't for sale yet."

"Do you want to build something?"

"My ex got it. Along with the other dog."

"*This* dog's pretty good."

She nodded. She'd stopped drinking her wine. Her glass sat full on the coffee table. I wasn't sure if this was a bad sign or a good one, or a sign at all.

"What happened with your ex?" I said.

"Are you really asking, or just talking?"

Lilian was a lot of work. "Really," I said.

She started telling me how they met after college. I loved her candor and her droopy blue eyes. I loved her house, the big Turkish pillows and thick carpets. A muted floral chaise longue sat in front of the bookcase. I loved the image of Lilian reclined there, reading. Rita would worry about dust mites. I wondered about my e-mail to Josh. I wondered if Rita was sitting in our living room right now with Homer Wilcox and an IRS cop.

"He loved the track," Lilian said, "which I knew going in, but I didn't know he planned to marry the track, that he planned a long loving relationship with the track, that he'd cheat on the track with some Lotto."

I was staring her down so hard my face started twitching.

"I decided I deserved better," she said, "and it took him two beats to agree."

"There must have been some good moments," I said. "Jasmine?"

"She's a great kid and my best friend. She was conceived after he hit a trifecta at Saratoga. I was the cigarette after the real sex at the track."

"Ouch," I said.

"You asked."

"I'm sorry. I mean about your marriage."

This time *she* looked away, to my great relief. "How's Rita doing?"

We sat silently until I said, "She's seeing someone else."

"Oh, Quinn, no." She touched my leg—"I'm so sorry"—working at eye contact again. "You must be a wreck."

"I guess," I said, and Lilian scooched closer. "Anyway, we're finished." She held my head to her shoulder. The tears soaking her blouse were mine, and very real, but I wasn't sure if I was crying about Rita or my taxes, about Luna preparing our bed while my father played darts, or about the possibility of something profound and spiritual happening to me seeming so laughable. What I was sure about was the way to smooth over it all: I lifted my head, looked Lilian in the eyes, and kissed her on the lips. She kissed me back with lips much firmer than Rita's, then she turned her head, and my mouth slipped down to her neck, salty from the day, a faint trace of perfume.

I reached tightly around her. I wanted to move in with her, marry her, have children. I hadn't snuggled up to anyone but Rita for years. Lilian was so lean, her long leg extending like a branch off the sofa to the point of her bony bare foot on the carpet. I pulled up a knee and turned to her, bringing our bodies together. I waited for her to lift her face, and when she didn't, I kissed her forehead. All those mornings—for years—as I spooned Rita, she sprang from my arms to read his e-mails. She woke up dreaming of him. My hand found the deep scoop in Lilian's lower back, my fingertips slipping inside the top of her jeans. Shifting again, I mussed her hair, so curly my fingers were entangled. I tugged her head off my shoulder and kissed her on the lips again, our mouths drawn open, the kiss warmer and wet. She looked me in the eyes: compassion and kindness. I looked away, and she dropped her head back to my chest.

I couldn't get Luna out of my head either. Her feelings would be hurt, sitting on the couch in the fur-lined teddy watching the spirit enter me on TV over and over. I was another guy who'd let her down.

I didn't want to let people down. I didn't want to be corrupt. "I *do* have faith in some things," I whispered. My voice sounded awkward and uncertain in the tight intimate space we occupied.

Lilian hugged me closer. I could do it. I just needed a break. I needed that feeling of sitting with Lilian and Jasmine over dinner. I needed to believe in things, to *want* to believe, even if they let me down. One by one I'd try to fix things, reapproach my life from a position of honesty.

I stretched out my leg and dragged my briefcase along the floor with my foot. Then I leaned down, popped it open, and slid her lease onto the coffee table.

I took her chin gently in my fingers and raised her lips to mine. Our tongues lolled over each other. This was what we'd both been looking for. Did she know all along? Twenty years ago, when she hugged me—it was the first time I recognized love.

Through her shirt I touched her flat, almost concave stomach, then I tugged her shirt to untuck it from her pants. But she touched her hand to mine and stiffened. Her head pulled away.

I sat back and rested my head at the top of the couch.

"Well, I'd better . . ." she said through a forced yawn.

On the ceiling there was a water stain. I tried to make out a shape—Mexico, Key West, Nixon, the Virgin Mary—but nothing came together. "You know," I heard myself saying. "I didn't have to renew your lease."

The tension building in Lilian seemed to dissipate: her decision was made easier, her intuition confirmed. She smiled distantly—for herself, her house and Jasmine, for her place in the world. Not for me. "Drive safe," she said.

Trisch's Corolla was parked on the sidewalk in front of our apartment. The living room curtains were drawn and the lights were on. As I took a drink from the bottle of Chianti, a blurry silhouette of Trisch rose from the couch, walked into the kitchen, and returned. I jumped the fence into Burden Park and sat in a dark shadow beneath a tree. With time I succeeded in unweaving and tearing off the bottom of the Chianti bottle basket; the basket sides flared out like a hula skirt. At one point, I saw movement behind the curtain, but I wasn't sure if it was Trisch or Rita or anyone at all. As I sloshed the last gulp around the bottom of the bottle, the hula dancer swirled.

After an hour I hooked my pinkie under the bottle's wicker handle and headed back for the fence. I walked a crooked line. My head wobbled. I got over the fence, but not without a three-corner tear in my pants.

From the front stoop of the apartment, I heard music. I listened some more. Footsteps sounded across the living room; I cowered, but the door didn't open. There wasn't a single parking spot as far as I could see. Some pedestrians passed. A few cars rolled by. After an hour or so, I left the Chianti bottle on the stoop under our mailbox and walked the two blocks to the tracks where I'd left my Land Rover.

I crawled into the back and grabbed my thick cotton beach blanket and brought it to the passenger seat. I cracked the windows and set the alarm. Then I reclined and bunched up the blanket under my cheek.

7. SUNDAY

I woke in a wine-stinking sweat, stuck to the seats; Buddy's pal at the dealership had talked me into leather. The sun beat through the windshield. I cranked the engine—it was 6:06—then drove along Water Street, looking across the park. It felt good to be moving. Trisch's car was still there. The curtains were closed. I rubbed the blur from my eyes—on the front stoop the Chianti bottle was gone.

A few blocks down, I double-parked and ran into a grocery for coffee. Driving off, the coffee slowly dissolving the ache behind my eyes, I flipped on some local talk radio. It seemed that David Newman had now described the miracle girl's visions to a reporter in more explicit detail. The commentators kept talking about the "physicality" of the visions, the "sensuality" and "love of God." It sounded pretty sexy. Evidently, there'd been some anger among the pilgrims—some at the press for sensationalizing this, some at David Newman for misrepresenting it, some at the miracle girl herself. "Is she talking to the Lord," one caller asked, "or getting her jollies?"

I drove around, feeling worse and worse for what I'd said to Lilian. At least I'd given her the lease. If the personal me was a schmuck, the professional me had done the right thing.

So the professional me was what I'd concentrate on. Marriages fell apart every day—and Rita and I weren't even married. Men said spiteful things to women all the time. From now on, I'd bury myself in my work and forget the rest of this mess. And I'd start with my seven o'clock appointment at Immaculate Heart. It was 6:59.

"What the fuck?" Chip said as I pulled up fifteen minutes late. Not even. "Waiting in this neighborhood I don't appreciate," he said. "Waiting for you, period."

I stood at the door of my truck searching for the key to the church.

"I'm working on a Sunday because of you," he said.

"No. *I'm* working on a Sunday because of *you.*"

"Buddy Jensen said today at the latest."

"Not *my* fault," I said. My head ached again.

"If you showed up the last time—"

"Right," I said, cutting him off. Chip was always like this; it had nothing to do with my being late. He was a sour small man who hated everything. A few years back he'd sued Habitat for Humanity after he hurt his shoulder tripping over a tool belt during an inspection.

The bronze key, its edges worn smooth, was for the side entrance. Chip followed me down brick stairs that hugged close to the old stone church. The lot next door was vacant, overgrown with weeds and littered with garbage, tires, a mangled shopping cart. Venable owned the lot. I kicked aside a Tide bottle and turned the lock.

The thick wooden door opened to a cool, silent space. Richly colored light spilled through the stained-glass windows, shining off the glossy backs of the pews, row after perfect row.

"This place is a hole," Chip said. "It'll probably collapse tomorrow."

"It's been standing since eighteen-ninety."

"Built by the Catholics," he said.

"The stone is twenty inches thick."

"The Catholics were in on The Galleria, too. The amazing collapsible balcony."

"Late-breaking news, Chip." It was no secret: a construction company in which the diocese was principle shareholder had the general contract for The Galleria. Frank's predecessor was on their board. All the promises for prosecution and accountability came to nothing. The company quietly went bankrupt and the scandal ended there. "What's your point?" I said.

"That Catholics are cheap and second-rate, and I don't believe they were any different a hundred years ago."

"Great historical insight, Chip." Saying his little snip of a name felt good—built-in condescension.

"The miracle and The Galleria are just highlights of the Catholic corruption that plagues Hudson City. This building's no different."

"What is it, Chip? You think the diocese arranged for David Newman to fall from the balcony twelve years ago so he could regain his hearing last week and the Church could call it a miracle to drum up business?"

Chip looked me up and down with a rotten face. "Who cares?" Then he stepped around me into the church.

Bugs were zipping through the overgrown lot. I leaned in the doorway watching them, cool musty air at my back, hot weedy air on my face. The boarded-up building across the lot was owned by Venable, too. No one wanted Immaculate Heart, which was why Buddy could jerk me around. This area was on the edge of the worst neighborhood in Hudson City. Really it was *part* of the worst neighborhood, but since so many of the buildings were vacant, crime dropped relative to the number of potential victims.

Venable wanted Immaculate Heart and some of the nearby buildings for the movies. They were involved in a joint effort with the city to attract Hollywood production companies here to shoot their urban blight scenes. Two blocks over, the city owned abandoned projects—two hundred units of late-Sixties brick apartment block, bashed-in steel doors, graffiti, paved over without a blade of grass. The web site promised,

"Realistic urban decay for your film in a contained safe environment. For the crew, inexpensive and comfortable Tri-Cities lodging. World-class restaurants and night life. Suitable for NYC, DC, Chicago, Detroit, LA, and other urban locations. Shoot without getting shot." Even though they'd never attracted the big films they were hoping for, there *had* been a few two-day shoots of a drug buy or a hooker, and the web site dubbed us "Hollywood on the Hudson."

The whole thing had been Buddy's idea. In the Eighties, Merchant Ivory had filmed a Victorian costume drama in Hudson City. At the south end of downtown near the river, there was a block that had escaped urban renewal: beautiful Queen Anne buildings with carved stone lintels, galvanized iron cornices, oriel windows, chiseled details over the doors. One tiny wooden building was squeezed down between the stone with its original sign—"Mandy Trusses." By accident and good luck, not much had changed on the block since Hudson City's glory days. Hollywood stuck pickle barrels over the fire hydrants, brought in truckloads of dirt to cover the pavement, a few horses, and stepped back a hundred years. Buddy's mind got ticking—if you can make a buck on century-old success, you can sure as hell make a buck on contemporary failure. "There's big money in poverty," he'd said to me once.

I heard some kids in the street and peeked around the corner to check on my truck. A bunch of eight- or ten-year-olds were looking in the windows. I pulled out my remote and hit a button. The alarm screeched and the lights flashed. "Stand back! Stand back!" a blaring voice ordered from under the hood. The kids scattered like birds.

I went back down the stairs and inside the church where the temperature dropped twenty degrees. From habit—a horse turning to the rein—my hand reached toward the well of holy water inside the door. A wrought-iron sconce cradled a milk-glass dish, empty except for the clear cellophane and red ribbon from the top of a packet of cigarettes. I snatched it up and dropped it outside.

My eyes adjusted to the dim colorful light. The power and water were shut off, but I flicked the light switch anyway. Cigarette smoke lingered in the air. I could see Chip's flashlight glaring over painted stations of the cross, cast-iron radiators, statues of Joseph and Mary. Very little had been removed—the crucifix was gone, and the organ had been sent to a church in the Catskills. But the organ pipes remained.

In the middle of the church I sat in a pew. My mother always made us sit up front—front right, in the third or fourth row. And we were always late for church, *always*. Well into the first reading, or even the responsorial psalm, she'd drag me up the center aisle, my hair still wet from the shower. While everyone watched, she'd kneel with great ceremony and importance at the end of a pew, make the sign of the cross slowly, pregnant with meaning. I'd follow, head hanging, week after week.

I walked up on the altar and looked out over the pews, trying to imagine having something to say to a congregation. But what did the priests ever say? All I could remember was the Sunday each year when the sermon was sacrificed for a gloomy annual report on the church's finances. Following the reading of the gospel, the priest would harangue the congregation for our stinginess over the collection basket. He'd cite our duty to God and the Church, the rising price of heating oil, and the decadent pleasures we all blew our money on. Then he'd squeeze in a quick rebuke for lateness. This was the one Sunday each year I sort of enjoyed because all the pious parishioners looked just as guilty as I felt every week. Otherwise—except sometimes for the music and vaulted ceilings—Mass was an hour of punishing boredom.

A sudden bang below me in the basement was followed by a string of curses from Chip. I looked up at the choir loft suspended below a round stained-glass window depicting a scene of John the Baptist in the River Jordan. The old organ pipes, dull in the light coming through the glass, stood to one side. Dust was suspended, perfectly still, in the round shaft of sunlight, and for the moment there wasn't a sound. I thought of the pilgrims twenty blocks from here massing for another day of their vigil, and I thought of the miracle girl. She was appearing to people all over Hudson City, but not to me. Lilian was right. She'd have no reason to.

A door in the basement slammed. I went around through the vestry and down the narrow dark stairs. Yellowish light filtered through metal grates and dirty windows into the basement. "Are you almost done?" I shouted.

"I hate this building." His voice came muffled through the wall.

A brown low-pile carpet covered most of the floor. One beige folding chair was collapsed at the center of the room beside two fluorescent tubes. A small altar was set up at one end of the basement, and beyond that a kitchen. I tapped my fingernails on the stainless-steel counter. There were two deep cast-iron sinks, yards of counter, a pass-through to slide out casseroles and vats of spaghetti sauce. It was a kitchen designed to handle a dozen women reheating dishes brought from home to feed a hundred.

Beside the kitchen was a small bathroom. Green water sat low in the toilet bowl, a floating cigarette butt. A metal shower stall with paint peeling off in flaps was in the corner, missing a curtain. The sink was a classic—a plumbing fixture, not a design project. There was a black spot through the porcelain from a leak that must have dripped for years. Next to the spigots, plated with pitted chrome, half a dried-up bar of soap sat in a depression.

I lifted my head and was startled by the face in the mirror, someone other than me in the dim light—gray skin, stringy brown hair, red stubble on my jaw, some white stubble too. The face looked haunted. If a spirit had entered me in the courtyard of St. Mary's, it must have been the devil.

In Key West I'd planned to reinvent myself. I was looking for a place to be anonymous, get a fresh start. When I failed, I came home and decided that if I had to be here I'd at least be rich, and when that didn't work out either, I ended up where I was now—staring at myself in the basement of an abandoned Catholic church. If I left again, where could I go? A small town out West maybe, where pretty girls were intrigued by anyone from someplace else. I'd get an honest woodworker job paying cash, a Craftsman bungalow with a front porch, a new name: kind of a cross between homesteading and the witness protection program.

I leaned in closer to the mirror—my eyes were bloodshot and swollen, my skin splotchy from the heat. The longer I stared, the worse I looked. I imagined Rita looking back at me, and I reached for the mirror and lay my hand flat on the cool glass over the image of my face.

Upstairs, I waited by the door, resting my head back on the wall, eyes closed. Standing there, I'd barely dipped into sleep when Chip tromped up the stairs and across the church. As he got closer, I smelled his cigarette and opened my eyes. I'd thought his hair had been wet, but I realized now it was gelled. Short slick hair, a deep tan, and a penny-sized patch of whiskers he'd missed shaving on the underside of his chin. He was a few years younger than I was and almost as short as Buddy, but he lifted weights and wore tight black polo shirts. He lived in a Venable singles' complex and loved to brag about all the women with huge "bazungas" he picked up at the complex pool and "porked."

"I finally realized what it is," he said. He took a deep drag and exhaled out his nostrils. "You're wearing the same clothes you had on yesterday for that bullshit miracle stunt on TV. And you stink. I'm sitting here waiting for you, and you're up all night on a bender."

"Did you see everything you need to see, Chip?" The headache was getting worse.

"Who the hell do you think you are?"

I closed my eyes. "Are you done here, Chip?"

"Trying to have a vision of the miracle chick so you can beat off to it?" He laughed, pleased with his wit.

When I opened my eyes, he was stabbing his cigarette out in the holy water sconce. I lurched, grabbed his shoulder, and threw him aside. He was lighter than I'd expected, and he fell against a pew. He threw down his clipboard, and came at me but stopped two paces shy. "Yeah?" He flexed his biceps. "You want some of this? You see these guns?"

"Do you have *any* respect for *any*thing?" I said.

He flexed again. I turned and started out the door.

"I'm getting you fired," he shouted. "That's exactly what I'm doing. You don't put your hands on my person." He pointed at himself. "My domain."

I was halfway out the door, the sun hot on my head. My whole skull ached.

"I'm going to call that nun and tell her if you're not fired I'll file a complaint with the city. You can't put your hands on an inspector. And I'll give *her* a piece. That nun who ragged me out like I was ten years old, for cussing. Sister Rosemary, that bitch—"

I clocked him hard at that, and he went right down. Pain sliced like a cleaver through my hand. He was crunched up on the floor, but he staggered to his feet, backing away, holding the side of his head. I'd been aiming for his mouth, but I hit his ear.

"You shit. You shit!" He was hysterical. His voice shot up an octave. "I'm going to sue your ass so bad!"

I backed out the door and he hurried by me, bent over, holding his ear. Part way up to the street he turned. "I'm going to sue you until you don't exist anymore. Till you're dust, till you're . . ." But he choked and started to cry, and stumbled up the brick stairs—gone.

I squeezed my throbbing hand into a fist, then straightened my fingers. It hurt like hell, but maybe nothing was broken. He was the first person I'd hit since junior high. And the strange thing was that my heart wasn't racing, I wasn't all hyped-up, or even fully awake really. It had seemed like the natural thing to do. The right thing.

Reaching into my right pocket with my left hand, I snagged the key and locked the church. It was a couple hours until Frank's Mass, and I thought I should show my support. But I couldn't go to the office without a shower and a change of clothes. I stuck my nose in a pit and sniffed: not good. My skin itched from layer after layer of sweat. And I needed another hour of sleep.

Home was out. My father's apartment, given yesterday's conversation with Luna, was out too. I didn't want to see Charles. He was shrewd:

he'd ask me about the audit and know I was lying. I didn't belong to a gym. And what about friends? Buddy, Frank, Rosemary. Trisch was *my* friend, too. Lilian. Patsy. None was the sort you'd bang on the door at two a.m. with a bullet wound in the arm saying, "I need to disappear for a while," and they'd close the shades without asking questions.

Other friends? Mike Malone, my lifelong best friend, moved out to Seattle just before I met Rita. Neither one of us was great about keeping in touch. My other Hudson City friends had left for college, or after college, and hadn't returned. Mostly down in New York, some in Boston, some on the west coast. There were a few others in town I counted as friends, couples Rita and I had dinner with, some of Rita's old pals.

I climbed the stairs toward my truck, just to get moving. I was thirty-five years old, not so young. I had to take control. My head didn't just ache. It was decomposing in a way that only sleep could cure. It had been so cool in the church, almost chilly. So I opened the back of my truck, lifted up the floor panel, and pulled out the tire iron. I threw the beach blanket over my shoulder, reached for the beach towel, and then decided to grab the whole basket—sunblock, a Frisbee, two sun hats, an old copy of *Time*.

Back inside the church, as my eyes slowly adjusted, I moved between the pews to the vestry. Then down in the basement, I dropped everything but the tire iron in front of the bathroom. One of the low-budget movies they'd filmed in the projects here was about squatters who, out of necessity, invent a new type of heater. They try to patent it, only to be cheated by their lawyer, who gets rich while they're forced from their squat to the street. I watched the movie, looking with great provincial excitement for locations I recognized, and I thought about the squatters now as I lifted a plywood hatch in the floor to expose the water meter. Down on my knees, I worked the tire iron under the strap that locked the valve. I snapped it off, turned the valve, and water rushed through the pipes.

In the kitchen, the tap spit rusty water and air. I let it run until the water was clear. Then I filled one of the sinks, turning the bar of soap over in my hands under the stream. The cold water was a relief on my jammed finger. I stripped down when the sink was full of suds, dropped in my shirt, boxers, and socks. I draped my trousers over the counter.

The church basement was so cool that the cold shower slowed my heart. But I adjusted in a minute and lathered up my hair and body. I felt great. I thought of the commercial for the soap called Zest.

I dried off vigorously, goose bumps popping up on my skin. Wrapping the towel around my waist I went to the kitchen and dunked and scrubbed my clothes. All I was missing was the washboard. I heard myself humming before I realized I was doing it. Then I remembered taking a bath one time while Rita sat on the bathroom floor, reading an article to me from a magazine. When she finished reading, she picked up the washcloth and began absentmindedly scrubbing my back and humming a melody that neither of us knew. We laughed about it and decided that the melody was in the collective unconscious of mothers and wives, a slow patient melody with the rhythm of scrubbing that reached back through generations of women. I've heard her humming the same kind of unidentifiable melodies as she rinses out her diaphragm; if I ask her about it later, she can't remember the tune or even that she was humming at all.

I wrung out my clothes, snapped the shirt, and looked for a place to hang them to dry, but the basement was damp, so I hooked my arm through the beach basket handles and took my wet clothes upstairs. From the altar I looked out over the church. The sun was brightest through the John the Baptist stained-glass window in the choir loft. I walked up the aisle and climbed the dark spiral stairs.

It was warmer up in the loft but still cooler than any other place in Hudson City without air conditioning, I was sure. I draped my clothes over the organ pipes, warm from the sun.

At the top of the stairs there was a narrow door with a skeleton key in its lock, a gold tassel hanging off the key. Inside were shelves of candles, long stick matches, sheet music, and music stands. I left the closet open and twirled the key around my fingers by the tassel.

On the near side of the window, out of the sun, I spread the beach blanket on the wooden floor worn so smooth through the years it felt soft. I don't remember lying down—only thinking I could rest for half an hour while my clothes were drying.

And I dreamed: My back was comfortably arched as I floated in space. A low slant of rose-colored light shined on me, and the smell of roses filled the air. A movie-montage of images appeared: the girl squatter worked on the heater with cold hands, nails bitten down to scabby cuticles; on a hotel couch Buddy and Frank wearing business suits drank Scotch from short tumblers, laughing, exhilarated, sleazy, their legs crossed and showing bare white calf above black socks; Nixon wept, the flag in his lapel askew. The whole time I was floating, in great comfort. The miracle girl hovered above me in a slant of rose-colored light. She reached a hand toward my chest, and the light became brighter and hotter, piercing my skin, slicing between my ribs and spreading through my body; the girl squatter gnawed at her cuticle until it bled, and when she moved her hand she was Rita singing, "Outbreak, outbreak"; Homer Wilcox licked his fingers and curled his mustache chanting, "Back tax, back tax."

My senses awoke one at a time. My eyes took hours to draw open, lids retracting for miles, gaining momentum until they finally clapped up in my head. I sat up and sweat trickled down the middle of my chest. The sun through the round window beat down on me like a spotlight. I smelled the beach. And when I could make sense of sound, I jumped up and dashed to the window. Through the stained glass I could see my lights flashing. The siren wailed. The voice ordered, "Stand back! Stand back!"

I ran for the stairs but realized I didn't have the remote—and I was naked—so I took two leaps back toward my pants. My heart was pounding. My watch read 2:45. I had to think, *Night or day?* I had to think, *What day?* I'd slept over six hours, and I'd missed Frank's Mass. The car alarm wouldn't quit. "Stand back!"

I took a deep breath and tried to calm down. I dressed. My shirt and boxers were dry and crisp.

I straightened up the beach blanket, took my hat and sunglasses from the basket: the hat had a floppy white brim, and with the sunglasses, I'd have a little anonymity.

In the reeds by John the Baptist's feet, a small section of the stained-glass window opened for ventilation. I twisted the iron handle and the hinges squeaked. Sun glared off my truck. The lights flashed, the siren wailed, but no one was in sight.

I went downstairs and out the side door, locking it behind me. A soft hot breeze blew across the vacant lot and against the church—the first breeze in a week.

I pushed the button on my remote as I rounded the corner, and the car alarm stopped. From this side, I couldn't see anything wrong. But as I got closer I saw the driver's side window was shattered, and there was a gaping wound in the dash where the stereo had been. Shit. I opened the door and brushed pebbles of safety glass off the seat with my hand. Still, not a soul was around. The hot wind was strange for Hudson City. I looked at the sky—the same hazy blue it had been for a week. Not a cloud.

A few papers swirled around my feet. I snatched up one sheet that wrapped around my leg: it was a tax form, *my* tax form, page one of my Schedule C. My briefcase was gone. I panicked, lunging for loose pages, but snagging only a few fired me up like a fever. I stopped, my heart pounding, watching a file folder skim along the street then spring open with a gust—a stack of receipts fluttered into the weedy lot. It was futile. And the records were useless anyway—evidence against me. They were a lie, my past. Maybe this was the fresh start I'd been looking for. I opened my hands and the crumpled pages flew off in the wind.

I floored my truck down the block. The AC was busted. Hot air blew through the smashed window. When I got to Hoosick Street, I wanted to turn uphill, out of town, out to the old day camp. I suddenly felt that all my childhood memories were being razed and dragged off, along with the arts and crafts cabin and the docks. I knew I'd left youth behind a few years back, but those slapped-up houses covering the old softball field seemed to bar even the fantasy of a return visit. It felt like the end of something.

Still, I found myself turning downhill, downtown, toward the miracle. After only five or six blocks, traffic was bumper to bumper. The clergy permit was still on the dash, so I double-parked on a side street, brushed a few pebbles of glass off my pants, and joined the crowds walking to Little Saigon.

It was three-thirty. I bought a newspaper from a cigarette shop and tucked it under my arm. I was suddenly starving, so I stopped at the first restaurant and ordered *pho* with crabmeat. The Vietnamese man served me noodles and broth from steaming vats, then threw in a handful of crabmeat from the fridge. I sat on a low stool at a low table. It reminded me of the day care. The soup was too hot at first and my face dripped with sweat. I was watching the miracle on TV and hadn't realized it was in Vietnamese until the man saw me watching and switched it to an English channel. It showed the fires down at West Point. No one had forecast these odd winds—"like Santa Ana winds," the commentator said, stoking the flames. A helicopter camera showed the smoke pluming over the Hudson River. Then it showed some of the ordnance in the fields exploding, and it was hard to know if new stuff was blowing up all the time, or if they were showing the same explosion over and over.

There were only a few people in the restaurant and I was terribly hot, so I took off the hat and sunglasses and wiped sweat from my face with paper napkins. A reporter interviewed residents of Hudson City who'd had enough. Neighborhood groups were sick of the crowds and inconvenience. Petitions called for the streets to be cleared for traffic. There were complaints about local government favoring Catholics, about the city money being spent. There were appeals to the pilgrims to go home. These hot winds, they said, were making people crazy.

The restaurant owner refilled my water from a pitcher dripping with sweat.

I sucked down noodles and drank broth from the bowl.

The newspaper cover photo was an aerial shot of the crowds. "4000 Expected by Today." I pulled the Sunday magazine from between the fold, and opened it at random. First I saw the light and my heart missed a beat: the rose-colored light slanted into the photograph exactly as it had in my dream. Then I realized the photograph was of me, fainting on the mound of flowers: legs buckling, lips parted, eyes rolled back, face tipped toward St. Mary's steeple and the cross on top. It was a picture of religious ecstasy. The light cut into the photo at a low slant, appearing, apparently, from nowhere.

I skimmed the article: "The man in the tie . . . A message . . . Pilgrims report the scent of roses."

The Vietnamese man set the water pitcher on the table. "You're the one," he said to me.

I put the hat back on. "It's all a mistake," I said.

"You have an obligation."

I stood to leave and shook my head, holding out a five-dollar bill that he wouldn't take.

"Tell them what she said," he called as I escaped into the street.

I moved among the pilgrims toward St. Mary's and the miracle girl's apartment. At the mouth of an alley, the smell of garbage carried by the wind hit me in the face. I pulled the hat lower and dropped my head.

I stopped at a phone booth and called Buddy on his cell. "I want to talk to you."

"Hey, miracle boy," he said brightly.

"We've got to straighten things out."

"Hope you don't mind I'm using your desk. You're very organized."

"Meet me in Rockefeller Park."

"Where are you, anyway? Your boss is a little pissed. And Rita called."

"Be there in half an hour."

"Bite me, Quinn. I'm busy. Your visions don't impress me."

I didn't say anything. Two Vietnamese men in oversized suits and narrow ties were jabbering into cell phones on either side of me. They spoke Vietnamese, but from their tone I understood that money was at stake. They could well have been talking to each other. "Please," I said after a long silence.

"I've gotta go down to the miracle in a few minutes. Meet me in front of Eddie's Lunch in an hour."

As the pilgrims got thicker, I bumped a man whose sweaty arm swiped my shirt. He smelled of a long day in the street, and I had the odd feeling of starting my day awake and fresh when everyone else was winding down.

I slipped into the next Vietnamese restaurant I saw—Pho Ha—and sat in back at a gold-speckled Formica table facing an aquarium and a white wall. It was nice and cool, and I was surprised the place wasn't busier. I ordered a Vietnamese coffee and opened the newspaper on the table. The picture of me and the slant of rose-colored light gave me a chill, even though I knew it was absurd. I must have seen the picture out of the corner of my eye early this morning—probably when I ran into the grocery.

The coffee came—an inch of sweetened condensed milk on the bottom of the small glass under thick black brew. I stirred it with the tiny stainless spoon and sipped—like hot molasses and a black beauty.

I read the front page. There were renewed concerns about Hudson City's infrastructure. There were sanitation concerns. Garbage was piling up in Little Saigon, even though the mayor had contracted a private company; king-sized blue garbage trucks rumbled in from Scranton, Pennsylvania, hauling off tons of waste. Several citizens' groups were outraged at the money the city was putting out, including the PTA, who had been told that music and art classes were eliminated because there wasn't another penny in city coffers. The mayor's office responded that this was a different coffer.

On the other hand, graphs and pie charts displayed the retail sales spikes in Hudson City businesses. Hotels and motels had earned their typical six-month take in the last five days. The mayor proposed an increase in the lodging tax, effective retroactively, to defray policing costs. Several private companies were donating man-hours and services to the city, including the *Tri-City Times,* Hudson Gas and Electric, and Venable. The diocese, it was reported, was supporting only the immediate needs of pilgrims.

I left the paper on the table and started a slow walk down the six or eight blocks to Eddie's Lunch, an island of pre-Vietnam Hudson City in the heart of Little Saigon. The strange wind tossed up the hem of a nun's gray habit, revealing her Nikes and pompon Peds.

The sidewalk grill in front of Eddie's Lunch was given a wide berth. Fat sizzled on the coals as the cook rolled and speared dogs and brats. His pug-nosed Irish face was as pink as rare meat. It must have been 150 degrees where he was standing. The wind was erratic—greasy smoke blew one way for a minute, then the other, then churned straight up into the air.

I filled a cup at the water station—"Compliments of Second National Bank"—next to a phone pole that was papered with travel agency ads for package trips to Vietnam. There were garish posters of Vietnamese pop singers and performers, a whole culture and social life I knew nothing about. One hand-lettered sign read, "We are a couple of Buffalo—looking apartment in Little Saigon."

Pilgrims with buns in outstretched hands fast-stepped like fire walkers to the grill then retreated to the cashier, a Vietnamese girl making change with blackjack-dealer speed. Dressed in a starched blouse and skirt and a conical wicker hat, she sat on a high stool, looking as cool as she might selling programs at a football game in November.

Buddy showed, half an hour late. "By the way," he said. "What did you do to Chip?"

A cloud of smoke blew over us.

"He hates you," Buddy said.

The wind shifted the smoke away, but I could taste the grease in my mouth and nose. "Let's move," I said, rubbing my swollen knuckle.

"He *despises* you. I don't get it." Buddy smiled broadly, scratching and shaking his head, astonished and delighted—as if he'd just seen an erotic contortionist perform the impossible.

I started walking toward St. Mary's and Buddy followed.

"He said he's pressing charges. He's getting a restraining order."

"Listen," I said when we were in the middle of the street. "No more special deals for Venable. It's all by the books now. I hope we can still be friends, but the kickbacks—"

"Favors," he interrupted. "Between friends."

"I mean it, Buddy."

"You *need* some favors, man. You're getting fired, and prosecuted for tax fraud and assault. Plus . . . well, I can't help with your problems in the bedroom, but I can smooth-talk the bishop, and I can deal with the IRS and Chip, too. I can make your problems go away."

Rita. Was she working? sitting by the phone? "The bishop doesn't trust you," I said.

"But he needs me."

Was she e-mailing Josh? It was late in London. Josh would be getting into bed with his wife, his kids snoozing. Was she wondering where I was?

"Does the name Josh Katz mean anything to you?" I asked. "At WorldMedia."

"Listen to you. *Josh* Katz. I suppose to you it's Ronnie Reagan, Duke Wayne, Marty Scorcese."

I looked at him like, *What-the-fuck*.

"Papa Hemingway, right? Dick Nixon."

"What?"

"Joshua Bell Katz? J. B. Katz?"

And I knew. Of course.

Two National Guardsmen who looked about seventeen years old were leaning against their Humvee. Several teenage girls chatted them up.

"War stories," Buddy said. "A man is nothing without them."

J. B. Katz. Unbelievable.

"Not a bad deal, the Guard," Buddy said. "Took too much time away from my kids, though."

I had a good picture of J. B. Katz in my mind—taller than I was, with shoulders that looked good in suits, thick dark hair splotched with gray, stylish glasses that belonged more to a movie star trying to look sophisticated than a media mogul who actually was. The kind of guy who could pass for forty even though he was ten years older. He looked intellectual and successful, somehow both squirrelly and dashing. He was the CEO of WorldMedia. Beyond rich.

Buddy was jabbering on about the military. He'd been in the Air Force briefly, and always tried to sound like he was a pilot—"Troop transports in and out of 'Nam," he'd say—but I think he was more like a baggage handler or stewardess.

Rita mentioned J. B. Katz only once that I could remember—when we first met, watching the little TV in my old kitchen, and Katz was on the news. She told me she'd met him in New York, that he'd moved down a greeting line she was in, shaking hands. He held her hand and looked in her eyes a moment too long, stood a half step too close, insinuating himself, his size and sexual energy. "Sexual," she said. "Charismatic."

"Cheerios for a buck nineteen at the commissary," Buddy was saying. "I'm talking the huge box—like you need handles."

Did she mention him to test the waters? Say a little so she could say she had?

"The U.S. military travels to the ends of the earth to enforce capitalism." Buddy was gesturing with his arms.

Surely J. B. Katz wormed himself into our lives at other times—on the radio or TV, in a magazine. Her breath must have quickened, her skin warming.

"Yet the military's the most socialist institution in this country. Never mind their health care, housing, pensions. I'm talking government-subsidized Oreos, filet mignon, Ben & Jerry's, tequila. Subsidized French wine, for God's sake. Levi's, Italian suits, Waterford crystal, brakes and transmissions. If any country offered all that to its people, we'd arrange a coup. Or invade." His arms were just about flapping. "The U.S. military is un-American."

Did Rita and J. B. Katz ever talk on the phone, or was a sound bite of his voice on the news a treat, like a whisper in her ear?

"My kids have more sneakers than Shaquille O'Neal. I just wish it wasn't such a depressing drive out to the PX."

The PX was at an air base on the verge of closing before it became a processing center for Vietnamese refugees. "Really?" I asked. "A dollar nineteen for Cheerios?"

His arms fell to his sides. "I have no idea. My wife does the shopping." He sucked his teeth. "But in front of the PX they make caramel corn. With peanuts. Fresh. And they scoop out a pistachio ice cream like I've had nowhere else. I guess I like things with nuts." He nodded like he'd just come to this realization. "I like to come upon the occasional nut." With a handkerchief he wiped his neck, front and back, even though he wasn't sweating. "Hotter than hell," he said.

"I mean it. No more petty corruption."

He stuffed the handkerchief back in his pocket. "We're at a great threshold in the future of this city. There's going to be a lot of wealth to spread around—for the city, Venable, the diocese . . . me!" He didn't try to contain his glee. "And you too, if you stop being such a putz."

"If it's an honest job with Venable, I'll take it. But I'll never get rich working for the diocese because I'm not taking your bribes."

"Now they're *bribes*."

"How could you report me to the IRS, you bastard?"

"Down, boy. I told you I can fix that."

"How?"

"Trust me."

"Ha."

We were walking into the carnival midway of miracle mania. "It makes me feel good," Buddy said, "to see people spending money in Hudson City. I've believed in this city, poured my heart into it, waiting for a break. And here it is. Don't spoil this moment talking about dishonorable intentions. You've been in this game a couple years. I've been day-in-day-out for over thirty years working to make this city a better place. There's not a single thing Venable does that's not good for Hudson City. Period."

"So sign me up. Hire me."

"We need you in the bishop's office, Quinn. Now more than ever."

"I'm not doing it."

"For coordination. A liaison."

I shook my head.

"Frank and I work well together," he said. "But you're like a son to him. I can tell. He'd take it wrong if you came to work for us. But I'll talk to him about salary. Maybe get you some commissions."

Next to Hai Than Laundry and Water, at Vu Bail Bonds, a sign in the window said: "Come in for Air Condition. Buy Christian Souvenir, Mary, cross, ect. Cold drink. Web access. Phone call. Channel 6 on 48 inch screen."

"What's most important is that this new relationship between Venable and the diocese not be spoiled. You can help us with that, greatly benefiting both companies." He couldn't help grinning. "Both . . . *concerns*, I should say. We're building an economic and a moral monopoly."

"How are you going to take care of my audit?"

"Get me the property and it's done."

"Take care of the audit and I'll give you back the contract for the lot at the camp."

"I don't negotiate with terrorists. Anyway, it's chump change. Take the lot. It floods."

"Does Venable really want to be known for evicting a day care to build a Home Depot?"

"Hell no. It's hotels we need. We're gonna throw up hotels faster than you can say two Hail Marys."

"What good's a hotel in the Heights?"

"The miracle can't stay here, Quinn. It's so depressed. There's no parking. Too far from the interstate. Too many Buddhists, if you know what I mean. The miracle expands to fill the city."

I couldn't tell if he was serious—that smirky face. "You're joking," I said.

"See," he said. "*That's* the difference," as if I'd fallen into his trap. "You're a joker. I'm a dreamer." He was going to stop at that, but then continued, hamming it up. "I've done some research, and the miracles with greatest growth potential and sustainability keep the visions, healings, and revelations coming. We'll give the miracle girl a quota. Put her on commission. We'll want the miracles to happen on that mound of flowers, of course. That was a beautiful stunt, Quinn. It was like you were working with me already. You sensed the direction this was going. We'll want to buy St. Mary's Church too—one of the first things you'll head up with the bishop. We'll need piles of crutches and whatnot. People get jazzed up with the miracles then take a tram to the real deal. A riverfront of shops and restaurants with the miracle theme. Vegas entertainers, Billy Graham, whoever. I'll hire IMAX, call it 'Miracle in 3-D? or is it 4?' And why stop there? We'll build a Christian theme park: Noah's ark, Jesus walking on water, Garden of Eden, replicas of the Vatican, a wax pope. Do you know there's a billion Catholics in the world, Quinn? I had no idea. It's like opening up China.

"Some look at these crowds and see sweaty lunatics wasting perfectly good vacation days and trashing this quarter's productivity figures." He took a Napoleonic taste of the air and cast his gaze over the heads of the crowd. "But I see people who believe in something with their hearts, people who know what they want and are willing to pay what it takes. I see the proverbial one billion Cokes a day."

"So, you're full of shit."

"I know," he said. "But I'm real close on that South Hudson Mills project—"

"Vacuum cleaner bags," I said.

"The fourth-biggest vacuum-cleaner-bag producer in the country, plus—"

"Miracle-theme-park dreams sucked into a vacuum-cleaner-bag reality. How do you face the day?"

"They've got HEPA filters now, different styles, domestic and foreign. This is a sizable operation and they've completely outgrown their plant in Woburn."

"Quite a coup if you snagged them," I said, openly laughing at him.

"You're so friggin' superior." His lips clenched. "My advice to you? Hook up with a sugar daddy in prison. Let him have you to himself so you can maintain your air of exclusivity."

I stopped laughing.

"I can make Chip and the IRS go away. Two problems solved for two favors. The first, as you know, is Eighteen-Ten Hoosick. The second is even easier. The investors for the South Hudson Mills project'll be in town midweek, and I promised them they could meet the miracle girl. I told them we'd do lunch, but I'm having trouble inviting her—"

"Jesus, Buddy, she's not a *geisha*."

"Nothing like that. But she's the new face of Hudson City, like it or not. She's our key-to-the-city girl. Memorial Day parade, she should ride in the Cadillac convertible. Ground breakings, give her the golden shovel. Ribbon cuttings, all her. My point is, she has a civic duty."

"How do they even know about her?"

"I sent them a few clippings and photos to supplement that dreary Chamber of Commerce packet. This is exciting stuff happening here, lots of good and wonderful. We want to be able to say, 'Yeah, come visit Hudson City. This is where she lives. And if you're a VIP, she'll join you for lunch.' What's wrong with that?"

I just shook my head.

"I've been wiggling the bishop for a sit-down with the two of them, but he's not biting. I thought you could—"

"You thought I could what?"

"Be inventive, Quinn. Assert yourself. " He put his hand over his heart. "Appeal to Frank. Tell him you see Hudson City finally becoming something after so many years in a slump. Tell him this city has finally been blessed. By what? Call it God. Call it luck. Call it timing. Call it the miracle girl!"

He glanced at his watch, and a cute woman, around Rita's age, looked at me. I pulled my hat down and walked off behind Buddy. I felt her watching my back.

We bumped through the crowd, stopping at the curb across from St. Mary's courtyard.

"You'd better get back to the office," Buddy said. "Vis-à-vis one hand washing the other, I'll want to talk with the miracle girl tomorrow at the latest."

I just wanted to play things straight from now on. I'd had enough of Buddy for today.

But he was still talking: "I've been picking up your slack for a day and a half. Frank needs data on the cathedral."

Did he actually imagine he could buy the cathedral?

"I'm getting a crew in there for a face-lift. We hired a guy off the Sistine ceiling job to head things up. World-class. He better be goddamned Michelangelo for what we're paying. Frank's so happy, he's like a baby. All boats rise with a high tide."

I had a headache again.

"I'm late." He started to walk away. "Talk to Frank," he said, then turned back. "And don't—" He stepped closer and lowered his voice. "Don't have any more visions. You snowed them once. Sometimes less is more."

"What makes you think my vision wasn't real?" I said. "Maybe I did have a spiritual encounter."

He chuckled.

"I could've."

"O.J. could be innocent." He squared his stance, pressing his hands together like he was praying. "I don't know a lot about the Catholic faith. But I'm sure that Christ's mom would think a little more about her messenger, Quinn. I say this in friendship because . . . well, O.J. is a prime example of delusions run wild." He looked at his watch again. "Go to the office, do your job, make your car payments—that'll be your contribution to the world."

. . .

People were looking at me again, so I pulled the hat lower and kept moving, elbowing through the huddles at the opening to the walled courtyard. I could tell by Floquet's singsongy tone that he was wrapping up. There were more TV cameras today, a few more reporters. Pilgrims were packed in more tightly. The miracle was growing.

"And God says in Acts, 'I will pour out my Spirit on all people.'" A pair of metal crutches and two white canes had been left on the mound where I'd fainted. "'Your sons and daughters will prophesy—'" Did Floquet look directly at me in that instant? Did he recognize me? "'—your young men will see visions, your old men will dream dreams.'" I think that he did.

I looked for the source of the rose-colored light. Up above the wall a dried-out wooden phone pole tipped toward the street. Power, cable TV, and telephone wires drooped from the pole to the buildings, flopping in the wind. Some cables were tight, some sagged; they went at angles, crisscrossing; there seemed to be too many—eighteen or twenty cables for a three-story triplex. It was a complete mess. A hazard. And nothing to account for the light.

"Let us pray." Around me, a thousand heads suddenly dropped. In the quiet, I could hear the Channel 6 reporter describing the scene live. Floquet stepped down from the podium, through the flowers, touching bowed heads and elbows and shoulders as he navigated the crowd.

The last time I went to Mass was with my mother on Christmas—the organ banging out "Joy to the World," a full choir, hundreds of candles, and the church packed to the rafters with well-dressed Catholics feeling good about themselves. And when the priest told us to pray, I dropped my head, closed my eyes, and decided to give it a go. I prayed for my own happiness. I prayed that Rita and I could love each other better. I prayed for my own happiness again. Then I lifted my head and raised an eyelid. Unless they were all faking it, everyone around me was still praying. But I couldn't think of anything else. I tried, hard. And as people began to shuffle, open hymnals, the sound of pages fluttering, I threw in "world peace" and "no more hunger," but it felt pretty half-assed.

I glanced at the front door of St. Mary's just in time to see Floquet shaking hands with several people, including the mayor and goddamned Buddy. For Christ's sake. They all went into the church and closed the tall wooden door carved with a labyrinth design. The last man to go in looked just like Homer Wilcox. I was losing my mind.

Then I thought, if it *was* Homer Wilcox, that was how Buddy would take care of my audit—yes, they were friends, of course. Buddy could control the IRS. At that moment, I didn't think there was a position more powerful. Was the mayor in on Buddy's schemes, too? And Floquet? If I let Frank know about this, I thought it might redeem me.

Heads were still lowered in prayer as I slipped away. The quickest route to my truck was left down Broadway past the miracle girl's building, then over Congress. The paper was right: the crowd was getting bigger. And the wind hadn't cooled things off—it had only stirred the air—an electric sort of heat.

I had to move sideways through the crowd as I got closer to her building, and I realized I'd made a mistake: the other way would have been quicker. I turned and looked back, then decided I was committed. There was no turning back.

They were singing a hymn in front of the miracle girl's building. As I got closer, I could see a dais being built over her stoop, coming straight out from the front door. The carpenters wore Venable uniforms.

Three policemen now stood around the door. Twice, I gathered from what I overheard, someone had tried to bust in and bring her out.

The hymn ended. Pleas were called to the window for her to appear. We all watched—hundreds of us—for the curtains to sway, the door to crack—but there was nothing.

The clergy permit was my badge—the truck sat where I'd parked it. I brushed away a few more pebbles of safety glass and got in. To avoid the crush of traffic between Little Saigon and the office, I took Hoosick Street around the university, miles out of my way, but I was sure it would be quicker. I turned down Van Rensselaer, passing the shop where Luna worked; she was somewhere back in the dark store—behind the stained-glass ornaments, chimes, and crystals—standing.

I parked at the end of the lot behind the diocese office, hoping no one would see my broken window. When I walked in the front door, Patsy looked up. She was holding a wet washcloth over one eye. Her face brightened. "That's so cool," she said. "Do you feel different?"

Frank's door was closed. The office felt eerily static: the brushed stainless crucifix with the copper Jesus still hung on the wall; the low porcelain drinking fountain spilled out ivy next to Patsy's desk. I leaned closer to her and whispered, "Has Frank or Buddy Jensen said anything about me? You know . . . unsavory?"

She looked at me blankly. "What's up with your cell phone? The bishop's kinda tweaked."

"It broke." The truth.

"You probably should have come to the cathedral. It was embarrassing. The TV camera left before Mass even started because there were like thirty people."

"I was tied up."

"The bishop was disappointed you weren't there." She removed the washcloth from her eye, and I reeled back. It was swollen red, yellow, gray. "Infected," she said apologetically. "My new piercing."

Puss oozed from her swollen brow. "It doesn't look so good."

"Surgical steel, my butt. I hate that mall. Everybody lies." She got up and I followed her into the kitchen. She ran hot water over the washcloth. "People are calling to see if we know who you are. The man in the tie." Folding the washcloth in fourths, she pressed it to her face. "The bishop told me to say we have no information."

"That's good."

"But what about it?" She squeezed my forearm. "Did you see some vision? And where have you been?" I'd never run into Patsy outside the office, and I wondered if we met at one of those clubs she went to, dancing and bumping in a mass under the laser lights, if she'd see me as her nerdy older brother or if we'd hit it off.

The bishop suddenly filled the doorway. "One question, John," he said, pointing his thick finger at me. "Are you in cahoots with Floquet?"

"You can't be serious."

"Don't fool with me."

Patsy rinsed out coffee cups with her free hand. Frank's breathing was louder than the running water. Rosemary edged by him with papers to photocopy. It was a Sunday and they were all working. Everything seemed normal but still felt different. I felt stoned—that weird heightened sameness of everything.

"Buddy Jensen, Floquet, and the mayor are in cahoots," I said. "*That's* what you should worry about. They're marketing the miracle."

"And you're just helping out a little? Staging your own vision?" He shook his head. "Shameful."

I'd tried to slug the men who had carried Frank off. That's why I'd fainted. I was sick of getting scolded. Patsy reheated her washcloth, steam rising from the sink. Rosemary laid a sheet of paper on the copier glass. They didn't want to miss a thing.

"I'll need your file on Five-Fifteen Trinity Street," the bishop said. "You can draw up a lease for Li'l Tykes Day Care. And clean yourself up, Quinn. You should come to this office presentable."

"Li'l Tykes is in Eighteen-Ten Hoosick," I said. "She's *got* a new lease."

"They're moving."

And it was all clear. "That's what you're giving Buddy, isn't it? You're selling him Eighteen-Ten Hoosick in exchange for refurbishing the cathedral."

Frank's face went red.

"There's no such thing as a little corruption, Frank. A little bit wrong."

Rosemary flipped a page. Patsy rerinsed the mugs. Frank made two fists, glowering, then he pointed at the front door.

. . .

I drove north—hot air blasting in the broken window, sweat running down my calves and face. I felt guilty for telling off Frank. The space at 515 Trinity was nicer and just around the corner from where the day care was now; Frank had found a solution that helped everybody. I shook my head. *Like a son.* Well he wasn't my father.

I passed Arby's. None of this mattered because I was leaving. They needed woodworkers in Cape Breton to maintain old fishing boats. I'd spend my days with hand planes and chisels working for Canadian dollars under the table.

At the turnoff I swung east, dry grass baked in the pastures. *If I could just cool off,* I thought, *I'd see everything more clearly.* I screeched left at a charred skeleton of a roadside bar that had burned to the ground years ago. Five miles later I banged down the dirt road, parked at a Venable chain, and walked the last few minutes to the old camp. At the water's edge, I dropped all my clothes and fell forward into the lake.

The water was silky and cool. I swam along the bottom, pumping my arms and legs, the water cooler and darker as it deepened. I made it out beyond the sand to the muck, then surfaced through a shower of refracted sun rays. Treading water and tasting it on my lips, I looked back at the beach. I was already out beyond where the docks and ropes had once marked the swimming area. I arched my back and floated, the low sun burning at the tops of the pine trees. I pictured the shape of my body—like a cliff diver falling, or like Rita in a back bend.

I swam out deeper, remembering the time Rita and I drove up to Bennington, Vermont, to a yoga supply store for a back-bending bench. Surrounded by little Zen fountains and tabletop rock gardens, headstand supports, and meditation pillows, she stepped out of her sandals and lay back over the arched wooden bench. Her shirt pulled up, exposing her belly button. "It's incredible," she said. "I'm in heaven."

On my hands and knees I looked up under the bench. I wiggled a slat. "The joints are loose," I said, "and they're stapled."

"It totally opens me up." She sighed. "It's like my chest is stretching, and my heart. It's just what I need after hunching over all day at the computer."

I looked at the tag: "Hardwood." Could be anything. Mostly sapwood, grainy and knotty, which I didn't mention. Rita, unfathomably, liked knots. She liked *pine* furniture. She liked *distressed* furniture. Unrepentantly.

"There's drips in the finish." I frowned. "For six hundred dollars. Let me make you one."

The scrolled end of the bench rounded into the soles of her feet. Her body curved up to the fulcrum, midspine, and draped down the other side. Eyes closed, hair cascading over the slats to the floor, her chest expanded with her breath. "I need it now."

"I'll make it now. You'll love it. You can't have this shoddy mass-produced bench. I couldn't bear it."

We left town with a box of seconds from Bennington Pottery—crooked handles and drooping lips. That was over a year ago. Rita had mentioned the bench a few times. And when I thought about it now, it seemed I was so focused on making a piece of furniture whose quality I found suitable, I hadn't heard the quiet frustration in her voice, the resignation.

On the way home from Bennington, Rita was taking me to a "special place," which was something we used to do—surprise each other like that on a Saturday. It took longer to find than she'd thought, and after driving forever in circles I became openly skeptical. Then we descended a hill to a sluiceway, the gate open wide. "Uh oh," Rita said.

But she insisted we park. We stripped to our bathing suits, and walked down to the edge of the reservoir. The grass met cracked mud at what should have been the water line. A hundred yards out, water the color of chocolate milk collected in puddles. Black rotting tree stumps were exposed. Laughing, I said, "This is *not* a special place."

She ignored me—"Let's go"—and stepped out into the mud.

"Don't be ridiculous, Rita. We can't swim here."

"We were going to swim *across,*" she said. "But we can wade. The place is on the other side."

The other side was a long way off—probably a fifteen-minute swim. Walking through the mud? I didn't know how long. "Let's just bail," I said. "Let's go home."

But Rita didn't stop. Ten paces away she was sinking in mud to her ankles.

"I'm not coming."

"Don't be lame."

"I'm sitting right here."

She turned around. "It's a great place," she insisted.

"If you want to mud wrestle, fine, but—"

"Come on," she said, and I sat down on the grass, sure she'd come back.

But she didn't. From the shade of a leafy tree I watched her slog through the mud for five minutes until she reached the water's edge, where she turned around and tried to wave me in. I didn't budge.

She marched on through the water, still sinking into mud, recoiling every few steps as she came down on a root or a sharp rock. The far side of the reservoir was thick with pine trees rising up a steep slope. Further east, low forested mountains humped up against the sky.

Sitting in the shade, I thought about Rita's stubbornness. She'd let me talk her out of the yoga bench, but she wouldn't surrender to a dried-up reservoir. And now, as I swam across the lake in the direction of lot sixteen, I thought about Rita's faith in memory, faith that a special place would be waiting, still worth the effort. A stubborn faith, like her stubborn dedication to a daily yoga practice, the stubborn principles she wouldn't bend. And I thought about me: cheating on my taxes, deceiving Frank about my deals with Buddy, deceiving Rita about it all.

When she made it to the other side, her tiny figure waved me over once more, then she disappeared into the shadow of the pines. She wasn't going to let me hold her back.

In half an hour I was impatient, in an hour pissed, in still another half hour worried. For five minutes I called to her, my voice echoing back, and then I started across. The mud oozed between my toes. When the murky water got waist deep, I stumbled over slimy tree trunks, roots extending like bloated legs.

Finally, on the other side, I looked up into the dark woods. I shouted Rita's name again, but she didn't respond. So I headed into the trees. I remember the pine smell, the air cool and humid, a feeling of remoteness. I decided to go up to the highest point and look from there, so I climbed the hillside, scaling a few rock formations, going around others. Even when I saw Rita's back, crouched on top of a small rock face, it seemed impossible I'd found her. As I started up the last incline, a stick snapped beneath my foot; she turned and saw me and put her finger to her lips. When I reached her she didn't rise or turn. I touched the top of her head; she squeezed my calf.

A stream ran down from the small mountains in the east, widening to a pool in the rocks below us. Swimming and splashing—I could hardly believe it—were two black bears. It was incredible. They rolled around on the rocks. They relaxed. One climbed a tree. They stripped leaves and berries from branches. They pawed each other, growled, sighed. One batted the other into the water with a backhand. Bear stuff.

"They like this spot," she whispered.

Rita had been there only once, eight years ago. But somehow she knew the place wouldn't let her down.

"I had no idea . . ." I said.

And in that moment she must have realized—the way she'd met my eyes, then looked off into the trees before turning back to the bears—she realized I hadn't believed in her.

At lot sixteen I stumbled out naked and vulnerable, tenderfooting over rocks and branches along the water's edge. From the first surveyor's stake, I paced out the land. It could be *my* land. Buddy already had the day care—all he really wanted was an audience with the miracle girl.

In the middle of the property, mosquitoes swarmed above a low spot, a puddle of standing water. Well, that could be filled and graded. I could build on the rise further back from the lake. A smaller footprint, for sure, but Rita and I didn't need lots of space. We just needed *our* space.

If Buddy succeeded in playing the miracle to investors, land and real estate prices would creep up in Hudson City. All over the country in the last twenty years, prices were rising. Never mind Manhattan or Boston, I'd been priced out of Ithaca, the Berkshires, Providence, and Lake George. Once I'd planned to look at summer property in Maine, but now I couldn't even get into Nova Scotia. As population grew, space shrunk. I was running out of time. Not so young. It just seemed possible that soon enough I'd be priced out of Hudson City.

It was dark as I drove back to town. Just past eleven Trisch came out the front door, and Rita followed. They were holding hands. From standing on that stoop at night, I knew they'd never see me under the trees at the back of the park. Rita was wearing a pair of my boxers, flip-flops, and the T-shirt she bought in Jamaica. Her hair was pulled back. Their voices traveled like electricity through the humid air—not words, only sounds—voices low, tired, restrained. They embraced for a minute or two, a slow side-to-side rock. Trisch patted Rita's back.

So many cars were parked illegally, Trisch had to back through an obstacle course down the sidewalk to the end of the block. When she dropped down the curb into the street, she rolled forward and tooted her horn. Rounding the corner her headlights slashed through the park, shining in my eyes for an instant.

Rita watched Trisch's brake lights glow at the end of the block and listened to the car accelerate then fade away. Instead of turning to go inside, she stretched her arms over her head, hooking her fingers around the back of her neck, her elbows jutting. I couldn't watch her do it without thinking of her at her computer—the stretch that helped her through hours in front of the screen.

She scanned our block and the streets around the park, maybe looking for my Land Rover. She took a deep breath, and I almost thought I could hear her exhale. I was fifty yards away, not even: close enough to toss her a Frisbee.

She twisted her hips back and forth. In my mind I heard her lower back cracking and her T-shirt moving over her skin. The layers of clothes on Victorian women and Japanese women in kimono slipping against each other, warm, silky—that is the mysterious sensuality of women. With Rita it was the movement of her breasts, her belly and hips beneath the fabric that sucked my breath short.

A few years earlier I'd found a card in a bookstore with a sexy painting on the front—two lovers embracing—and on the inside was a poem:

Whenas in silks my Julia goes,
Then, then, methinks, how sweetly flows
The liquefaction of her clothes.

Next, when I cast mine eyes and see
That brave vibration each way free,
O how that glittering taketh me!

I crossed out "Julia" and in the same swirling script wrote in "Rita," then sent it to her anonymously.

She didn't mention the card for nearly a week. I thought it had been lost in the mail. When I asked her about it, she flushed and smiled, then snuggled against me on the couch. An hour later I was in bed reading when she came silently into our bedroom wearing a silk bit of lingerie only as long as her hips, wrinkled from its exile at the bottom of her drawer. She crawled on top of me and made love slower than I've ever known, her breasts swaying beneath the silk.

After, when we lay in each other's arms, I asked her if she remembered the poem, and she recited it just above a whisper as the candlelight flickered on her cheek and nose. The next day, the card was on her bulletin board. And now I realized: she hadn't mentioned the card because she wasn't sure it was from me.

Still holding the back of her neck, she looked up at the sky and released a long sigh that I *did* actually hear. I looked up, too. Lots of stars, no moon yet. Or the moon had already set. I've never figured out how the moon works, never understood why I sometimes see it in the middle of the day.

The door clapped. I looked and the front curtain swished. Rita was gone. I sat awhile longer. I'd liked that—the two of us looking up at the sky together.

Some time later, when the city had quieted, I made my way across the park, my back stiff, and jumped the fence. As I headed down the sidewalk toward our apartment—there had been no movement for hours, but she'd left the light burning in the living room—I fingered the skeleton key in my pocket. When I got to our stoop, I withdrew the key, flipping it around my fingers by the gold tassel. I left it on the threshold, leaning against the door.

As I neared Immaculate Heart, my pulse quickened. Two in the morning, but people were out, children too. There was music. There were cots on front porches. The air here felt hotter and heavier. I got looks: a white man in a Land Rover in the middle of the night.

But the buildings surrounding the church were dark. The sidewalks were deserted. I circled the block before parking, set The Club and alarm despite the broken window, and hurried through the spray of streetlight illuminating the small brick plaza between the curb and the church doors. In a few quick strides I was covered in darkness, descending to the side door. It was a dangerous place, but I'd noticed that the church had not been vandalized, and I hoped that if I didn't stray too far, I'd be given the same immunity.

I slipped inside and locked the door then touched my fingertips to the dry holy-water dish. I made the sign of the cross, then I laughed. Was I making jokes for my own benefit? Not a good sign.

I held the scroll top of a pew, giving my eyes time to adjust. The stained-glass window in the organ loft glowed from the street lamp outside, projecting color into the rafters high above my head. Skimming my palm along the pews, I felt my way down the aisle to the vestibule and the staircase. My hands reached out along the walls as I kicked stair risers to find the next step, winding up to the loft.

The scene of John the Baptist, dressed in a hide, pouring water over Jesus' head, began at the floor of the loft and extended to the slope of the roof. I stood in front of John the Baptist, ten feet tall, his waist at my eye level, the River Jordan rushing around his calves. Christ sat on a rock with his feet in the water, his head bowed.

I plucked my towel off the organ pipes, stiff and dry, and fumbled through the dark closet for a candle and the long stick matches. With a candle lit, I went down to the basement and took an icy shower. I could smell the lake on my skin. Like a frog.

Back in the loft, I straightened the edges of my beach blanket and lay down in the field of light, more color than I ever thought about—more color than I'd ever see in a day. It made me want to believe in something.

In my dream Homer Wilcox banged a foot-high stack of papers on a conference table where I sat with Richard Nixon. Nixon's expression said, *This doesn't look good*. He was sweating. There was a second bang and I pulled back from the dream as if I were floating above the room, then I woke in a free fall, grunting.

I sat up with a start. It was still dark outside, though the streetlight through the stained glass seemed brighter. Another bang. I jumped to my feet and dressed silently. With an unlit candle and a match, I hurried down the loft stairs.

More noise was coming from the basement. A braver man might have rushed down to investigate, but I cowered by the side door, fingers on the dead bolt, in case I had to make a run for it.

There was a crash—my heart missed a beat—but I didn't run. I stayed crouched, a quick pulse snapping at my temples. It hit me that I was about six blocks from where Rita's father was murdered. A long anxious silence was broken by the creaking of a door, then silence again. I watched the far corner of the church where the basement stairs emerged beside the vestry. High up that wall was a statue of the Virgin Mary, the white stone faintly dappled with a collage of color from the stained-glass windows—a Peter Max Virgin.

Then there was a light. A dim beam moved steadily around the corner—a small flashlight, I realized, held in someone's hand, a hand I imagined to be enormous, the paw of a large soulless man who would torture me with quiet indifference. I doubted now that I could get out the door and up to my truck, unlock The Club, and start the engine before he caught me. So I waited.

The weak light shone around the church. It shone toward the altar, then fixed on the Virgin Mary, washing out the stained-glass colors. Then the figure moved down the aisle on the opposite side of the church, as slow as the procession of a priest and altar boys past the stations of the cross. Under a window where some streetlight filtered in, I could suddenly see the brim of a baseball cap, the line of a back, a bulging duffel bag.

I cowered and listened, the dead bolt in my fingers, waiting for the flashlight to round the corner toward me. Instead I heard feet climb the organ loft stairs, and a wave of relief swept through me: I could be safely speeding away before even the fastest man could race down those spiral stairs and out to the street.

I watched the intruder, tall and thin, move across the loft and freeze, staring down at my beach blanket, I knew, and my towel hanging over the organ pipes. After a moment the figure stepped directly in front of the stained glass, removed the cap, and although I saw only a silhouette, a wave of recognition gave me the chills. I rose from my crouch, holding the end of a pew. The silhouette stepped closer to the window, touching the glass with both hands, then turned, and in front of the dazzling color I saw the profile. And I knew. Anyone would. The miracle girl.

I cleared my throat. "Don't let me scare you," I said loudly, knowing she was deaf but still feeling the need to say something. "Hello," I said more loudly, and she turned, a feline tension in her body. Then she dropped to the floor behind the wall.

I didn't want her to run, and I didn't want her freaking out up there either. I felt responsible. So I hurried down the aisle to the organ loft stairs to assure her she had nothing to fear from me. As I reached the top, I caught a flash of an object in my peripheral vision. I turned toward it as it crashed into my head. I staggered. My head dropped and my eyes pressed shut. I swatted, slapping away an arm, and something hit the floor with a boom. When I forced my eyes open, everything was a blur. She dashed around me to the stairs and I lunged for her. She ran the other way behind the organ pipes. I could hardly see her, but I was pretty sure she had one foot over the waist-high wall, ready to jump.

I held up both hands, open palms. "Don't do it!" I shouted. "I'm not going to hurt you!" The next throbbing wave pounded my head, each punch a little weaker. My cheek stung, one eye burned. I tasted blood in the back of my throat, sweet and syrupy. She shifted more of her body over the wall, and I held my hands up higher. "Don't!" I shouted again. Then I carefully touched my eyebrow, and my fingertips came away bloody. At my feet lay the weapon—a pineapple bleeding out a small puddle of juice.

Now all I tasted was pineapple. I smelled it, breathed it, flashed on memories of glazed Easter hams festooned with pineapple rings, hand-feeding pineapple chunks to Rita in Jamaica.

She was straddling the wall. I knew it could go either way. I lit the candle that I'd dropped when she hit me, and held it in front of my chest, moving closer to the window, illuminating my face. "I won't hurt you," I said, my lips exaggerating the shapes of the words. "I know who you are. I won't hurt you. I know you." I said it over and over like a chant, the throbbing in my head starting to subside. She eased over this side of the wall enough to suggest I was doing the right thing. "I won't hurt you." She leaned toward me to read my lips, and I saw the other candle at my feet, the one I'd blown out before going to sleep. I lowered myself to the floor and sat cross-legged, lighting the second candle from the first and holding them, one in each hand, at my knees. "I know who you are."

She paused, one hip on the wall, her eyes darting from me to her bag to the stairs, then she slipped down, both feet back on the floor of the loft. She stepped into the full glow of light from the window—green, opal, ruby red illuminating her cheeks and nose, forehead and chin. A scarf wrapped around the top of her head, and her shiny black hair plumed like a fountain, the ends of the tight curls brushed with the light. She came closer and grabbed her flashlight off the floor.

I rested one votive on my knee and rubbed my eye. Blood trickled down my cheek. Or pineapple juice.

She wore a black short-sleeved T-shirt, cargo pants, and Converse high-tops. She gave me a wide berth, ready to bolt. If she ran, I wouldn't chase her, but I hoped she'd stay. I wanted her to sit awhile. I wanted to talk with her—or find some way to communicate. I was already rehearsing the story: "She practically knocks me out with a pineapple, and it's her, the miracle girl, in the middle of the night, and we sit there together until dawn." And who, I wondered then, would I tell the story to?

She stepped closer, her flashlight raised in one hand to strike. She was a ropy strong woman nearly as tall as I was. If she could rattle me with a pineapple, I wondered, what could she do with a metal flashlight? She reached toward me, watching my eyes and lips. I kept perfectly still, the candles in my fingers propped on my knees.

Her hand moved under my chin. Her face was threatening; she cocked the flashlight higher.

"I won't hurt you," I chanted, again and again.

She touched my throat.

And as I spoke, she held her hand there, feeling the vibrations, watching my eyes. I could smell her skin. Then she lowered the flashlight. Her shoulders, her stance, softened.

She withdrew her hand and made a sign. I shook my head. She signed more slowly, and I shook my head again. So she slipped a notebook and pen from her pocket and began to write.

When she dropped her eyes and head, tipping the pad toward the window, her face flooded with the kaleidoscopic light. Every mix of color imaginable reflected on her skin. I could see that amazing eyebrow. I could see why all of Hudson City was dreaming about her. She was heavenly.

She tore off the sheet of paper and floated it to me. Her handwriting was neat and forceful; I angled it toward the window: "You're the asshole with the phony vision."

I shook my head.

She nodded, signed something, and scowled.

"Listen," I said, and when I lifted the candles closer to my face, hot wax spilled over my fingers. I yelped and dropped them, and they snuffed out when they hit the floor.

She picked up her flashlight and beamed it in my face, then she pointed at me and nodded like she knew I was a liar.

I didn't want her to leave. It suddenly seemed important for her to like me. I closed my eyes and looked directly into her flashlight beam. "I only fainted." I formed my lips around each syllable. "I never said I had a vision." The flashlight shined through my eyelids. "The first I heard about it was on TV."

Suddenly a siren wailed. "Stand back! Stand back!" I jumped up and peered through the cutout in the reeds. My lights flashed. Three men hunkered around my truck, their big old Cadillac parked in the middle of the street, its trunk open. *Ha,* I thought, *the radio's already gone, suckers.* And then with a crash I heard over the siren, the front end of my truck hit the pavement. While two of the men spun lug wrenches at the rear wheels, the third popped the hood and snipped around the engine with wire cutters. Eventually he got the right one—the alarm cut off like a slice to the throat. "Shit," one of them said in the sudden quiet. "I hate those things." They hurled my tires into their trunk and sped away.

I turned from the window. Standing had brought a rush to my head and pounding to my temples. My eye was stinging again. The miracle girl tapped my shoulder and pushed a note at me: "Do you have a car? I need a car." She hefted her bag and pulled on her black cap. She was starting to get on my nerves.

I took my keys from my pocket and held them out. She snatched them up—not even a smile. "Where?" she mouthed, raising her shoulders and palms in a question.

"Right outside," I said. "Careful with the upholstery. It's leather." I pointed out the tiny window, and she stepped in front of me to look. Her shoulders sank when she saw my truck—anger pinched her mouth and eyes. "It's all yours," I said. I spoke fast out of the corner of my mouth. She took a step toward me to get my face in a better light. "And who are you anyway? You've gotten a little mileage out of phony visions yourself. Where's your Absolut Miracle T-shirt?"

She stared at my lips after I'd stopped talking, like someone hanging on my words, then made another abrupt sign. The throbbing in my head had settled down, but my brow and cheek still stung. And my eye hurt, my actual eyeball.

She was writing another note, but I was already sick of her notes. I grabbed my towel, lit a candle, and took it downstairs. In the bathroom I set the candle on the sink. I couldn't see much in the mirror, which was probably good, because what I could see was red, swollen, and dripping with blood. I ran water over a corner of the towel and dabbed at it. The pineapple skin had cut me in five or six places. Then I wet half the towel in the cold water, wrung it out, and pressed it to the right side of my face. I leaned back against the wall and closed my eyes. I tried to think. I tried to think about what I was doing here. I was on the run from Rita, the IRS, and a city full of fanatics who thought God had whispered in my ear. I was hiding in the bathroom of a decommissioned church basement from the most famous and sought-after woman in Hudson City. And she had clobbered me with a pineapple.

The towel got warm, so I rewet it and held it to my face again. Did I have a job anymore? Did I have a life? Did Rita really believe that her e-mail affair wasn't a betrayal? Had I really believed that the kickbacks from Buddy were kosher? Was Rita becoming Jewish so she could share her religion with J. B. Katz? One more time I cooled the towel and pressed it to my face, then I headed upstairs. I set the candle in the holy-water dish and went outside. My truck was a wreck. I peered under the hood. From what I could see, the alarm wire was the very last wire in the entire truck that he cut. It looked like a sea creature with hundreds of tentacles barnacled onto my engine. Repairable, I thought. Insurance, I thought. I slammed down the hood and took a step back. It looked awful. Tires really made an SUV.

Inside the church, I bolted the door closed and went back up to the loft, mostly hoping she'd be gone.

But there she was, kneeling on the floor with the flashlight, examining a map spread at her knees. She must have felt me coming—she looked at me but didn't shine the light in my face. As I came near, she quickly folded up the map and rustled it into her bag. I sat on the beach blanket and made an expression like, *Now what?*

Looking around, fidgety, taking stock of her stuff, she was very unlike the serene woman whose long back I saw at her kitchen counter making a sandwich. Very unlike the mysterious woman, *magical* even, who put Frank into a trance. Nothing like the woman these few thousand pilgrims had come to be near, whose face had taken over our newspapers and TVs, who claimed she'd healed the sick, restored hearing to the deaf, chatted with the Virgin Mary. She clicked her pen repeatedly with one thumb and bit the nail of the other. Then she wrote a note: "Are you the only one here?" I nodded, and she wrote: "I need to stay."

She seemed to be all through beating on me, so I nodded again. "Whatever."

She stuck her pen in her pocket. End of conversation.

I dragged my beach blanket away from her, spreading it out beneath the organ pipes. Sleep was tugging me down. I curled onto my side, my back to her, and pinged the small treble organ pipes with my fingernail. I followed the ringing into sleep.

I dreamed in color and woke hours later, my left hip numb, and I rolled to my other side. It was still dark. The miracle girl was tucked into the corner of the loft next to the stairs and the closet—right where she'd been standing when she hit me with the pineapple. She sat with her knees pulled into her chest. One arm was curled around her shins, the other had fallen beside her, palm up and open on the floor. Her head was tipped to one shoulder, eyes closed.

8. MONDAY

Sunlight warmed the backs of my legs—a slow awakening in which my dream about the miracle girl seeped into a long period of half-consciousness. I knew I was in the loft, in the church, the sun was coming in, but I didn't want to let go of the dream: the miracle girl was clicking her pen, sitting in front of my jigsaw puzzle at the dining room table, poring over my taxes, and I was trying to see over her shoulder to learn the secret calculation that would save me from the IRS.

For a long moment I thought that it had *all* been a dream, that I was still alone in the loft. Trying to blink away the blur from my right eye, I rose up on my elbows, smelling pineapple juice. I turned slowly to look over my shoulder: there she was, cutting the pineapple into pieces on my Frisbee.

I sat up, picking sleep from the corners of my eyes. I combed my fingers through my hair and straightened my shirt. I had to take a leak but felt self-conscious, so I sat cross-legged on the blanket and took a hunk of pineapple in my fingers when she offered. She ate too, the fruit piled between us on the Frisbee, her jackknife blade propped up on the rim. We looked past each other, awkwardly. The knife, its blade and fake bone handle glistening with juice, was Boy Scout issue.

Eating with our hands in silence from the common platter, juice dripping down our wrists, swallowing mouthfuls of the fruit she'd clubbed me with—it all felt ritualistic, like eating an enemy's heart. Was this act—eating the weapon with which she'd suppressed me—my admission of defeat, or a signal for a truce? Either way, the pineapple tasted delicious and sweet. I couldn't think when I'd eaten last.

Outside, the city awoke—the morning's first siren, a kid shouting to his friend, the bass from a car stereo rattling the glass. I heard some birds. And as we ate, I stole glances at her: she'd seemed so serene in the photos, mesmerizing to Frank. But she was obviously anxious. Mostly though, I was amazed that it was actually her. The miracle girl was sitting with me and sharing a pineapple. How was it possible? Not that I believed in the miracles, but she was famous and beautiful and mysterious and she'd come to my loft. *My* loft.

As if she read my mind, she wiped her hands on a bandanna and wrote a note. Tearing it from the pad she looked up at me. She ran her finger across her eyebrow and down her cheek, then nodded toward the side of my face, circling her fist over her heart, which I understood to mean—more from the expression in her eyes—*Sorry.*

The note said: "Why are you here?"

I smiled and shrugged.

She raised her palms and eyes like, *Yeah, yeah, but why?*

"Listen," I said. She watched my lips. "It's complicated. There's problems at home, problems at work."

She wrote: "Why not a friend's."

I shook my head.

She took her time with the notes. I touched my eyebrow—the ache spread through my temples. "I need to get away," the note said.

I opened my hands and nodded toward the stairs.

She clicked her pen, thinking.

"Excuse me," I said, my bladder about to burst. I grabbed my towel off the organ pipes and took the long walk down to the bathroom. Two votive candles were burning on the sink—night-lights left by the miracle girl. I flushed and stripped and stepped into the shower, the cold water a relief on the side of my face. I washed and stood at the mirror. My eye looked okay, but it was swollen and red. The scratches down my cheek from the pineapple skin had scabbed over. I looked like I'd tumbled in the rosebushes. The bathroom smelled warm with paraffin.

What was she *doing here?* seemed like a reasonable question. How did she get in? What about the pilgrims? When I returned to the loft, I asked her.

She started to write on the small pad, then stopped, pulled a full-size notebook from her bag, and started again. While she wrote, I hung up my towel and put on my socks and shoes. I looked through the small opening in the window at my truck. All four wheels were gone. The rear end was propped up on an old car seat, and the front bumper was crushed against the pavement. My insurance would pay, but still, it broke my heart.

She slapped the floor three times, and I turned from the window. She handed me the notebook: "Last night, very late, we invited dozens of people into the apartment. I stayed in my room while my mother spoke to them. A friend of mine was in the third group. She slipped into my bedroom, we switched clothes, and I left with the rest.

"I got my first communion in this church. I didn't know it was closed. I came in through the coal chute. When I was little, we used to sneak in that way all the time. There was a sweet old janitor here who caught us one day. He shooed us off, but the next time we tried, the chute had been swept clean and there was a piece of cardboard on the floor to land on. I've been thinking about this church ever since this started. I don't know what it was, but something drew me here."

At the bottom she wrote: "How did you get in?"

When I finished reading, I looked at her, smiling. "With a key."

She watched me for a moment, waiting for me to say more, then grimaced. She wrote furiously: "You're one of them?" Her eyes narrowed.

"Who?"

"Floquet." Her pen gouged the paper.

I laughed and her face got angrier. "I work for the diocese. For the bishop. Buildings and properties."

Any trust we'd built turned sour. I was glad we'd eaten the pineapple.

For several minutes she looked away from me, anxiously plotting her next move. And I tried to think through mine. But she was working herself into a panic—her breathing speeded up and she twisted and pulled her fingers until the knuckles snapped—so finally I touched her, and when she looked I said, "Don't worry. You're safe here."

Her dark eyes fixed on me, then she wrote, "I need a car. I have some money—not on me—but I can get it to you."

"Listen," I said. "I think you're in trouble. You pulled some shit, and it's gotten out of hand. Unless I steal you a car, I'd have to rent one. So how do I know you'll get this car back to me?"

She grabbed my wrist and throttled my arm, forcing me to look into her eyes, which were insisting, *I promise. Believe me.*

I told her I'd be back as soon as I could. My head was killing me. First order of business, a cup of coffee. I unbolted the door and when I touched the knob, it was hot. I cracked it open—the sun was low and fierce. The heat would not be breaking today.

I started walking. Several guys were hanging out on the next corner, so I crossed the street with purpose midblock and kept going. They looked my way. A car slowed. A conversation on a stoop halted. I felt very white, stumbling on a piece of loose concrete in the sidewalk. Clumps of weeds grew in the cracks. Brick-sized hunks of concrete were busted away.

Up ahead, five or six men were smoking in front of a corner store—A and P Grocery. I crossed back over the street and quickened my pace. I was sweating. I remembered hearing about A and P—the owner said they'd had the name for three generations and he was waiting for A&P to try and get him to change it. He said he expected they'd have to pay him a great deal. Every five or ten years the local news would run the story, but the A&P lawyers never called.

Two more blocks and I was on Hoosick Street. Traffic was slow and heavy heading downtown, and I felt safe again.

At Tri-City Plaza I went to the Grand Union, got a coffee and plain doughnut from the deli counter, and grabbed a paper. I sat at one of the tables surrounded by cakes frosted in garish colors and packed in striped boxes with clear tops. The coffee was thin and smelled like cornmeal.

Page three: "John Quinn of 482 Water Street, until now known only as 'the man in the tie,' is employed by the Tri-Cities Roman Catholic Diocese." Fuck. I read the speculation about why I couldn't be found and why I worked for the Church. Had I felt a calling? Was I deeply religious? The bishop had declined comment. Floquet had only said, "The Lord blesses those who are blessed." There was more description of the rose-colored light, witnessed by hundreds of pilgrims, and descriptions of my body buckling, my feet lifting off the ground above the flowers as my chest filled with the spirit, my head tipped back, and I gently collapsed. Video of the event had proved inconclusive. And at the bottom of the article, another quote: "I love him. He's away right now." Rita.

I went outside to a pay phone in front of Kmart and called her. It went straight to voice mail, and I hung up.

I opened the Yellow Pages to auto rentals and tried three biggies and a local. They all laughed. There wasn't a car to be had in Hudson City.

Then I called in to our messages. A coin-op Little Cowhand Bronco grinned at me. *You have twenty-two new messages.* "Hello, Mr. Quinn. This is Homer Wilcox from the Internal Revenue . . ." I skipped ahead. "Hello, Mr. Quinn. This is Jerry McAllister from the *Tri-City Times.* I'm hoping . . ." I skipped again. "Hi, Quinn. It's Patsy. The bishop is blaming . . ." "This is Cindy Burnside from WTRI-TV News . . ." "Homer Wilcox again . . ." "Tom Hart calling from 'Tri-City Triumphs' . . ." "Homer Wilcox . . ." "It's Patsy . . ." "Homer Wilcox . . ." I slammed down the phone.

I kicked the bronco. The air was heavy in my lungs, like diesel fumes—hot air with a high lead content. Breathing hard I plugged coins into the phone and called Buddy. "Here's the thing," I told him. "Can you really take care of the IRS for me?"

"Let's just say I have some influence with your auditor."

"Well, take care of it, and we'll figure out later how I can return the favor."

"You know what I want."

"Don't be a prick. The bishop told me he's selling you the day care property."

Buddy laughed. "I want a sit-down in that girl's apartment, Quinn. I want you back in this office working to score me an invite."

"She's not even in the apartment. Don't you know? She's left town."

"What are you talking about? She can't leave town."

"Gone."

"I just saw it on TV. She's—"

"You *think* she's in there."

"How do you know this? Where is she?"

"You wanna work with me, or not?"

"She's not going back to Rhode Island," Buddy said. "She *needs* to live in Hudson City."

"I know where she is."

"Where? Now."

"She wants to be left alone."

"She can't be left alone. She has to . . . She . . . I know if I could talk with her, if we could just break bread."

"But she doesn't talk."

"She doesn't have to. I'll do the talking. She just needs to *be*. And she'll make it all happen."

I let a long silence stretch through the phone. "Here's the deal—"

"You're a liar anyway. I don't believe you."

"I want a letter from the IRS, from Homer Wilcox, saying I've been audited and cleared. Then I'll talk to her and see if she wants to meet you."

"She can save us. She must know that."

"Then," I said, "no more special deals. *And* an interview with Venable."

"If you're lying . . . I swear to God, Quinn—"

"Have the letter dropped at my house. With Rita. Today." I hung up. Then I dialed the office.

"He fired you yesterday," Patsy said. "I typed the letter. But then he hired you back."

"Just connect me."

He was shouting before the phone got to his mouth. "Where in God's good name—"

"Frank," I said. "Listen, I can take care of this whole miracle if you want."

"Who do you think you are? You have a job to do here. You are unreliable, immature, you punched a city official—"

"I can do it, Frank. I can squash the whole thing. I mean it."

"Did they give you drugs when you fainted? Are you on drugs?"

"I just want to know I'll be forgiven."

"Forgiveness is a sacrament. There's no deal-making."

"Whatever, Frank. If I can get this monkey off your back, will you . . . I don't know. Will you just forget about all of this?"

"Of course, John. The Lord has—"

"Good. I won't be into the office, but I promise you I'm working on it. You'll see." I hung up and called Rita but got the voice mail. "Screw it." I decided I'd go over there and tell her to expect the letter from the IRS. She could consider it the last favor she'd ever have to do for me.

. . .

The walk took about forty minutes. I walked slowly, stopping in a grocery for a bottle of water. I had to start taking better care of myself. When I turned the corner around the Armenian church, I saw a Channel 6 News van across the park, its satellite dish extended on a boom above the telephone lines. My first thought was that parking had really gotten impossible, then, quickening my pace, I thought there'd been an emergency, something with Rita. It took five or six steps before I stopped dead, realizing the reporters were waiting for me.

Stupidly, I jumped behind a phone pole. They were a full block away across Burden Park. I didn't see anyone prowling around the street; no doubt they were sitting in their air-conditioned van eating sandwiches and drinking sodas. Probably watching satellite TV.

Two blocks north there was a pay phone in front of the firehouse. I hurried over there and dialed Rita again. Voice mail.

I decided to take a risk. I swung a three-block loop around the back of our apartment and cut in through the alley. Garbage heaped out of Dumpsters and barrels, a sour smell sticking to my sweaty skin. Air-conditioners were chugging. A spray of cool water hit my arms and the back of my neck; I looked up where a gray-haired woman in a nightgown was watering plants on a third-floor fire escape.

Ahead I could see our back stoop. The fan was spinning in Rita's office window. Part of me wanted to catch her in the middle of an e-mail to J. B. Katz. Even better, I wanted to find the two of them together in her office, embracing. Fully clothed. I couldn't take any more than that, and that would be enough: it would be done. She'd be guilty. I'd be humiliated, but I'd get the sympathy. Rosemary and Frank would cut me some slack, and so would my parents, and hopefully Lilian. Even Trisch would have to admit that Rita was to blame.

My chin at sill level, I looked in through the chop of the fan blades, straight through to the living room where Rita was sitting on the edge of the coffee table, elbows propped on her knees, talking on the phone. I watched her for a few minutes, although I couldn't hear her voice over the fan. The fan was sucking out, blowing toward me. I smelled our house, our home, the dusty wood floors and plaster walls, the particular smell of our kitchen—coffee, bread, cinnamon, and crumbling linoleum. Rita didn't move.

Finally, I called to her, then called louder, which startled her. She held the phone to her chest, looking over her shoulder at the front door, then toward the kitchen. I called again and her face jerked toward me. I waved my arm, and she came, never standing fully upright, squinting through the fan and the screen. "I'll call you back," she said as she kneeled at the window.

Now I smelled Rita: her shampoo, an imitation of strawberries that smelled more delicious than the real thing, the steamy crescents under her breasts, and her breath when she was tired or had been crying, a thick smell, like olive oil.

She switched off the fan.

"Was that J. B. Katz?" I said in a loud whisper.

She shook her head, pressing her lips together.

"A letter's coming from the IRS. Just tell me you'll get it to me."

"What happened to your eye? Oh my God, Quinn. What's going on?"

I'd forgotten about the welt, and now it hurt again. "Will you get me the letter?"

"I'll do anything for you," she said.

"It's a little late for that."

"Is it?" she said very softly. "Too late?"

I reached up and grasped the black iron bars beside my face. "Why don't you e-mail your boyfriend and ask him how I should feel?"

"I'm sorry, Quinn. I'm so sorry. But if you'd let me explain—"

"Explain what? I wasn't chatty enough so you had to go out and find some Brit to discuss what you had for lunch and the meaning of love?"

"It's not like that."

"And all the dreams you don't remember."

"Look, I knew him before we even met. It was right after my father died—"

I leaned into the bars and actually laughed. "That's supposed to make me feel better? That you've been having an affair with a married man the whole time we've been together."

"It's not an affair, Quinn. We just e-mail."

"I figure ten secret e-mails per day equals two fucks a week."

Her breath caught. I'd hurt her.

"You need therapy," I said. "Or maybe spiritual guidance. I could hook you up with the miracle girl if you want."

She started to cry. "It's completely separate from you and me."

"We've had some laughs, Rita. I'll come by for my stuff one of these days."

"Don't go. We've got to talk."

"Tell Josh he's got a pansy name."

"Don't be an ass, Quinn."

"Loves," I said and turned back down the alley.

I was dripping with sweat when the automatic doors back at the Grand Union whooshed open—a rush of cold air flooded over me like water. Moving briskly through the aisles, I grabbed crackers and pretzels, a jug of grape juice, bananas, and nectarines. I ordered two turkey and Swiss sandwiches from the deli counter, paid for it all, and went back out into the heat.

A block from the church I could see my truck rocking back and forth, kids on top. I walked faster, then started running, the groceries heavy at my side. "Hey," I shouted at them: four kids were jumping on the hood and roof. The front bumper ground into the street. "Get off there!" And they stopped, looked at me, and laughed, holding their ground. They were only about twelve years old, but I suddenly wondered if one of them might have a gun. I kept running at them, screaming, "Get off!" They stood low, legs bent, waiting to see what I'd do, and when I reached into my bag to hurl a nectarine at them, they bolted, disappearing into a tight alley.

I stood looking up at the church. From the outside, the massive stained-glass disk hovering above the three front doors was muted, the colors muddy. I thought I saw the miracle girl pull away from the tiny pop-out window.

I unlocked the side door and went in, so overheated from running that the church didn't even feel cool. Sweat collected in my eyebrows and spilled into my eyes. The cuts were stinging. I wiped my face on my sleeve and looked up to see the miracle girl standing at the wall of the loft.

When I reached the top of the stairs, I smiled. Her face jutted forward, expectant. "There's not a rental car available in the whole Tri-Cities." And when she was waiting for more, I shook my head, slicing a hand through the air.

She slapped the top of the wall. Still looking at me, her face turned angry.

"But I brought lunch." I held out a sandwich.

She flicked her thumbs then tapped one palm with the other hand, giving me a look of disbelief. When I shrugged to say I didn't understand, she seemed disgusted that I still hadn't learned sign language after our many hours together. She wrote, "That's it?!"

"Well, no." I looked at the floor but kept my mouth pointing her way. "I'm on about ten wait lists." It was actually three. "Avis might get a compact in. And there's a chance at Rent-a-Wreck, down by the river."

She shook her head, and turned her face away. She'd changed into a clean shirt—a navy blue T-shirt. I held out the sandwich again, and finally she took it.

We sat facing each other, the bag of pretzels between us. Blue and yellow light shifted across her face. I thought about whether she looked more black or more Vietnamese. I couldn't tell about the color of her skin—I hadn't seen her yet in daylight. Her eyes were big and dark. Her nose was broad and flat at the bridge. Her face was square, with prominent cheekbones. Her full lips had the penciled shapely lines of Vietnamese women. She was nearly as tall as I was, narrow shoulders and hips, small hands and feet. Watching her eat the turkey sandwich, anxiously tapping two fingers on the Chuck Taylor emblem on her Converse high-tops, she seemed, more than anything else, American.

Buddy was right—she'd be a great multicultural symbol for Hudson City. If I could convince her that hanging around a few more days would heal the city, she might just have lunch with him.

Until then, she and I would be sitting around the church with no place to go anyway. If she wanted to leave, fine. I was going too, as soon as my Land Rover was back on the road. I'd upgrade the stereo, maybe get bigger tires. Pop on a new front end, buff out the scratches. My life at that moment seemed salvageable.

When she'd finished half her sandwich, she wrote on the small pad, "How long have you lived in here?"

I laughed. "I don't live here," I said. "It's just a couple days. I found out my girlfriend's been cheating on me since before I met her."

She shook her head and mouthed the words, *I'm sorry,* as she made the sign. She seemed to really mean it. I was a little proud of myself for reading her lips.

We were silent awhile, or *I* was silent awhile. She picked up her second half. I listened to us chomp crispy white lettuce and crunch pretzels. "Another breakup," I finally said.

She raised her head and then her eyebrows so I'd repeat it.

"I just said that I thought Rita and I were going to make it. But . . . poof." I made an explosion sign with my hand. "She's really the first woman I thought I wanted to go the stretch with."

Again, she made a puzzled expression, not only with her face but her shoulders and spine.

"She's the first woman I wanted to marry," I said, knowing that wasn't really what I meant, but I didn't know how else to say it. I'd never want the Church or the government certifying my relationship with any woman I loved. I started to say that, but *that* didn't sound quite right either.

"Why not the other girlfriends?" she wrote.

"Some were boring. Kind and good-hearted, smart enough, pretty, but dull, dull, dull. I ran into one of them at a wedding, and she's telling me about her job and her kids and her amazing tax lawyer husband, and I say, 'Do you ever have kicks?' and she says, 'Oh, yeah. Last summer I was at another wedding and the band was great and I was talking to this guy and it turned out that he was really into the history of educational theory too . . .'"

The miracle girl was laughing. A full-faced lovely laugh, her bright eyes fixed on me.

"The fun ones had problems too. One of them never heard of Martin Luther King. Another one didn't know what Parisians were. Another one, and this was in college, used to steal umbrellas from the dining hall lobby if it started to rain while we were eating. 'It's okay,' she'd say. 'Everybody does it.' She was a philosophy major."

She looked down at her sandwich and took a bite. "Are you following?" I asked.

Chewing, she put her sandwich down on the paper and sliced one hand across the other palm which I took to mean, *Some.*

I was glad to be talking and didn't mind—if she didn't—that she wasn't getting it all. Her lips quivering when she inhaled, the eagerness in her eyes as she watched my face, were a relief. Was it really her?

"Then there were the needy ones. The summer before my senior year in college I was painting houses. I broke up with a woman I hadn't been seeing very long, and for days she came to the job site and hung off the bottom of my ladder begging me to reconsider. It got sort of embarrassing—with the other guys, I mean. Another one used to sit by the bathroom door when I was in there. She was literally jealous of the time I spent with the toilet. I used to drive down to Poughkeepsie to see her. The weekend I finally broke up with her, I threw my bag in my car, but my battery was dead. So I rolled my car out of her driveway, and I'm pushing it down the street and hopping in to pop the clutch, but I can't get up enough speed to start the engine. By the time I'm a block down the street and I've tried three or four times, she's gotten into *her* car and she's following me at half a mile an hour. We go on like this for a couple blocks. Me pushing and hopping in and the engine groaning, her following ten feet behind."

I stopped there. The miracle girl's hands unfolded, one over the other.

"You mean what happened next?"

She seemed to nod, mostly in her eyes.

"I never got it started. I pushed it ten blocks before I steered it to the curb, and left it there half sticking into the street."

She raised her palms. *And then?*

"Walked over to her car and got in. She drove us back to her place."

Yes?

I scratched the back of my neck—the sign for "mea culpa." "You know," I said. "What else could I do? I followed her inside and we had sex."

She rolled her eyes, but in a nice way, as she wrote on the pad. I took the note. "Did you break up with them all?"

"God, no," I said. "Mostly, women break up with me. Or maybe half-half." I made the slicing sign across my palm. "One of them dumped me for a whining folk musician who was a clown on weekends. Like for birthday parties."

She made juggling motions with her hands.

I pointed at her. "That's him."

She wrote, "Folk like Dylan and Michelle Shocked? Not so bad."

"Not quite," I said. "He played long ballads about cleaning up the Hudson River and the importance of empathy. He wrote a song called 'Inclusiveness.' Bad. Trust me." I could tell she didn't get that last bit.

She handed me a note. "And this one?"

"Rita?"

She nodded.

"We haven't really had the big breakup scene yet. I guess it'll happen when I move out."

She waited. Rita talked about the "active stretch" in yoga, when she'd extend a muscle and appear still, but inside her body the muscle lengthened, opening up space. During the miracle girl's silences, her face and body almost rippled, our communication continuing.

"Rita's great though," I said without really thinking. "She's funny and smart. Smarter than me. She has . . . you know . . . integrity. That sounds bland, but she actually believes in honesty in this grand kind of way. There was always this unspoken thing like she was a better person than I was. Or that's what I used to think. I don't know. You think you can believe in somebody, and then you find out you're a putz. It's like, Can you ever trust anybody again?"

I waited for her to write a note, but she didn't.

"I always thought she was devoted to me," I said when it seemed like that was okay with her—I mean, for me to keep talking. "With the old girlfriends, the idea of really being committed seemed ridiculous. How could you have that much faith in another person? They were too unpredictable. I mean, everybody is. But Rita was a real in-sickness-and-in-health kind of deal." Saying that made me think of Rita sitting and crying in the tub in six inches of warm water, blisters stinging. "Maybe she just couldn't forgive me for some stuff," I said. "Maybe that's why it always seemed she was holding a little bit back."

She watched me and again didn't respond. I figured I'd gone on long enough. I looked at my watch—12:30. Taking my hand in hers, she turned my wrist to see the time. Then she gently touched my cheek, just below the biggest of the cuts, and made a "thumbs up."

I touched my eyebrow and nodded. "We'll be here awhile," I said, picking up the Frisbee and twirling it on my fingertip.

She made a sign like dialing a phone then holding a steering wheel.

"They said don't bother till tomorrow, but I could try tonight." I twirled the Frisbee again and it spun off my finger. I never could do that trick.

I went downstairs through the church, heading for the bathroom, twice stooping over to pick up the Frisbee after it went spinning off my finger. On my way back through the vestry I stubbed my toe on the iron foot of a candelabra and nearly tripped. The Frisbee flew out of my hands and landed on the altar steps. With the chairs and communion table removed, it looked more like a stage. I walked out to the center, where the priest would stand. It was easy to imagine the pageantry of Christmas Mass: wreaths and poinsettias, strict rows of boys in choir robes, the opening chords of "Joy to the World" bellowing from the organ pipes, candle flames glinting off gold communion plates and the chalice of wine. On the back wall, where the crucifix used to hang, a cross of paint lighter than the rest of the wall almost seemed to glow.

The Frisbee spun off my fingertip and hit the hollow floor. I picked it up and looked toward the loft. I couldn't see her, so I stomped my feet a couple times, and her head popped up from behind the organ loft wall. I waved the Frisbee, then wound up and let it snap. It rose as if in an updraft, up into the shadows in the eaves, a splotch of yellow that gently descended right into the miracle girl's open hand.

She twisted her body and flung it back. Without moving my feet, I caught it an inch in front of my chin.

I launched it again, and it shot up, off to her side, and—cling, clang, clong—struck three organ pipes in descending tones, before ricocheting against the window. Her next toss hovered high above my head, then tipped back as it dropped, and I quick-stepped to the edge of the altar, snagging it before it crashed into the pews.

I hit the organ pipes a couple more times. She forehanded her next shot: the Frisbee flicked off her index finger, glided in the darkness high up in the rafters, then floated down to me through the stained-glass light. My God.

My next toss was low, careening into the loft wall and flubbing in the back pew. I held up my arms in apology.

When I got up to the loft, she was sitting on the floor, curled against her bag, writing in a notebook. She looked up and smiled, then went back to her writing. I took off my shoes and my watch, emptied my pockets, lay back on the beach blanket, and stretched.

It wasn't like I was handing her over to Buddy and Frank. I could control the situation. I could do it in such a way that they'd be satisfied and she could still get to wherever she was trying to go. It wasn't like I was selling her out.

As I drifted off to sleep, I saw the Frisbee spinning, floating, coming to rest in her hands.

I woke to slurping sounds. She was sitting cross-legged against the loft wall, notebook resting in her lap, writing furiously and chomping on a large piece of fruit, so large she could barely manage it with one hand. It looked like a big mango—the skin was greenish orange—but the meat was more like cantaloupe, and the shape was plumper and bulgy—a pregnant mango. Juice dribbled down her wrist and dripped on the floor. She'd changed into shorts; she was barefoot.

I rose up on an elbow. She was holding the fruit on the palm of her hand, steadying it with her fingers like you'd hold a basketball over your head. She bit the bottom, at the heel of her hand, sucking at the juice, a long trickle hitting her knee. I'd never seen anything like it.

She looked over at me, smiled, and kept on writing.

I pretended to drift back to sleep, curling onto my side, but really I was watching her, engrossed in the fruit and her nonstop writing. When she got to the last line, her hand lifted, snapped over the page, and set back down writing all in one motion—like a swimmer doing flip turns. It reminded me of Rita—the fluid motions between yoga poses. Rita was always good with her body and hands: she chopped garlic like chefs at Benihana, wrapped gifts like the ladies at Bloomingdale's; she could mat pictures, cut hair, paint molding and mullions, and carve jack-o'-lanterns that came alive.

My stomach started churning, and I curled up tight, hoping the turkey sandwich had been okay. I thought about the mayo and the heat, then I got up and went down to the bathroom holding my gut.

I decided that I didn't have ptomaine poisoning, but I *did* use the last of the toilet paper. And the bar of soap was down to a sliver. In the kitchen I looked through the cabinets and then through a mop closet, but the place had been stripped clean. It felt a little awkward. It was *my* church, and I felt like a bad host. In the loft, I told her I was going to the store for some essentials.

She'd finished the fruit. I looked for a pit or seeds, but there was nothing. "What do you need?" I asked.

She motioned phoning and driving.

"I'll call," I said.

Although my truck looked abandoned, instead of temporarily crippled, it seemed too risky to call for a tow. My face wasn't that recognizable, but my name was in the news. If I were discovered in the church, I didn't know where I'd go. As soon as the audit was cleared up, if I didn't hit the road, I'd find a new apartment. Maybe I'd get a place down by the river. I'd be single again. I'd have women in for dinner and they'd admire my state-of-the-art stainless-steel kitchen. The furniture I built would be arranged to ensure good flow and complement the space.

The sun was still high in the sky. It was three o'clock. The humidity must have been one hundred percent. In half a block of busted-up sidewalk I'd broken a sweat. Another block down, the fire department had attached a sprinkler to a hydrant: kids and adults played in the fan of water. The sun cast a hundred mini-rainbows through the spray. Delighted shrieks. Wet and shiny black skin.

They watched me approach, the youngest ones looking like they thought I might be there to shut off the water. As I passed on the opposite sidewalk, a girl tried to splash me and when I jumped out of the way, everyone laughed. It was good-natured, though; there was a collective feeling of relief that I seemed to be part of.

A and P Grocery was just beyond the hydrant. Some older kids hung out in front, ice cream on sticks melting as fast as they could wolf it down. "Nice hat," one of them said to me.

"Oh, thanks a lot," I said, trying to play along.

"Oh, thanks a lot," another one mimicked, and they all laughed.

I went into the store. I couldn't see anything, it was so dark. The door shut behind me, and the stale air-conditioned smell reminded me of the office. My eyes slowly adjusted.

In the back, by the beer coolers, I found toilet paper and soap. The miracle girl's face stared at me from the cover of *Hudson City Magazine*, a Chamber of Commerce publication full of ads for local restaurants and bars, and ads for shopping-and-a-show bus tours down to New York. I picked up a copy and dropped everything on the counter. The cashier punched prices into her old-fashioned register. When she smiled, I saw her gold front tooth inlaid with a silver cross.

As she slipped the miracle girl's face into a bag, I held up my finger, and dashed to the back of the store to grab a toothbrush and a tube of Crest. Then I grabbed another toothbrush. I passed them to her hands, and she rang them up.

When I came into the church, I glanced up at the loft, but couldn't see her over the wall. I headed straight for the bathroom with the toilet paper. Halfway down the basement stairs, I froze—I heard a retch, a gasp. I retreated a step, then heard the retch again and realized it was her, vomiting. I rushed down two steps, then stopped. She wouldn't want my help. *She must hate me,* I thought. My own stomach felt better, but I'd given her a sandwich that had made her sick. I went up to the loft and waited.

When she came pounding up the stairs, I braced myself. I hoped she was out of fruit she could attack me with. She seemed like such a celebrity—temper tantrums allowed and expected, the privilege to slap faces.

But when she got to the top of the stairs, she only raised her eyes and held up her fists like she was steering a car. She was carrying a toothbrush travel case and a tube of paste.

I'd forgotten to call. "Nothing," I said, not wanting to stray too far from the truth.

She watched my eyes, waiting for more. I looked away, knowing she suspected I was lying.

"Look," I said. "It might be a few days."

Her eyes narrowed and sharpened.

The afternoon grew hotter, the miracle girl filling notebook pages while I read about her in *Hudson City Magazine* and yesterday's paper. As the bath of light crept from one side of the loft to the other, we slid across the floor ahead of it until we were sitting side by side on the beach blanket right next to the organ pipes. The sun was shining on her toothbrush and a small washcloth laid out on top of her black bag. The toothbrushes I'd bought lay together on the Sunday comics. I touched her wrist and said, "Do you want to look at the paper?" and then I pointed, hoping she'd notice the toothbrushes, notice that I'd been thoughtful.

One article showed her graduation picture from SUNY New Paltz, 1991. Her face was a little younger, rounder. She looked on the edge of a smile in the picture. Or, more like a second after the shutter snapped she exploded into laughter. A cheesy article about David Newman retraining his voice was meant to inspire and warm the heart but came off pathetic: on the protein diet to slim down for his comeback, he was photographed in a sweatshirt, its neck torn *Flashdance* style, his hair newly bleached and spiked.

The second young man to have his hearing restored was reported to be suffering insomnia, headaches, and anxiety. He was distracted and confused by the clamor of the city. Car stereos, bus engines, and barking dogs burrowed and squirmed under his skin. He was training as a computer programmer, but now he couldn't sit at the keyboard for more than a few minutes—the whir of the hard drive made him crazy. He openly wished he'd never gotten his hearing back.

Like David Newman and the miracle girl, he'd lost his hearing in an accident. All three had several operations, and when they failed to regain more than one percent of their hearing, doctors said there was no hope. "However," a hearing specialist interviewed for the story said, "there are hundreds maybe thousand of cases in the research where patients regained hearing spontaneously with no medical explanation, but where divine intervention is not cited."

All over Hudson City kidney stones were dissolving, tonsils were shrinking, tight joints were jiggling free. The miracle girl appeared mid-flight to an old man tumbling down the stairs; at the bottom he brushed off the dust and went on his way. She continued to appear in dreams, and as I read this I realized she'd appeared in mine too.

A reporter had dug up David Newman's initial descriptions of the woman who'd appeared to him when he was in a coma. At first her face was shadowed, he'd said, but then, as if she was self-illuminated, a sunny glow shone from beneath her skin. He'd said it twelve years ago, and as I looked at the miracle girl now, it could not have described her better. He hadn't mentioned the shape of her eyebrow, but he did say there was music coming from her, "music in her face."

I tapped her shoulder and she stopped writing. Stretching her wrists, she read the article about David Newman, then rolled her eyes. So I turned back a page and showed her the article about the boy who wished he was deaf again. She read this one more closely, then pointed to herself. *Me too,* she mouthed.

"What?" I said. "You wouldn't want to be able to hear?"

She nodded.

"C'mon," I said, a look of disbelief.

She flipped to the back of her notebook and wrote on a blank page. "I navigate the hearing world fine, but deaf is my identity, my culture."

"But don't you want to hear a waterfall or the wind in the trees?"

She scooched her back toward the window and took my chin in her hand, turning my face to the light. Then she signed for me to repeat, and I did, her soft fingertips on my face.

"I see color—light—flow—frenzy—power in a waterfall," she wrote. "The sound—a roar?—not so subtle. I feel wind on my skin—hair—lips, I feel it flutter my clothes, swirl in my ears. Hearing would be a distraction."

Then she held up a finger—*just a minute*—turning back to the beginning of the notebook. She pointed to a paragraph and I read: "I never really knew what sound was until I heard the voice. When I was little, I used to press my forehead to stereo speakers to feel the beat. I'd rest my face on the car door to get the rumble of the road. But other than those times, I've been very happy being deaf—I'd never want to lose it. And this voice that I think I've been hearing isn't going to change that. I won't let—" She'd stopped writing midsentence. Then halfway down the page she'd started in again. "The only sound I ever knew was the explosion, and I'm not sure, but I sometimes think I'm still hearing it—all day every day—the mine exploding beneath my mother's feet, the sound of my mother's death ripping through my ears." I handed her back the notebook.

"But talking," I said, two fingers flicking from my lips. "Communicating."

She wrote, "Most of my friends are deaf. We sign. Even if I could suddenly hear and speak, I'd still sign with my friends. English is so linear. It takes forever to say anything, one word plodding after the next. I don't even like reading. With one gesture, my face, my body, I can say what takes a long dull sentence in English. Sign language is 3-dimensional, it's deep."

"But what about the limitations of sign language?"

Her brow darkened.

"Limitations," I repeated.

Throwing up her hands and throwing back her head, she looked at me like I'd offended her. Then she flipped back to the middle of her notebook and started writing again. I waited, thinking she was going to show me something, but she shifted her body so I couldn't see. I *had* offended her. "Sorry," I said, but she wasn't looking.

I got up for a drink of juice, and when I sat back down, I tapped her knee. "So why are you writing all this English, then?"

She slapped her chest and mouthed, *It's my story.* Then she wrote, "That smarmy Floquet is making it his own."

"You know," I said, "and I'm only saying this because I like you—" Then I stopped short when I heard Buddy Jensen in my voice. "Look. You brought this on yourself."

Her eyes and cheeks bugged out, and she made a fist. I held up my palms in defense.

She sized me up—the curve of my slumped back, wrinkled shirt (twice washed in the sink downstairs), hair shampooed with the hard chip of Ivory, stubbly chin, and eyes alternately avoiding and scrutinizing her face. With some reluctance, she turned to a page near the front of her notebook and held it up: "I didn't announce this to the world. Floquet did. Something happened to me. Maybe I'm losing my mind. I know it's a possibility. I had come back to town to see my doctor. I had a CAT scan, and the next day David Newman got his hearing back, and the day after that my doctor said there was nothing wrong with me. Then I made the mistake of telling Floquet.

"I feel things—I felt things—in my body. And I heard a voice. I'd known the vibrations of voices, but I never knew the fullness of a voice, the music, the intimacy of it until I heard hers. It was a voice as colorful as any painting, any landscape, and at the same time clear and fluid as water. The voice was like a stream, deep in a forest in the summer. Crisp and fresh. I don't want to hear it."

I looked up at her, tilting my head onto my hands like sleeping. "Maybe you were dreaming."

She shook her head and wrote in the margin, "I read signs and lips in my dreams."

I thought that maybe she *was* losing her mind. She wasn't faking this to get famous. She believed it was real. I pinched the next page and raised my eyes to ask permission. *Okay?*

She nodded.

Words were crossed out, sentences added in the margin and placed with long arrows. Her handwriting was rounder and inkier than the notes she'd rushed. "It has happened four times. First I feel a tug at my shoulders, a gentle pull on my limbs, getting lighter and lighter until it's like breath, someone blowing softly on my skin, moving up the nape of my neck then down my back. Very slowly—what seems like ten minutes or more, time lengthening—the room (it has happened all over the house) perfectly still, middle-of-the-night still, the air cools me, the gentle blowing behind my knees, between my toes, inside my thighs, over my belly and chest, blowing through my hair to my scalp. When it blows over my face, I close my eyes and I see water rushing and behind it a warm rose-colored light. Then the single stream of air becomes many—little tornadoes moving over my skin. Five, then ten, then hundreds of them making my skin constrict. And then the pain begins: thrashes across my back, dead weight crushing my shoulders and buckling my legs, stinging scrapes on my forehead, searing agony in my palms and feet, a cold slice at my ribs. I fear it. I try to bear it, but I give up every time and pray (I actually pray which I don't do, which I haven't done since I was little) that I'll die.

"And every time, I think I'm dead. But then I'm lowered feet first into a warm pool—a large bath really—and relief soaks through me, but before I've physically recovered, the water begins to rock the length of the tub, shifting side to side, tiny rippling vibrations. The vibrations build, whirlpools twirling beneath the surface, a tidal pull at my breasts and belly, a pull inside me, drawing me out, loosening my arms and legs in their sockets, opening a space inside my body. And then I feel a presence, neither male or female but a physical being above me, below me, over me, inside me. Not penetrating—but suffusing me, and I feel a tiny flutter in my pelvis that rises into my womb. The fluttering builds as the water ripples over my skin, jostling my breasts. The fluttering spreads down my legs and up my spine. My lungs flutter and my breathing gets short and heavy, and the flutter won't stop. It's faster and deeper and I feel the thump of my heart and I think I shout out, and an undertow surges through my body completely emptying me out for an instant, then a wave rushes through me with the smell of roses and something bitter, like anise, and a feeling of utter joy. My heart swells with it. I think I laugh out loud. And that's when I hear her voice, clear and ringing, the voice of love.

"It all happens and somehow only a moment has passed. The third time, my mother and I were reading in the living room. She got up and asked me if I wanted some iced tea. I said no. She went to the kitchen and when she returned with a glass of tea for herself—a minute or two, she said—I was splayed out on the couch, my clothes soaked with sweat, the voice still sounding in my ears, but as usual I couldn't remember the words.

"I know the Passion so where I feel the pain, the quality of it, could be all in my head. But it's so intense, so awful, if I bring it on myself . . . What would it say about me?"

I closed the notebook and stared for a moment at the cover. I didn't know how to respond. I didn't know how to help her. "Why would God pick you?" I finally asked.

She shook her head, an undertone rising from her throat. Her silence was so natural that sound coming from her was as physical as flesh. I realized our knees were touching. In some ways I was starting to believe her. As she opened to another section of the notebook, I could smell her skin—earthy and fresh—like a husk pulled from sugar corn.

"I was born because America dropped soldiers in Vietnam. I hope that my parents loved each other, but I'll never know. My survival defies all odds. That is miracle enough. If God has come to me, if Mary has spoken to me, it's no different from what millions of others experience in meditation and prayer—anyone, anywhere, any religion. I don't believe I've been singled out. The miracle is that I lived, that I'm here at all."

When I'd finished reading, she took the notebook back and wrote, "Please. I'm trapped here. I've got to get away so this can all blow over."

"I'll try," I said, meaning it.

She looked at me in a way she hadn't before, and it made me wonder if *I* looked different. Then she wrote a note asking why I believed I'd had a vision.

I explained again that I'd only fainted. "I guess I'd love it though," I said. "If something like that *could* happen. Could happen to me."

She squeezed my cheeks, gazing into my eyes. Her breathing quickened, and I wondered if she could hear it.

The miracle girl kept on writing her story, so I went downstairs for a cold shower. I took my time coming back up through the church, touching stone moldings, wooden grillework in the confessionals, steam radiators with chipped silver paint, white marble statues—toes, calves, and knees.

"Are you hungry?" I asked her in the loft. The sun sat low in the sky. "It's seven-thirty."

She nodded. *A little.*

"Why don't I get some sandwiches?"

She nodded. *Okay.*

I'll phone.

Thanks.

At Tri-City Plaza I called for rental cars—still nothing. So I dialed Buddy. "What about my letter?" I said. "She's real amenable, Buddy. She wants to help the community. I told her all about you."

There was a pause, long enough that I knew I'd gotten to him. "Mr. Wilcox said he'd draft a letter PDQ." Just hearing his voice got my heart pounding.

"When will Rita have it?"

"She probably has it already. If not, then tomorrow morning. Why don't I come and meet the girl now?"

"When the letter is in my hands."

"Quinn. A little trust."

"In my hands, Buddy."

I hung up and tried Rita. *I'm unavailable* . . . You'd think she *might* want to hear from me. You'd think she *might* stop e-mailing her boyfriend for ten seconds.

I didn't want to walk all the way across town to our apartment before the temperature dropped a little, so I bought drinks and sandwiches—no mayo this time—and went back. When I opened the side door, I could see her in the loft, standing in front of Jesus in the stained-glass window; it looked like John the Baptist was pouring water over her head. Without a scarf, her hair spilled to the sides. She held up her T-shirt with one hand and looked down at her belly, watching her other hand caress her skin.

I kicked the door closed. The vibrations traveled up to the loft, and she jerked her head toward me, dropping her shirt. I waved.

Again, we sat facing each other and ate. I told her there were still no cars. She clenched her hand, holding a tight fist for a few beats, then relaxed and took a bite of her sandwich.

She was thinking about her options, I was sure. She wouldn't wait forever for me to turn up a rental car. Did she even trust me? Why would she?

As the light through the window dimmed, we finished our meal. She'd washed out her scarf, and it was hanging on the thin treble pipes to dry. Her hair was still wet from the shower, and she twisted it into a knot at the top of her head.

I tapped her arm, and when she turned, a few coils of hair sprang out.

I held up a finger, then motioned like a hand moving around a clock, then like dialing a phone. She understood—*I'd go call again in an hour*—and she smiled—*Thanks.*

"Didn't you have a plan?" I asked, but it was too dark for her to read my lips, so I reached for her pen. We lay side by side on the beach blanket propped on our elbows, wax from three votives running like lava along the wood floor.

She wrote quickly. "Police put up No Parking signs—Fire lane—then towed the whole street—my car. I put my head down and just kept walking. When the crowd thinned, I looked up the hill and saw the church."

"Where are you planning to go?" I wrote.

She looked me in the eyes and shook her head—*I'm not telling.* Then as if trying to make up for it, she turned back a few pages in the notebook and slid it toward me. I tipped the pages toward the candlelight.

"In junior high, we lived at the bottom of the hill. I got my first communion and confirmation in this church. Week after week I'd write down my sexual sins of the heart—nothing I'd actually done, only things I'd imagined—and I'd pass the notes to an old priest in the confessional in this church. He'd say, 'Shame on you,' order fifty Hail Marys, demand I never think dirty thoughts again. And now, it's here that I'm trapped."

At ten p.m. I was walking past A and P Grocery again, the fire hydrant still spraying. Fifteen or twenty people, mostly kids, were dashing through the water. They hardly noticed me. I'd become part of the new landscape of miraculous heat and visions and sleepless nights.

The miracle girl had been nervous when I left. She didn't like the dark. She walked with me to the door, shining her flashlight, rotating the dead bolt back and forth several times. As I turned out the door, she pulled back on my arm and made a sign: her right hand reached forward then circled back to her left hand, cupped at her chest. I hoped it meant, *Hurry home.*

As I passed Tri-City Plaza, I could see downtown all lit up. Sporadic sirens and a rumble of activity rolled up the hill, imitating Buddy's vision of a lively Hudson City: a gentrified downtown with innovative restaurants, sidewalk cafés, and jazz clubs full of yuppies with deep dot-com pockets. A city purged of surf and turf.

Avoiding Little Saigon I went left at Congress Street toward downtown. The streets *were* bustling. Restaurants, for what they were, overflowed. Card tables and shiny plastic lawn furniture stood precariously on uneven sidewalks—pilgrims eating pizza in the heat, Indian and Chinese food, burgers and subs. After ten on a weeknight.

I put on my sunglasses and joined the line at Uncle Sam's Hot Dogs—the city's famous four-inch dogs served up in mini-buns. There was miracle buzz in the hot dog line, and as I progressed toward the door, I got the gist real fast: the miracle girl had disappeared. Or she was sick, or overcome with the spirit. She'd gone to Bethlehem or Saigon, Lourdes or Mexico City. She'd died. She'd ascended. "Anything's possible," a reporter on the TV said. "She may still be in her home."

"She's gone back home," one man said to his wife.

"*Está en Roma,*" a Hispanic woman behind me told her friend.

"In Rome to meet the pope," I heard in English behind them.

"They'll be making her a saint," came the reply.

I got a root beer and three chili dogs, and continued down Congress Street. Even Second Street News, the army surplus, and pawn shops were open. And busy. This *was* a boom. Inside a vacant storefront, tables were set up with cookies and lemonade and Venable brochures.

At the Armenian church, I looked across Burden Park: the TV van was still parked in front of our building. I went left up Canal Street, past the firehouse, and in five minutes was creeping through the alley to our bedroom window. I leaned into the bars. Rita was sitting on the edge of the couch in the living room, staring at the TV. There was no sound.

"Hey," I said in a stage whisper, and she jerked her head like she was waiting. The lights were low, but I could see she'd been crying.

She came and kneeled at the window, touching her fingers to the screen. "Why don't you come inside?"

"Did you get the letter?"

"Please come in so we can talk."

"You can stew in your guilt all alone, Rita. Did the letter come?"

"We can work that out. We can work it all out. People go bankrupt. People pay off fines."

"It's jail we're talking about."

"Buddy made you cheat, didn't he?"

"Don't even say that word." I looked away. "Anyway. No. He didn't make me. I knew what I was doing. So make your judgments."

"I love you," Rita said. "Please. I'll tell him it's got to stop."

"Why haven't you already? You're obviously e-mailing him all day when I'm trying to call."

"I had to turn the phone off. It rings for you nonstop." She pressed her hand forward, stretching out the screen. "Please, Quinn. You've got to forgive me."

"Look. Is there a letter or what?"

"Come inside," she said. "Come home."

"I need the letter."

"Just come in for it. Come in for the night."

She had it! I was ecstatic. "Shit, Rita. Give it to me."

She turned her face away. "There's no letter. Nothing came."

"Dammit!" My head dropped.

"We can deal with this together," she was saying. "Don't you see that that's what our problem has been? I really don't feel like we're truly together in anything. If we love each other—"

"That's such bullshit," I said. "I practically worship you. The way you move and laugh. The way you breathe." She let the anger from my voice fall away before she continued.

"I know you do, and those things make me feel so good. But I always feel like you love who I am to you right now. You love what you see in this moment. But you don't really love everything I might be, or everything I could be, ten years from now, fifty years, or next week. I don't know how else to say it. You need to believe in my absolute core because everything else could change. You have to trust my heart." She pushed her hand harder into the screen. "And forgiveness—"

"Don't try and turn this around," I snapped. "And while we're on forgiveness, I've been doing some thinking, too. Our *problem* is that you've never forgiven me for . . ." I hated even saying the word, ". . . for herpes. Have you? You *claim*—"

She burst out crying.

"You claim we've moved on—"

"No," she said through her tears, shaking her head. "No, I haven't."

I was silent. I'm not sure I'd really believed it was true. I just wanted to accuse her of something.

I pressed my hand flat to hers through the screen, to the hundreds of neatly aligned, tiny squares of her skin. I wasn't sure what to believe. I left her there crying, and trudged down the alley into the darkness.

Someone was on the pay phone by the firehouse, so I called from a booth in front of Uncle Sam's. The air was greasy and hot with Indian food and burgers. People looked desperate, like they couldn't stand another night without sleep. A man who seemed famished but too hot to eat sat on the curb with the floppy point of a pizza slice drooping in front of his mouth.

"I've got the letter right here in front of me," Buddy said.

"You give it to me first. Then you can meet her."

"I can't work in this atmosphere of distrust. Lunch tomorrow. The Dutch Tavern. Noon. Bring her and the letter's yours. Otherwise, you're on your own, chump."

"You—"

But he cut me off. He had a way of turning the tables on me so quickly. I held the receiver to my ear, a recorded voice urging me to hang up and try again. Pilgrims were beginning to leave Little Saigon, confused, angry. As they realized the miracle girl had deserted them, there was no focus for their prayers and hopes. They'd been set adrift.

With ice cubes rattling in two king-sized Sprites, I began up the hill.

I wasn't sure, but as I rose out of downtown, the night seemed a notch more bearable. The hot wind still came up in occasional gusts, but with traces of slightly fresher air. Like swimming through cool patches in a lake.

The church's doorknob was hot. But inside—the miracle was holding true—cool sacred air. I bolted the door and headed toward the stairs. The church was quiet and dark. I thought she might be sleeping. Or she'd left. I missed her a little.

I walked with light feet, open ears, eyes raised toward the loft. The ice had melted and the paper cups, dripping with sweat, were quiet. And then, out of the corner of my eye, I saw a head pop up soundlessly from between the pews. A dim light from the window silhouetted her—her wild hair restrained again with the scarf, her flaring cheekbones and delicate chin. She'd been hiding, and I knew she'd been scared. But now, seeing me, she sat on the edge of the seat and collapsed forward, her hands pressed together as if in prayer.

I sidestepped between pews, crossed the center aisle, and sat down beside her, the curve of the pew familiar on my thighs and back. I touched her arm with the sweaty cup, and she turned her face. There in the darkness—light spotting the tip of her nose, the crest of her cheek, an earlobe—she saw the Sprite, and I saw the bright white of her broad smile. She touched her chin—*Thank you*—her wide eyes sparkling. I hated myself for thinking what a natural she'd be for advertisers. She settled back beside me and we sipped our drinks—flat, watery, and chilled—looking over the rows of empty pews, past the confessionals and communion rail, at the dark altar and the faint white cross on the wall where the crucifix had hung.

She slipped down in the bench and propped her knees on the hymnal rack. I rested my feet on the kneeler. Slowly, her head leaned closer to me. I was protecting her. She was relieved to see me. I reached my arm around her. Breathing deeply, falling toward sleep, she laid her head on my shoulder, seeming to trust me. But how could she when betrayal was so easy?

How could Rita trust me if she'd never forgiven me? Just when she forgot an outbreak, another one came along. She wasn't always angry, but it was lurking in her, like the virus—fierce and painful during an outbreak, dormant and simmering the rest of the time.

The miracle girl suddenly lifted her head, brow furrowed. She turned up her palm—*What's wrong?*—then she laid her hand flat on my thudding heart. How could Rita believe in *my* heart?

She flicked her finger under my chin then pointed at her chest. *Tell me.*

I shook my head and looked away, but she took hold of my jaw and pulled me back. Gazing into her face I said, "Sorry," then closed my eyes and brought her head back to my chest.

I thought of Rita's face darkened by the window screen. She gave her heart to J. B. Katz which could only mean there was less for me. She was playing at being lovers with another man. How could she commit to me fully, how could she be open and available to me, when part of her, every day, went to him?

If I didn't go to jail and if I ever built a house, I'd build a simple structure with no dark corners where lies and justifications might hide. Despite everything, it was easy to imagine sharing that house with Rita.

At my throat I felt her hand, and I realized I was humming. I stopped. She tapped my neck, and I started again. No particular tune—something I figured out as I went along.

And I hummed like that for quite a while, my hand on her back, feeling her breath deepen. With time, my tune seemed to fill the church—as if my voice had steadily billowed up to the rafters and was now settling down over us.

Finally, she lifted her face and pointed to the empty soda cup, holding her bladder in exaggerated agony.

I nodded. "Me too."

So I followed her downstairs. It was almost completely black, but by now we both knew the half-steps, turns, and doorways by heart. I stood waiting in the darkness. Smudges of light at the small basement window wells defined themselves as my eyes adjusted. My legs were tired from the long walk down the hill and back up. I stretched my arms, my neck, my spine. In the most peaceful moment I'd known in a week, I took a deep breath in the darkness, listening to her pee tinkling into the bowl. I smiled—delighted that I wasn't deaf.

She came out, made a sign, and went up the stairs. I washed my face and the back of my neck. The hand towel she'd left on the peg smelled of her skin.

In the loft one candle was lit, and she was lying on the blanket in front of the organ pipes. I sat beside her. A car came down the hill and turned in front of the church, its high beams shining through the stained glass and passing over us like searchlights. She touched a pillow she'd made for me from a few of her T-shirts. I lay back, and she curled against me, then lifted her eyes and made the motions of a symphony conductor with her finger. I started to hum and she smiled. She laid her head on my chest, her hand at my throat, and before I closed my own eyes, she was asleep.

Voices startled me awake. Her arm was tight across my body. A long horrific screech of metal on metal rattled down my spine. She lifted her head. "It's okay," I mouthed, and stroked her back with one hand as I slipped the other arm out from under her. The voices clattered through the night again. I jumped to my feet and looked through the small window. A battered white van was parked in front of my Land Rover, its rear doors open. My own doors had been removed and leaned in a neat line against the van's tire. The passenger seat was handed out of the truck and into the back of the van. Taking aim with my remote, I pressed the alarm button over and over until my thumb cramped. Nothing. They took the floor mats and steering wheel. They took the sun visors, bumpers, and grille. They took the hood and assorted engine parts. I watched them check twice for tools left behind before they put on their blinker and eased away from the curb.

For a while I stared out through the window. A black stain of coolant pooled beneath where the radiator should've been. Insurance would call it a total. They'd get the remains, and I'd get a check. My stomach turned, and I took a deep breath of night air. And I noticed the air smelled fresher. It was cooler. No question. The heat had broken.

I turned from the window just as she turned her back to me, reaching up under her T-shirt. With a flourish, her elbows ducked inside the sleeves, and she performed those quick moves that no man will ever fully understand—straps, clips, and arms sliding, shirt rising up her back exposing the gentle dip of her spine—then she tugged her bra from under her shirt. How could anything be so sexy?

She dropped the bra on her duffel and pointed to her bladder again, embarrassed. Her bare feet padded down the stairs then down the aisle while I straightened the beach blanket and arranged our makeshift pillows. And as I dropped to one knee, a boom startled me. I rushed to the wall and looked down into the darkness. I couldn't see anything but rows of pews. I heard her groan and raced down the stairs to the front of the church. Writhing on the vestry floor, holding her foot, she cried—like tortured whimpers coming through a clenched throat. She had kicked the heavy iron base of the candelabra.

"Are you okay?" I said, useless, since she couldn't see my lips in the darkness, stupid, since she was in agony. I touched her foot and she slapped my hand, so I signaled *getting up*. With one arm over my shoulder, her other hand reaching from pew to pew, we hobbled the length of the church then up to the loft.

I lowered her to the beach blanket and lit a few candles. Blood flowed between her toes. She looked up at me, and I made a sympathetic face then rubbed my hands together like washing. I dashed down to the bathroom with one of the huge soda cups, filled it with water, and came back up with the soap.

I lifted her ankle onto one end of my towel, then sat on the floor and trickled water over her quivering foot. The blood rinsed away, and fresh blood seeped from a jagged cut between two toes. I shrugged, *Not too bad,* trying to reassure her. Gently, I took her toes in my fingers and began washing at the tips, working down to the cut. She winced, but not so much that I thought she might have broken a bone. I rubbed my finger between her toes along the cut, and far from hurting her, it seemed to provide some relief. So I lathered the soap over the sole of her foot, and worked the suds around her heel and ankle, her smooth curving instep. When I massaged my thumbs into the soft spot in her arch, a shudder ran through her, a peaceful sigh in her throat.

She lay back and her head knocked the organ pipes, so we shifted a few inches down the blanket. I rinsed off the suds, the water soaking into my towel, then I patted and squeezed her foot dry. The bleeding had mostly stopped, but I grabbed a clean napkin from dinner and rolled it up between her toes, as if I'd painted her nails.

Her breathing deepened. She lay still. I poured the cool water over her other foot, then worked the suds into her skin, around her ankles and each slender toe. A low moan rose from her chest. I rubbed my thumbs deeper—her moaning like a chant.

I rinsed and wrapped her foot with a dry corner of the towel, still pressing my fingers and thumbs through the terry cloth into her skin. I stroked the injured foot, and her breathing quickened, her body quivered. "Are you okay?" I said, but her head had tipped back, eyes closed, her spine arching. Heat rose from her skin. I held her ankles. Her moans turned to cries rising up the organ pipes, a pulsing chord filling the church. Her body shook, and now I felt it too—the resonance in the pipes, glass, and rafters vibrated under my skin. And then her cries turned to voice, shaping something like words, a true voice, a nameless melody rising from her, trumpeting out the organ pipes, ecstatic music.

She sat up suddenly, her face terrorized, covering her ears. "What?" I said. "The voice?"

She shook her head violently. As I reached for her—her eyes darting around the loft—I realized what was happening.

"You hear me," I murmured, and she pressed her palms harder to her ears and began to cry.

I crawled beside her, and she put her head to my chest. I held her, humming quietly, hoping I could tether her with the sound of my voice.

She hadn't spoken, but there was the sense of words—like Rita talking with Trisch the night before across the park. The cadence and tone of a familiar loved voice—beyond words, more than words.

As I rocked her in the candlelight, the air blowing in the window cooled, and soon I heard a light patter of rain. She lifted her head and turned her face toward the stained glass. She smelled the rain, eyes closed, and she let the raindrops blowing inside sprinkle her face. Turning to me, she opened her eyes, and with my fingertips, I rubbed rainwater into her skin.

9. TUESDAY

In the night, she woke with every sound. I didn't know what to do, except hold her. At first light, when I woke, she was sleeping on my shoulder, a sweatshirt over her head. A gusting wind brought rain clattering against the stained glass, and she jolted awake. My heart thudded at the look on her face, then she jumped to her feet and dashed across the loft. She grabbed one of the big Sprite cups and retched into it. I went to her, but she waved me back, then stumbled downstairs holding the cup under her chin. From above I watched her hurry down the aisle, favoring her injured foot.

From the cover of *Hudson City Magazine,* her face stared up at me—the glossy paper crinkled with rain. Drinking from her water bottle, I tried to make sense of it all. For two weeks there'd been news reports of doctors admitting all they didn't know about spontaneous restoration of hearing. But to have seen her body on fire . . . What had I witnessed?

Peeling an orange, I heard her uneven step up the stairs.

"Are you okay?" I said when she was closer.

Fine.

"Really?"

She nodded, and looked at the wet spot on her T-shirt. Then turning away from me, she lifted the shirt over her head. Her long lean back, the beads of her spine, her sloping shoulders and neck, the shorts barely hanging on to her narrow hips—she had the body of a lemur.

Her back still turned, she put on her bra and a clean shirt. She opened her shorts, and halfway through tucking in her shirt, she stopped and held her stomach. I thought she might be sick again. But by the way she smoothed her hand over her belly, her head dropping easily to one side, then zipped and buttoned, I understood.

I held out my hand and pulled her down on the beach blanket beside me. I looked her in the eyes, and she looked away. A car splashed by too fast, its motor racing, frightening her. I squeezed her hand, waiting until she met my eyes. "You're pregnant," I whispered, and she burst into tears.

I was holding her, her face against my neck. In her sobs I heard her voice again. We were on the floor, sitting awkwardly, rocking. The rain fell harder, and I wondered if she could still feel the patter, now that she heard it. I wondered if it hurt more to hear her own cries.

When she stopped crying, she reached straight for her paper and pen. "You've got to get me out of here," she wrote.

"But even if I get a car . . . where are you going?"

She wiped her eyes on her T-shirt sleeves, then looked me square in the face, shaking her head. Then she wrote, "No one can ever know I'm pregnant. Promise me. Please. Or what's happened with my hearing. It's not me I'm worried about—think what a life it would be for my child—what these pilgrims would make of it. The last two weeks of my life is what my child would endure for years."

"I promise," I said. "But what about the father?"

She shook her head.

"'No' there isn't one?"

She sighed, a little annoyed, and wrote, "Friend of a friend of a . . . He said his sister-in-law was deaf. He signed—very poorly—but it charmed me. Afterward, he starts sobbing, confessing he's married. And that it's really a deaf daughter." *Okay!?* she gestured, and tore out the page. The rain poured down.

"I'm just trying to help," I said.

Her eyes went wide, fists raised: *Then do it! Get a car!*

I nodded, my hand flat on my heart, meaning it. "As soon as it lets up a little, I'll go."

She picked up her water bottle, swished the half-sip I'd left in it, and waggled the bottle at me. Then she took it to the basement sink for a refill. I put my face to the window at John the Baptist's feet. In the rain the skeleton of my truck looked more abandoned than ever. Rivers rushing in the gutters seemed powerful enough to sweep it away. How could I hand her over to Buddy? How could I even suggest it?

When I turned from the window, she was there. In one gesture she raised her eyebrows, shrugged her shoulders, touched her belly, and took a drink: *The only thing I know about pregnancy is you're supposed to drink lots of water.*

I pointed to myself, then her, then cradled a baby and pointed far off.

She shook her head: *No. I'm sorry.*

"How are you going to escape this? They'll find you. I can take care of you." And in a flash I glimpsed an entire life with her—lying low for a while, she'd change her hair, put makeup over the mole at the tip of her eyebrow. I'd make a cradle for the baby. "Please, Sue."

And she read everything I'd thought. "No." She spoke it. I knew it was final.

Half a block from the A and P Grocery the rain came on even harder. I ran down the sidewalk and jumped into the doorway. The hydrant was still spraying over the empty street.

They only had tiny collapsible umbrellas, worthless in a good gust, so I ended up with a poncho. It was green and plenty big, a picture of Mickey Mouse on the front, and Mickey Mouse's back on the back. His ears stuck up from the hood. Humiliating but cheap—$7.99. Then I was off again, sweating inside the plastic.

At Tri-City Plaza I went into the supermarket for a large coffee and cinnamon doughnut, and took them out to the pay phones under the roof in front of Kmart. I called around for rental cars. Not a chance. One agency used the word "exodus." One offered to pay my bus ticket to anywhere I wanted if I'd bring back a car. "But I dunno," he said. "I hear there's no bus tickets either."

I popped the last hunk of doughnut in my mouth, sipped the coffee, and mixed it around. On that same show where I'd seen the Tet festivals in Vietnam, they did a segment on the Forbidden City in Hué, almost completely destroyed in the Tet offensive. They showed tank-sized holes through the city walls, the base of a pagoda surrounded by rubble, ponds green with lily pads. One temple had been rebuilt. It was during the monsoon, and tiled roofs hung out over wooden walkways that stretched all the way around the building. The monks could meditate then move along the covered walkways behind a thick curtain of rain dropping from the edge of the roof.

That's what I thought about as I looked out from this covered walkway in front of Kmart, rain pelting the parked cars and gushing like a broken water main from a clogged downspout. In Vietnam they collect and bless the rainwater for festivals, then use it for ritual washing. I thought of Sue in the loft, touching the inside of the stained-glass window, listening to sheets of rain rinsing it down.

I grabbed the phone and called Buddy. "What's taking you so long?" he demanded. "It's all unraveling, Quinn. This whole thing is losing credibility. I need the girl today. My life is in her hands. And yours is too."

For a moment I didn't say anything. The line of cars *out* of town was stopped dead. "I'm at Kmart," I told Buddy. "Hurry up."

"Traffic—" he began, but I didn't want to hear his voice.

Back in the supermarket, I ordered her a sandwich with extra pickle spears. I got her a bag of carrot sticks, a liter of water, and a bottle of kiwi-raspberry juice. I picked up a bottle of vitamins. On the baby aisle I found a rattle.

Buddy's white Seville slipped on the wet pavement when he hit his brakes. He powered down the passenger window and waved me over, his wipers beating frantically, flinging water at my poncho.

I sipped my coffee. "C'mon, c'mon!" Buddy shouted from the driver's seat. I'd never seen him so torqued. I looked at all the cars backed up leaving town, and I thought how betrayal was only a problem when you believed in something. Did they believe in Sue, or was it something else?

He leaned across the front seat and pushed open the passenger door. "We're meeting investors at the Ramada in forty minutes. Lose the poncho and get in, Mickey."

"You know," I said. "I'm gonna have to go get her, and we'll meet you back here."

"No friggin' way." Buddy's face shot red. "Get in. Now." He pointed at the passenger seat.

"Can't be done."

"Don't fool with me."

I'd never loved the rain so much as I did at that moment. The way it filled up the air so completely, so evenly. The way it was everywhere.

Buddy punched the wheel and the horn blew. Then he got out of his car. "Why?" he demanded, in my face. "Tell me why."

"She doesn't completely understand that she's meeting you. If she sees you, she could bolt."

Buddy liked the explanation for involving coercion. "I'll hide in the backseat. I'll hide in the goddamn trunk." He was desperate.

"My way, or the highway," I said.

"I swear to God, Quinn." He was shaking his head. "I swear to God." He poked my chest with his finger. I hopped in his car and hit the gas, leaving him behind.

There was no way I'd make any progress going up Hoosick, so I took a left toward downtown. Pilgrims were sleeping in the backseats of cars stuck in traffic. The drivers looked numb, drained of life. As I got closer to Little Saigon, the streets got thicker with pedestrians wearing clear plastic ponchos. The ponchos seemed to expose them, like a lens allowing a glimpse through their clothes and skin to their dispirited hearts.

Pilgrims huddled in groups, some weeping, some shouting out at the sky—like the aftermath of a hurricane. I took a right to loop back up the hill on the back streets. A man stood on a corner with a sign: "I still believe."

I parked in front of the church and dashed inside. Peering up at the loft I couldn't see her. The patter of rain on the roof made the church sound emptier. Abandoned. With a sinking feeling, I walked toward the altar and vestry, and listened at the top of the basement stairs for the shower; but there was nothing, and I realized she was gone. She knew I'd show up with someone like Buddy. I was worse than Buddy. Worse than Floquet. At least they wanted her for something they believed in; I'd wanted her to save me from myself.

I hung the wet poncho over the candelabra by the basement stairs, and set her lunch and Buddy's car keys on the floor. A shiver cracked through me—I was suddenly chilled. If she'd only trusted me.

As I headed down the side aisle past the confessionals—carved wooden boxes where a doddering priest had made Sue ashamed of her awakening sexuality—the sun slowly broke through the rain clouds, brightening the stained glass in the loft. I took in the sight one last time.

The sun grew even brighter, the colors in the window as vibrant as I'd seen them, and I stepped into the jeweled light, lifting my face, eyes shut, soaking up the heat. When I opened my eyes, sunlight glinted off the organ pipes, and I heard them resonate. A low mellow hum. I squinted through the glare, but the light brightened and the sound from the organ pipes gained strength, the vibrations moving like hands over my shoulders and down my back. The light turned rose-colored, and the air turned sweet. I stared ahead, ready for the organ to roar with music, waiting for whatever might be there.

The hands moved around my chest, over my pounding heart, the smell of roses thick in the air. And a hand was on my face, tugging at my chin. I turned. Her hair wet from the shower, shoulders bare, skin shiny and dark, she smiled at me. My beach towel was hitched up over her breasts, spotted with blood from her toe.

She signed and mouthed, *I had faith in you,* and she jingled Buddy's keys. *Thank you.* Then she jingled them again—seeming to enjoy the sound. I kissed the top of her freshly shampooed head. Roses.

A powerful gust rattled the windows. I looked at the loft, and the sunlight was gone. Rain drummed on the roof.

I turned back to her, but she wasn't there anymore. A paper bag crinkled. She was sitting in the confessional biting into her sandwich.

She was in the priest's box so I sat next door in the confessor's seat, and watched her through the screen, savoring the sight of her as she chewed. Her eyes scanned the vaulted ceiling, looking, it seemed, for the thump of rain. Did she think there was more possibility in her new world of sounds? She tore off a hunk of sandwich and passed it around to me. She teased her hair with her fingers and walked her toes up the smooth wood. I ate the sandwich. She passed me her juice. I took a sip and passed it back around.

For just a moment I rested my head on the wood and closed my eyes, and when I opened them, Sue stood before me, wiping her fingers on the hem of the towel. "It's the white Cadillac out front," I told her. "I think that's what the Virgin Mary drives." Then a gust of wind banged the windows, and she covered her ears, startled.

I reached for her, nodding—*Don't be afraid*—and she squeezed into the box and sat across my lap. She took my hands and placed them over her ears, then she hugged me, breathing deeply.

I held her and thought about the beginnings of a baby inside her, its tiny heart fluttering. Maybe that explained it all—the visions, the visitations—simply a new life, the possibility of a new life, within her.

And maybe that's what was happening with me, too. Up in the loft, the window was dark. The organ pipes looked dull and dusty. I hadn't had a vision. I was sure of that. But for that one moment when my chest expanded, the sunlight warm on my face, I'd believed in the possibility.

I removed my hand from one of her ears and hummed to her, almost silently. Maybe that's what Rita meant—loving the possibilities in each other. Through the towel I massaged around each bead of her spine, moving slowly up her back, humming like a prayer, a vow, our eyes closed, rocking gently on the little wooden seat of the confessional.

And then our peace was shattered—like the roof caving in. Across the church the door slammed open. In a black trench coat, holding a black umbrella like a spear—it was Frank. I lunged for the confessional door, but it was too late. He saw us immediately, and he was nearly toppled by a cameraman whose floodlight filled our little box like a stage. We shielded our eyes with our hands, frozen for a moment. Flashes popped. With my hand held out in front of me against the light, I saw figures running toward us between the pews. We jumped up, her towel fell, and she grabbed Buddy's keys, running naked for the vestry.

The stampede charged after her. The last I saw of her, she grabbed the rain poncho off the candelabra and her naked butt shot down the stairs. I ran to the vestry doorway and spun around. A young guy in a canvas jacket loaded with film, cameras dangling from his body like weapons, quick-footed across the backs of pews. I spread myself out in the doorway, gripping the doorjambs, readying myself to fight them off. But when the young photographer hit the floor at a run not two arm's lengths from me, I shouted with a voice that shook the deepest organ pipes, "Enough!" and he stopped short. The pack pushed forward. "You've stolen her life!" I bellowed. They shot pictures of me, but they wanted her, and I held them back.

"Let her at least get dressed!" But they kept pushing. "You want a naked photo? Is that what you want?" I ripped open my shirt, unbuckled my belt, and let my pants and boxers drop. "Here you go!" The TV camera fought its way to the front, unconcerned with edits. And then, through the rumble of reporters, whirring of cameras, and rain pounding on the roof, I heard the same sheet-metal boom I'd heard two nights before—the old coal chute.

"You're trying to make her something she's not. Leave her alone." The brilliant spray of flashes blinded me. I couldn't see anything but light.

Frank finally pushed through to the front. "Good Lord, John," he said, a bobbing microphone knocking our heads. As he took off his trench coat and covered me up, the young cameraman knocked me with a shoulder and forced his way through the door. Before I could regain my balance they were all rushing past, stumbling, trampling each other, racing down to a dark musty basement after something they couldn't believe.

10. TEN DAYS LATER

The tenth day of rain. The bishop turned at the altar and directed our attention to his niece, gliding with her father down the aisle. Rita squeezed my hand. The cathedral looked good: a skim coat of plaster with a fresh layer of eggshell paint, gold and midnight blue details repainted, and no new water stains, despite the weather. Venable had paid for it all including some patchwork on the roof. But the art restorer had never materialized, the heating hadn't been touched, and the skim coat had bubbled a little already—in a year, or a month, I imagined sheets of it peeling away.

Frank addressed his niece and her groom. He welcomed his relatives from Ireland, his dear friends, all believers. Up toward the front I could see the back of Rosemary's head. She was sitting next to Patsy and her boyfriend with his blue spiked hair. Buddy was somewhere too, I was sure. But Floquet had been officially defrocked and, I learned from Buddy, was going on the road as a motivational speaker.

Buddy's car had been found at a Burger King on the New York State Thruway—a note on a paper napkin saying "Thanks," a full tank of gas.

I told him she'd gotten away from me, that I'd done everything I could, and he knew I was lying. But he'd lied too. Homer Wilcox was just a Venable accountant. Buddy had never called the IRS.

And by that time Miracle Mania had ended. The pilgrims had turned on her, of course. She'd gone from virgin to whore in one quick shot on the evening news: nudity in the confessional was too much for them to bear. The bishop, in a strange sort of forgiveness, thanked me for helping to bring it all to an end. "So you're saying," I asked him, "that at least I can ruin a girl's reputation?"

"The Lord's minions are many and varied." For the first time ever, I heard some of Rosemary's irony in his voice.

At the reception Rita and I danced—high-stepping to Celtic music. I knew she missed her e-mailing, I knew she thought about him during the day, but I think she'd made peace with the clean break. And I thought about Sue—wondering if she'd settled in with friends and if the morning sickness had passed.

And I thought of the moment when I looked up at the loft and believed *not* in the Virgin Mary speaking to me—not that at all. It was a glimpse of possibility, a moment of faith. Rita kicked off her shoes and did spins in her black dress. She stumbled and fell into my arms.

The sky was so dark with clouds that when Rita and I got home around five, she lit candles on the mantel, shadows flickering up the walls, a familiar smell of paraffin in the air. We moved through the apartment silently—using the bathroom, getting out of our wedding clothes, listening to the rain clatter on the windows. The kettle whistled and a moment later the smell of flowers filled our apartment. I went to the kitchen—she was putting away a box of herbal tea—rose and hibiscus.

She held out a cup to me.

I shook my head, and she watched me fill a glass of lemonade from the pitcher in the fridge. She watched me closely these days, half-expecting a water-to-wine trick or a quick consult with the Virgin. She checked that the loaves in the drawer came from her bread machine, that the fishes I brought home had receipts. I had been intimate with the miracle girl. Rita, like everyone else, wanted to know if anything had rubbed off.

When her tea had cooled, she took my hand, leading me to our bedroom. We made love as the rain and wind pelted the window with such force it seemed to rock the room. I smelled her skin and lips, listened to her breath as we lay together, the apartment growing darker.

At dusk, she got up and put on her robe. I watched her walk across the living room to the bay window, the robe flowing behind her. She'd given up on Judaism, admitting that she really hadn't thought it through, but now, as part of her yoga practice, she meditated each morning and night. As she released her breath, I listened to her round, open "Ohh . . ." Candles flickered. I drifted in and out of sleep. And when I knew she was almost done, I rose from our bed, walked over and kneeled behind her, my chest pressed to her back, my hand touching her throat. "Ohh . . . Ohhh . . ."

We were beginning again with that single sound.